THROUGH BITTER SEAS

THROUGH BITTER SEAS

PHILLIP PAROTTI

CASEMATE
Philadelphia & Oxford

Published in the United States of America and Great Britain in 2023 by
CASEMATE PUBLISHERS
1950 Lawrence Road, Havertown, PA 19083, USA
and
The Old Music Hall, 106–108 Cowley Road, Oxford OX4 1JE, UK

Paperback Edition: ISBN 978-1-63624-308-5
Digital Edition: ISBN 978-1-63624-309-2

A CIP record for this book is available from the British Library

Printed and bound in the United Kingdom by CPI Group (UK) Ltd, Croydon, CR0 4YY
Typeset in India by DiTech Publishing Services

For a complete list of Casemate titles, please contact:

CASEMATE PUBLISHERS (US)
Telephone (610) 853-9131
Fax (610) 853-9146
Email: casemate@casematepublishers.com
www.casematepublishers.com

CASEMATE PUBLISHERS (UK)
Telephone (0)1226 734350
Email: casemate-uk@casematepublishers.co.uk
www.casematepublishers.co.uk

For Jim, Nancy, Rob, and Helena

Through bitter seas we wandered, toil without joy.

—Words once heard on a ship's bridge in the Pacific

1

When the *Akonapi* first came off the ways, she didn't have a name, instead, she had a number, *YP74A*, the *A* thrown in to distinguish her from *YP74B*, her sister ship—a vessel built by the same ship-building yard in San Diego and launched with her on the same day in 1940. Both of them were designated for use by Millard Mallott and Sons, a firm which maintained a sizable tuna fleet that had earned a solid reputation for bringing home a steady catch from the waters west of Peru. New and in excellent condition, the vessels had been commandeered by the U.S. Navy following the attack on Pearl Harbor. Their immense engines, matched with their 469-ton displacement and 131-foot length, gave them what the Navy believed to be viability for use as seagoing utility vessels and tugboats in forthcoming operations.

YP74B, by whatever quirk motivated the Navy's Pacific Service Force, had been dispatched to San Francisco as soon as she'd been commissioned and reconfigured as a tug. *YP74A*, steaming in company with transports and supply ships, had been dispatched in the opposite direction and sent to Pearl Harbor under the command of a warrant officer, a chief machinist, a man whose considerable technical expertise as an engineer was nevertheless found to be deficient for both navigation and fleet operations. He was relieved without prejudice once the task force reached Pearl and replaced with the sandy-haired Lieutenant Junior Grade Ted Hyde, who had experience with both. Hal, properly named Harold B. Goff—a newly commissioned ensign straight out of midshipman's school in New York—had joined the ship's company at the same time, the Navy having concluded that if watches were to be stood and even a vessel like a YP kept under sufficient control, at least two officers were required to oversee the ship's operations, nothing about previous experience or competence having been considered. There was a war on; people had to come up to the mark and learn on the job.

Fortunately for Hal, Ted Hyde, following his own early commissioning during the summer of 1940, had spent more than a year serving as the assistant first lieutenant aboard an attack transport; so Ted, as Hal was invited to call him, did have experience, as a watch stander, as a navigator, and with a plethora of other duties ranging from rigging and booms to the handling of small boats. With the august calling of command at sea, he had none, but Ted turned out to be a quick study and sure to pass along to Hal everything that he learned and did. By the time *YP74A* reached Australia and moved north to join the invasion force off Guadalcanal, Ted's firm but congenial methods had welded the crew into a tight family. In fact, given the state of morale which Ted had engendered, while the vessel remained on the Navy's list as *YP74A*, the crew had gone so far as to dub her the *Akonapi*, adopting the name of a Native American tribe in imitation of the larger ATFs, the fleet tugs, which also accompanied the invasion force. Needless to say, *Akonapi* did not appear on anything resembling official correspondence, for which *YP74A* had invariably to be used; nevertheless, the ship's boatswain's mates had fashioned a small wooden nameplate and continued to hang it from the rail that surrounded the bridge save for those occasions when a senior officer's visit happened to be scheduled. Regardless, both Ted Hyde and Hal took as much pride in the nickname as did the crew, and like the rest of their men, used the name whenever speaking of her among themselves.

c~

In fact, the *Akonapi* did not take part in the initial invasion of Guadalcanal. Instead, having reached Port Moresby in August 1942, she lingered there for six or more weeks—towing barges, pushing lighters, assisting ships in offloading or transferring cargoes from ship to shore—and did not go near Guadalcanal until well after the Battle of Savo Island. Finally, in late September, she was sent north, towing three lighters loaded down with boxed rations—such mundane items as toilet paper, mortar rounds, barbed wire, canvas—and three army officers who were to do advanced planning for the arrival of the Americal Division which, it was thought, would eventually join or relieve the Marines on the island. Rather than Guadalcanal, the *Akonapi* found herself based on Tulagi, thirty-two miles across Iron Bottom Sound from the island where the fighting happened to be taking place. There, occasionally, with so many supply ships moving in and out, she acted as a tug, helping them to move alongside and away from the makeshift pier that had been erected for their use. But as a rule, her main service took place at night when, with barges or lighters in tow, she made the trip across the Sound, moving supplies of one kind or another from Tulagi to the expanding perimeter that the Marines maintained on Guadalcanal proper.

Armed only with a single 20 mm Oerlikon with which to attempt to defend herself from air attack, as both Hal and Ted knew, the *Akonapi* would be a sitting duck for anything like a Japanese surface vessel or a submarine. While Hefling, the ship's gunner's mate, had demonstrated his proficiency in shooting at towed sleeves off the coast of Hawaii, no one on board felt confident that either the man or his 20 mm could contend with a Jap Zero, Val, or Kate bent on bombing or strafing them, particularly if they had a string of lighters

3

in tow. Their main protection, and they all knew it, turned out to be their size and the covering that the darkness of the night might afford them. Full and even half moons were their enemies; fog and cloudy nights, no matter how thick the soup, were the only things that could provide them with comfort on their trips to and from Guadalcanal, and even those, in the event of a close encounter, could not be relied upon.

Push came to shove for the *Akonapi* on the night of Thursday, November 19, 1942 at around 0315 in the morning, when Ted was on the bridge conning the vessel back across the Sound with two empty lighters strung out behind them. The initial problem turned out to be the moon, which was waxing gibbous and almost full beneath a cloudless sky without a hint of fog or mist showing anywhere. At the time, Hal happened to be back on the fantail where he'd been sent to check on the crew manning the towline, a slight chop having given Ted second thoughts about how the towline might be reacting under the strain.

"Baker, how's she lookin'?" Hal asked the boatswain in charge of the tow back aft just as another sailor, a man standing nearer the rail, had thrown up his arm to the west and shouted, "What the *hell* is that?"

Hal snapped his head in the direction the man was pointing and knew at once that he was looking at the vague outline of a Japanese submarine, its dark silhouette fully visible in the moonlight no more than one thousand yards distant. Momentarily, the shock of what he knew he was seeing caused Hal to freeze, but when the boatswain exclaimed "Shit!" in a voice almost loud enough to be heard on the bridge, Hal came to himself and barked at the sound-powered phone talker to report "Jap sub to port!" By that time, Ted had apparently already seen the sub for himself, given Hefling the order to open fire, and the 20 mm had started pumping out rounds with a staccato report. The tracers showed that the rounds were going out high, even as white dots, apparent Japanese sailors, began to emerge onto the sub's main deck and congregate around what Hal imagined to be their deck gun. Then, in what seemed like mere seconds, the Japs loosed their first round, the report sounding like the crack of doom. The round passed straight over the *Akonapi*'s bow. Fifteen seconds later, at just about the time that Hefling finally got the Oerlikon onto the target, the second Jap round slammed into the *Akonapi*'s superstructure, exploding the bridge and the compartments forward with such a fearful concussion that every man aft was thrown straight onto the deck. Before Hal could pick himself up, a third round struck them amidships; suddenly Hal found himself in the water and heard the towline snap almost directly over his head as the *Akonapi* began to settle. Very quickly, the ship went under, the suction strong enough to take him partway under himself, wrench his legs badly, and strip the shoes from his feet.

Relying mostly on the strength of his arms, his legs giving him sharp and searing pain, Hal resurfaced. Gasping for air, he did the only thing he could think to do: he used his arms to propel him toward the nearest lighter which the Japs had apparently not bothered to take under fire. In the process, he became aware that the boatswain who had been on the fantail beside him was also in the water, and with his help, Hal finally reached the lighter and got a grip on the remains of the towline so as to keep himself from sinking. How the boatswain got up onto the lighter, he didn't know, but the sound of voices eventually alerted him to the fact that at least two other men were up there with him. Then, clearly, he heard Baker shout, "Here, give me a hand! We've got to get Mr. Goff up here!" With effort, the three men began to hoist him up the side of the lighter, Hal gripping the towline for all he was worth until they finally pulled him over the side and helped him down onto the deck.

Once out of the water, Hal imagined that he had passed out from the pain, his lower back making him feel like he'd been struck by

5

a truck. How long he remained out, he didn't know, but when he came to, lying on the deck, he estimated the sun to be at a 45-degree angle from the horizon and imagined that it might be as late as eight o'clock in the morning. The pain he felt continued to go beyond anything he'd ever experienced. According to the boatswain, he'd also received a major gash across his buttocks, possibly from flying shrapnel, possibly from something he'd struck when they'd been blown from the *Akonapi* in the moments before she'd gone down. They'd done their best, the boatswain said, to stop the bleeding by stuffing a wet dungaree shirt down the back of his trousers where the gash had been torn, but without first aid equipment, that turned out to be the only thing they could do for him aside from elevating his feet and covering him with a cargo mat to try to prevent shock from setting in. Hal found that he was able to thank them for what they'd tried to do, and then found that if he tried to lie perfectly still—something that was hard to do considering the chop that morning—he could alleviate the pain he felt to at least a minor degree.

By noon, all four of them—Hal, the boatswain, and the two other sailors, the only members of the *Akonapi's* crew who had survived—felt like they were dying of thirst beneath the broiling tropical sun. It might be a chilly November in Boston, Hal thought, but around Guadalcanal, out in Iron Bottom Sound, the heat felt right on a par with what might be expected around Houston or New Orleans or somewhere up the Amazon in the midst of a summer swelter. Shortly after the sun reached its blistering zenith they were rescued, a destroyer headed for Tulagi finding them, taking them in tow, and pulling them on into Tulagi where Hal was removed on a stretcher to the tents of the Navy's base hospital. Once there, Hal Goff never saw Guadalcanal again.

⌒

Hal's sojourn in the Navy's Tulagi hospital didn't last long. After administering a local anesthetic, a surgeon who made crude jokes about Hal's bleeding ass sewed him up, gave him strict orders to lie on his stomach, and shipped him straight off along with more than 200 wounded Marines to New Caledonia. There, still unable to stand or walk, he found himself taken aboard a hospital ship and shipped straight back to San Diego, to "the Pink Place," the sailor's pet name for Balboa Naval Hospital. After four more weeks of recovery and rehabilitation, he regained his ability to stand and walk and, after more rehabilitation, to both swim and run. Finally, three days into February 1943, he found himself ushered into a four-striper's office, the four-striper being a tall, sallow Navy captain named Hickson who offered him a seat in front of his desk, bent his head over Hal's file, and finally looked up to say, "From all reports, Mr. Goff, you seem to have recovered. Feeling fit, are you?"

"Yes Sir," Hal said.

"Expecting some convalescent leave, are you?"

"If the Navy is willing to grant me some, Sir?" Hal replied.

"Have some place to go where you can show off that Purple Heart, do you?" Hickson said without showing so much as a trace of a smile.

"Yes Sir," Hal said, after a moment's hesitation.

"The Navy authorizes you twenty days of convalescent leave, Mister, with one day travel on either side of it. What that means is that you may swan around at will until 1200 hours sharp on 25 February 1943 at which time you will report yourself to the personnel office at Atlantic Fleet Headquarters, Hampton Roads, Norfolk, Virginia for reassignment. Here are your orders and travel authorizations," he said, hefting a manila envelope and pushing it across his desk for Hal to pick up. "Mind how you go. You don't want that gash on your hip opening back up, and don't be late for reassignment. The Navy takes a very dim view of anyone who fails to meet a commitment."

"Yes Sir," Hal said.

"Right," Captain Hickson said. "That's it, Mister. You're dismissed." And as though brushing a fly from his line of sight with a mere wave of his hand, Hickson sent Hal packing.

In a manner of speaking, Ensign Hal Goff USNR had told Captain Hickson a whopper, a porky, an out and out lie; he didn't have any place to go for the purpose of showing off a dubiously collected Purple Heart or for any other reason that he could think of. Hal's parents had died six years before in an unfortunate accident on the highway connecting Champaign-Urbana with Rantoul, Illinois, when a drunken Air Corps corporal from Chanute Field plowed straight into them after crossing the center stripe. The uncle who had taken over Hal's upbringing through his last two years in high school and then seen him almost all the way through his degree at the University of Illinois had died at the beginning of his senior year there, leaving him just enough money to complete his education, and after that, his only real homes has been temporary, the midshipman's school in New York and his confining stateroom on the *Akonapi*. New York as a place to spend his leave offered more than a plethora of exciting activities to hold his interest, but even with three months of back pay in his pocket, he judged Manhattan far too expensive for a leave extending to almost three weeks. San Diego seemed to sport a fine climate and offer plenty of attractions to go with it, but as far as Hal knew, the city seemed to be overflowing with such a multitude of sailors and Marines that he felt doubtful that he could even find a seat in a restaurant or an empty stool in a bar. In the end then, with a B-four bag filled with the clothing allowance with which the Navy had reequipped him, he boarded a train, slept sitting in his seat part of the way to Chicago, changed trains in Chicago, and pulled once more into the twin city of Champaign-Urbana, the place his journey had started nearly a year before, and made his way to the same boarding house where he had dossed down in college. Mrs. Rogers, the elderly landlady, greeted him with a smile and even agreed to give him his old room back, with breakfasts, for the length of his leave.

"I won't ask you where you've been," Mrs. Rogers said, "for I don't suppose you're allowed to say, but I recognize that ribbon you're wearing. You've seen action, haven't you?"

"Only in a manner of speaking," Hal said.

"Well," Mrs. Rogers said with a smile, "I won't ask further. The ribbon says enough. Same rules as during your student days: breakfast at seven o'clock sharp, the doors are locked at 10:00 pm, so if you come back late, you'll have to let yourself in with your key, and no girls allowed in the upstairs rooms. If you do bring a girl in, you're free to entertain her in the downstairs parlor, and if you want to eat in at night, you're to let me know by noon so that I can have something on hand for you. Remember all of that, do you?"

"Yes," Hal said with a smile, "I do."

"Good," Mrs. Rogers said, returning his smile. "It's good to have you back, Hal. I don't know where you've been or what you've been doing, but you'll always be welcome here, and I hope your time with me will give you a good rest."

"I'm much obliged, Mrs. Rogers," Hal said. "A good rest in these surroundings is going to do me a world of good."

And in keeping with that program, Hal carried his B-four bag straight upstairs to his old room, stowed his uniforms in the same armoire that he had used across his four years as a history major, and slept straight through the afternoon in an attempt to begin his recovery from the rigors he'd left behind him.

2

By the time Hal rose from his bed, got back into his blues and his overcoat, and emerged onto the street in front of Mrs. Rogers' boarding house, the winter sun had already gone down and a light snow happened to be falling, without wind, so that the tiny flakes settled on the sidewalks without depth. Surrounded by silence but finding the air cold, Hal raised and buttoned the collar of his overcoat and set off at a brisk pace. He headed three blocks up the street for South Goodwin, turned the corner, opened the door beneath the faux wooden balcony railing and French doors that adorned the upstairs facade of the owner's apartment at Pren's, and walked straight into same college hangout where he had formerly taken so many of his meals.

As far as Hal could see, nothing had changed. On his right the darkly finished counter with the kitchens behind it looked the same as did the booths on the left, and in the dimly lit, extra-large high-ceilinged room that bent to the right when one walked deeper into the establishment, Hal could already hear a pickup combo playing an arrangement of "Don't Sit Under the Apple Tree." Indeed, he could even see one student, having sweated the label off his beer bottle, fixing it to the top of his wallet before tossing the wallet, flat, straight up toward the overhead in an attempt to stick the label to the high ceiling. College traditions, Hal decided, died hard, if they ever died at all. With a smile to no one but himself, he unbuttoned the collar of his overcoat, turned to the man behind the counter, and ordered a hot pastrami sandwich and a beer. Once those were delivered, he walked straight down into the larger room where the combo continued to play. Noticing that the room was only about three-quarters full at the early hour, he found a booth just inside the entrance, seated himself, and quickly tucked into the pastrami. After all the Spam he had been forced to eat in the Pacific, it tasted particularly satisfying.

Hal had only eaten about half of his pastrami sandwich by the time the little band finished with the Andrews Sisters number and, to his surprise, the trumpet player and the saxophone player—ambitious music majors, he imagined—launched into an imperfect version of Glenn Miller's "Sun Valley Jump." Sensing movement to his side, Hal glanced to his left and was just in time to throw out his arm so as to prevent a person who had stumbled from falling all the way to the floor, regardless of the fact that the books the person carried had spilled straight onto the deck. The sudden weight on his own arm had been nearly enough to jerk Hal straight off his seat. If it had, both of them would have gone down, but they did not. In the wake of the event, Hal's whole attention was drawn downward toward the floor and the spilled books, so that he only looked up finally when the girl—for it was a girl who had caught his arm—said, "Oh, I'm so sorry!" and quivered somewhat unsteadily as she tried to recover herself.

"Here," Hal said, coming off the bench and leaning over to pick up the girl's books. "Take a seat for a moment so that you can catch your breath."

Mildly shaken by her near mishap, the girl did so, quickly sitting down on the corner of the bench across from where Hal had been seated where she remained almost but not quite breathless.

"Oh, I'm so sorry," she said again. "What a fool I must look. I'd glanced over at the band, and I shouldn't have. Thank you so much. You've saved me a nasty fall and a heap of embarrassment."

"Not at all," Hal said. "It could happen to anyone, and it has certainly happened to me more than once. Feeling better?"

"Yes," the girl said, showing him a smile.

She seemed older than Hal had realized upon first hearing her voice but pretty as far as he could see in the dim light, with dark brown hair, brown eyes, and wonderfully shaped lips.

"Student, are you?" Hal asked.

"Yes," the girl said, "graduate student."

"Studying … ?"

"English lit, if it doesn't sound too conventional," the girl said, beginning to recover herself and speaking with more poise.

"I don't know what your plans may be," Hal said, "but may I offer you a coffee, or a beer, or a sandwich, or something?"

Momentarily, Hal could see that the girl hesitated, not knowing what she might be getting herself into.

"No strings attached," he said quickly. "I've been on trains for the past two days and haven't spoken to a soul the entire time. My name's Hal Goff. I went to school here myself and only graduated in '40, in history."

"But you're now in the Navy?" the girl inquired.

"Yes," Hal said, "just back from the Pacific."

"I'm Bianca Colombo," the girl said, showing him a straightforward expression. "My friends call me Bea, and you may too, if you like. I came in for a coffee because I've just spent a long afternoon at the library and need some fortification before I go back to it. I don't know about you, but reading Laurence Sterne has been a bit of a trial, if you see what I mean."

"I'm sorry to say that I've never read Sterne," Hal laughed, "so I'll take your word for it. And please, you just sit tight. The coffee's on me. Cream and sugar?"

"No," Bea said with a smile. "Thank you, but I'll take it black, for the fortification it promises."

"So," Hal said, returning to the table a few minutes later with two coffees and setting a mug in front of her before once more taking up his sandwich, "are you from Illinois originally or from out of state?"

"I was born and raised in Herrin," Bea said, sipping her coffee, "down near Carbondale. There's a sizable Lombard community down there, all of them having come over from villages around Milan. My father and his brothers own a construction company. And you?"

"I grew up here," Hal said. "Went to Urbana High and started here at the U. of I. as soon as I graduated from high school."

"And you're home on leave?"

"In a manner of speaking," Hal said.

"In what manner of speaking?" Bea asked.

"My parents passed before I started college," Hal said, after swallowing a bite of his sandwich, "and the uncle who was raising me died during my senior year here, so for the length of my leave, I'm putting up with Celia Rogers, in the same boarding house where I lived during my college years. It's over on West Nevada Street, not far from here."

"One hears of sailors having a high time in places like San Francisco, Chicago, or New York," Bea said. "Why here? Why not one of those?"

"Ha," Hal grinned. "If I were only on leave for a day or two, one of those places would have done quite nicely, but even with three months' back pay, I don't know any ensigns who could afford twenty days in such expensive surroundings, unless, of course, they resorted to soup kitchens and sleeping on park benches."

"Point taken," Bea said, once more removing her lips from her coffee cup. "The Navy does not lavish you with money, then?"

"It does not," Hal laughed. "It doesn't make paupers of us, but it is not out to make millionaires of us either."

14

"So were you drafted?"

"I was not," Hal said.

"Pearl Harbor stimulated you to do your patriotic duty, then?"

Hal took a breath. "Hitler, Mussolini, and Tojo have to be stopped," Hal said firmly. "And that's all there is to it."

"I agree," Bea said. "And you were in the Pacific?"

"I was," Hal said.

"So how did you get back so soon? From what I've read in the newspapers, that thing at Guadalcanal continues to be a horror."

Hal hesitated. "The long and the short of it," he said finally, "is that my ship was sunk out from under me."

"Oh no!" Bea said, caught off guard and instantly exhaling. "Did everyone survive?"

Again, Hal hesitated. "No," he said at last, "only four of us."

"Oh my God!" Bea said, suddenly stretching out her arm and touching his hand, her face contorting. "Oh my God! I'm *so* sorry. I'm so, so sorry. I ..."

"There's no way under the sun that you could have had any idea," Hal said, giving her hand a reassuring touch. "It's a lamentable fact, and painful, but there's a war on, and whether we like it or not, such things happen. We have no choice but to pick ourselves up and keep going. That's why Hitler and Tojo have to be stopped. It's the only way any of us are ever going to get back to normal."

Momentarily, there was silence between them, Bea shaking a little.

"My parents," she said finally, "and everyone I know in Herrin absolutely hate Mussolini. Before he came to power, apparently, most of them used to go back every year or two to visit family, but once he was made prime minister, none of them would ever go back again, and that's when my parents put in their papers to become American citizens."

"I know plenty of Germans who feel exactly the same way about Hitler," Hal said. "They believe him to be the most evil disaster to strike mankind in their lifetimes."

"Yes," Bea said finally, "I think he's even worse than Mussolini. So, if I may change the subject, where do you go from here, after your leave ends?"

"Truth told," Hal said, altering his expression to a grin and giving his head a slight shake, "I don't know. After my twenty days are up, I have to report to headquarters in Norfolk for reassignment, but from there, I don't have a clue where they might send me. And you, where are you in your course?"

"Barely started," Bea said, looking up and recovering some of her composure. "I only graduated in December, so I'm merely weeks into my course, leading, I hope, to an eventual Master's in English. If I do well—if I don't make a hash of it—I might convince my parents to allow me to go on for an eventual Ph.D. I think I'd like to teach somewhere, in a small college perhaps."

"It might surprise you to hear me say so," Hal said, "but that's what I had in mind as a career path for myself. I'd had my sights set on a Master's in history and a small college as well, but the frank fact is that I didn't have the money to continue, and with the war coming on, all of my plans went on hold. Later, perhaps, I'll be able to get back to them."

"You're joking about the teaching career, aren't you?" Bea said, a quizzical smile shaping her lips.

"No," Hal said, feeling slightly taken back by the question, "I'm not. What makes you think I'm not serious?"

"Oh, nothing in particular," Bea said at once, hastening to cover her misstep. "It's just that most of the men I've talked to keep going on about establishing a business, making advances in engineering, or doing successful coaching in sports. You're the first man I've met who has honestly talked about college teaching."

"But, I gather, you've met one or two who've talked about it dishonestly?" Hal joked.

16

"Well, at least one," Bea grinned. "And his motives were as dishonest as his claim."

"Small wonder," Hal said, "but mine aren't. Two or three times while I did my years here I found myself invited into professors' homes, and from what I could see, the lifestyles they led looked more than attractive, particularly when the subjects that they taught continued to hold their interest."

"You mean as long as they had a passion for what they were teaching?" Bea asked.

"Yes," Hal said, taking a bite from his pickle. "You have that kind of passion for literature, do you?"

"I do," Bea said, the pleasure she took in her subject suffusing her face. "And are you that way about history?"

"I certainly was while still in school," Hal affirmed, "but at the moment, I seem to be living it rather than studying it as a subject."

"Can't be avoided, I suspect," Bea said.

"No," Hal said.

"Speaking of which," Bea said, taking a last sip of her coffee, "if I'm to avoid a disaster on tomorrow afternoon's exam, I'd best get back to the library and press ahead with *Tristram Shandy*."

"Pity," Hal said.

"Yes," Bea said, starting to gather her books, "but there's nothing for it. Do I must or suffer the consequences."

"I think you've hit upon the inevitable," Hal laughed. "Mind if I walk you back?"

"Not in the least," Bea said, tucking her scarf around her chin while the combo launched into a slow-moving version of "Moonlight Serenade."

"Might you be free tomorrow night?" Hal asked as the two emerged from Pren's and started toward the library.

"I might be," Bea said, after taking a moment to consider. "What did you have in mind?"

"Dinner?" Hal said. "A movie? A campus event? Whatever might be to your taste."

"Just as long as it doesn't break your bank and throw you onto the street, I think," Bea said. "I shouldn't like to be responsible, Mr. Goff, for causing you to freeze on a park bench hereabouts."

Hal laughed. "I said that the Navy doesn't make us millionaires," Hal said, "not that it leaves us destitute. Suppose we say dinner?"

"Lovely," Bea said. "Around sevenish?"

"Perfect," Hal said. "So where do I fetch you?"

"614 Washington," Bea said pertly, "at Mrs. Frear's. That's about one block over from where you're staying with Mrs. Rogers."

"Why, how very convenient," Hal grinned.

"Yes, isn't it," Bea said, showing him a subtle smile.

Because it snowed again lightly the following night, and because the two of them were necessarily walking, Hal took Bea to Skaggs for dinner. Located just off Green Street but to the southeast of what the students had always called "Campus Town," Skaggs had been in business since the turn of the century but happened to be an establishment in whose surroundings Hal had never before taken a meal. Neither elegant nor inelegant, neither expensive nor inexpensive, Hal knew Skaggs to be a place the faculty often frequented when they wanted both a bottle of wine and a good meal at a moderate cost. As a student, the French cuisine which the restaurant advertised had been beyond his means; now, with three months' back pay in his pocket and a young woman who seemed more than worth the expenditure, Hal had no hesitation in guiding Bea through the entrance and taking up the table that had been reserved for them.

"I've heard of Skaggs," Bea said, unfolding her napkin, "but I've never been here before. What do you recommend?"

"I think we're going to have to wait to see the menu," Hal chuckled. "This is my first time as well. As a student, I wouldn't have dared to show my face in here. I don't know whether or not you can tolerate wine, but would you care to split a bottle?"

Bea laughed. "I'm Italian, Hal. My father and his brothers buy their grapes from a vineyard in New York and put up eight barrels each year. I can not only tolerate wine, but I've seen it made. I've been drinking wine with meals since I was three."

"Bless you," Hal smiled. "Have you a preference?"

"The closest thing to the wine we make seems to be Zinfandel," Bea said. "So suppose we go for something different and opt for white? An inexpensive Chablis, I think, or a Chardonnay won't break the bank, and I doubt that either would make us walk away with a wobble."

"You're on," Hal said.

"Have you enough French to deal with the menu?" Hal asked when their waiter appeared.

"*Fruits de mer* translates as Fruits of the Sea," Bea said, "which must mean fish, scallops, shrimp, and so forth."

"And *canard* is duck," Hal said. "Ever had any? Covered with kirsch-soaked Morello cherries?"

"Never," Bea said. "Sounds perfectly delicious, don't you think?"

"With souffles to finish?" Hal asked.

"Perhaps *a* souffle, with two spoons," Bea said. "I hope I'm not vain about my waistline, but I shouldn't like to waddle out of here any more than I wish to wobble."

They sat for three hours over the meal that Skaggs prepared for them that evening, talking easily, enjoying the duck, the souffle, and the wine, and only started back after they'd finished the last drop of what had turned out to be, as Bea had foretold, an inexpensive but thoroughly satisfying bottle of Chardonnay.

"Thank you," Bea said as the two raised the collars of their coats and walked away from Skaggs beneath more of the lightly falling snow. "That's the best meal I've had since first coming up to Urbana."

"Beats breakfast at the drag house, does it?" Hal quipped.

"Whatever are you talking about?" Bea said, a confused expression coloring her voice.

"Mrs. Frear's," Hal said. "She doesn't wake you each morning with a cup of coffee and a hot buttered croissant?"

"No, she most certainly does not," Bea laughed, "but where does the word *drag* come into it?"

"Ah," Hal said. "Sorry, got beyond myself. Met a brother officer at Tulagi, an Annapolis man. Dating at Annapolis is apparently called 'dragging.' Because, I think, the midshipmen and their dates have to walk everywhere. Girls who go up to West Point for a weekend apparently put up in some kind of ritzy hotel when they stay overnight. The girls who go down to Annapolis for a weekend apparently stay in boarding houses run by sweet elderly women like Mrs. Rogers and Mrs. Frear, and the boarding houses are therefore called 'drag houses.' One imagines a circus arrangement with five or six girls all bunking in attic rooms and trying to put on their makeup in front of a single mirror."

"Sounds appalling," Bea laughed. "I've heard of Flirtation Walk and the high jinks that the cadets and their girls get up to there. Does Annapolis have something like that too?"

"I think not," Hal said. "Apparently, public display of affection— and that would include even allowing a girl to go so far as to take one's arm while walking across ice or through snow—will result in a midshipman being instantly put on report and assigned a punishment tour. Not to worry, however, because from what my friend said, the parlors in those drag houses are old, dark, and only dimly lighted."

"Rather like the parlor at Mrs. Frier's," Bea laughed.

"Oh," Hal said, "I didn't know."

"I'm pleased to say," Bea said, "that the three of us who live at Mrs. Frier's have each a private room and a private mirror, so at least we have that advantage over those drag houses that you have mentioned, but I think it only fair to tell you that Beth and Sally, the other two boarders, both of them seniors, refer to our parlor as their *web*. But then," she said, drawing an immediate laugh from Hal, "what else could one expect from a couple of undergraduates?"

❧

On the following evening, during a two-hour break from Bea's studies, Hal took her to see the Veronica Lake and Frederick March comedy *I Married a Witch* at the CO-ED Theater in Campus Town; the day after, because Bea had research to do and a paper to write, the two limited their time together to a long lunch taken at Pren's. On Hal's fifth evening back in Urbana, the two once more had dinner together, this one more modest than the meal they'd shared at Skaggs, and then took in a performance of two one-act plays staged by students from the university's drama department.

"Tomorrow?" Hal asked as he prepared to leave Bea standing in the *web* at Mrs. Frier's.

"Can we do lunch again, at Pren's?" Bea asked. "I have another paper due and that means hours in the library before I can even begin to write."

"Fetch you at eleven o'clock, here?" Hal asked.

"Yes," Bea said, reaching up and kissing him lightly, much to Hal's surprise. "I'll be ready."

But on the following day when Hal arrived at Mrs. Frier's, Bea wasn't ready. In fact, she wasn't even in the room. She was gone.

"She received a telegram late last night," Mrs. Frier said, "summoning her home. There's been a death in her family. She took the early train this morning. Beth is going to inform her professors, but she's left this envelope for you, Mr. Goff. What with your leave ticking away as it is … well, I'm sorry for the both of you."

"Not to worry," Hal said. "She had to go, of course. I absolutely understand that."

"I have Mrs. Rogers' telephone number," Mrs. Frier said, "and I imagine that Bea will call you the moment she returns. I rather think you've struck a spark there. Bea's spirits seemed to have brightened since you arrived."

"Thank you for the thought," Hal said. "I'm sure that I don't have to tell you that she's brightened mine in the same way."

For the six days that passed before Bea returned, Hal cooled his heels, literally, for with the steady dusting of snow which seemed to sweep nightly over Champaign-Urbana the temperature hovered below freezing. Hal had no choice but to make the best of it, and he did, going to hear a chamber group play selections from the Brandenburg Concertos on one evening, watching the Chicago Blackhawks play an exhibition hockey match against an Illini club on another, and once, even with the snow falling, walking all the way to Urbana's Princess Theater to see Spencer Tracy in *Northwest Passage*. Other nights, following a hastily taken supper at Pren's, he seemed content to sit, relax, and drink a few beers while listening to whatever pickup band happened to be playing for the evening. Things weren't as exciting, he knew, as they might have been in New York, Chicago, or San Francisco, but after thinking the matter over, Hal decided that he didn't care. For the time being, after Tulagi and the sinking of the *Akonapi*, they were, he thought, exactly what he needed, or would be once Bea returned.

Bea, Hal realized within hours of her departure, had dropped upon him, figuratively as well as literally, like some kind of gift from the heavens. Upon his arrival in Urbana, as he had stepped from the train and gone in search of temporary lodgings with

Celia Rogers, his first encounter with Bea had been the last thing that he could have imagined. He had not returned to Urbana looking for a girl, romance, or anything of the sort. What he'd wanted, what he'd needed, amounted to nothing more than a refuge, a retreat, a place to which he could withdraw in order to lick his wounds and put his head back together before the next unheralded onslaught which the war threw in his path. Bea had turned out to be a gift, and as far as Hal was concerned, he didn't feel the least bit inclined to look the gift horse in the mouth. Moderating the warmth he felt when his thoughts continually turned back for her as he looked forward to her return, he waited with all the patience he could muster but silently cursed the swiftly moving hands on the clock.

Six days after Bea had gone away, Hal returned not long after sundown to an early meal at Pren's with the expectation of spending the remainder of his evening reading the first volume of Winston Churchill's *The World Crisis* which he'd picked up earlier in the day and left resting on the end table beside his bed. But before he could even reach for the handle of the outer door, the interior door opened, and Mrs. Rogers spoke to him at once through the screen.

"Your young lady has returned," she said forthrightly. "She called about half an hour ago, and she would like to see you."

"At Mrs. Frier's?" Hal asked.

"Yes," said Mrs. Rogers.

"I'll go right over," Hal said, starting to turn.

"Mr. Goff," Mrs. Rogers called out.

"Yes?" Hal said, turning back.

"At times like this," Mrs. Rogers said after a moment's hesitation, "extending a little comfort is sometimes the best medicine."

"Yes. Thank you," Hal said. "I'll do my best."

As far as Hal could tell, Bea had been sitting quietly in the *web* when Mrs. Frier first opened the door for him and directed him toward the parlor. But aside from the three steps he took toward the hall entrance, Hal never got there before Bea rushed into the foyer and threw herself into his arms, hugging him to her and continuing to hold him with more strength than he'd imagined that she possessed. Mrs. Rogers had been right—a little comfort was needed—and to the best of his ability, Hal returned the comfort that was called for, holding Bea as tightly as he dared while feeling her quiver against him.

"It must have been bad," he said gently, finally, without letting her go. "Want to tell me about it?"

"It *was* bad," she whispered in his ear, "very bad, but it's better now, now that you're here."

Under any other circumstances, Bea's sudden declaration might have surprised Hal, or even shocked him, but given the week he knew she'd just been through, he imagined that her words had been stimulated by her grief and elected not to question them.

"Would you perhaps feel a mite better sitting down?" Hal asked.

"No," she said, refusing to let him go. "No, I just want you to hold me for a minute longer, and then I want to walk. I need to be outside."

"All right," Hal said, quietly continuing to hold her in a way that bound her to him and would convey whatever comfort she sought from him.

By that time, Mrs. Frier had diplomatically retired to the kitchen, and when Bea finally became aware that her landlady had gone and that the two of them were alone, she suddenly lifted her arms up around Hal's neck, drew his head down, and kissed him so passionately that she nearly threw the two of them off balance.

"Goodness!" Hal said with a smile when she finally eased her embrace.

"You won't know it," Bea said, once more hugging him tight with her cheek to his chest, "but thinking that I would be coming back here to you is what has gotten me through this past week."

24

"That's very thoughtful, I'm sure," Hal said. "If I'd had the slightest inkling that you had need of me, I would have taken the train down and tried to stand beside you."

"That makes you a dear for saying so," Bea said, kissing him once more, releasing him, lifting her coat from the coat tree, and slipping it on. "Let's go out and walk, and I'll try to tell you about it."

Moments later, hatted and gloved, at the foot of the steps where they started to walk, Bea took Hal's arm and said, "You were right. It was bad, *very* bad. In fact, it was pure hell. She was my cousin, Concetta Colombo, Connie to those of us who loved her. We were fourteen months apart, Connie being a year older and a year ahead of me in school, but we were raised together from the time we were infants, so she was as close to me as a sister. I'm going to miss her terribly."

"I'm sorry," Hal said, knowing even as he said it that it didn't help and that he really didn't have a thing to say that would.

"My aunt and uncle are beside themselves, as you can imagine, but there wasn't a thing that they or any of us could do. Connie had rheumatic fever, you see, as a child, and her heart simply gave out. On Wednesday she seemed fit as a fiddle and went straight in to work in the same way that she had been doing for the past six months. She was a loan officer at the Williamson County Bank, fresh out of Southern Illinois in Carbondale with a good degree in business. Her fiancé picked her up for lunch, and the two of them went to the Illinois Cafe which is a favorite in Herrin, and she'd no more than ordered when she suddenly collapsed. The owner called an ambulance, and they took her straight to the hospital. There she lingered for an hour or two, and then she was gone."

Once more, as Bea broke into sobs, Hal folded her to him and held her. "I'm sorry," he said again, and felt crushed, knowing that he could do no more.

After a minute or two, Bea recovered herself, let Hal release her, wiped her eyes, and took his arm so that they could resume walking.

"The great pity is that she had so much to live for," Bea said. "She and Al were to be married in June, at San Carlo Catholic Church in Herrin, and they'd already planned to honeymoon in Florida. Al is superintendent at Peabody's No. 9 mine outside Marion, so he's well paid and had already sent in a down payment for their house. Connie's job as a bank officer may have been entry level, but according to my father, he thought she would probably be president there by the time was thirty-five, given what the stockholders had told him. I could go on about it, but I won't. For our family, it is simply a tragedy, which is the best that can be said about it, and I don't suppose that any of us will ever fully recover from it."

"Time is a great healer," Hal said, speaking softly, knowing that he had merely voiced a platitude.

"Has time made a difference to you?" Bea asked. "With regard to the loss of your ship?"

Bea's question suddenly made Hal think about Ted Hyde and the rest of the crew with whom he'd served aboard the *Akonapi*.

"Some," Hal said truthfully, "but I don't suppose anyone can shed something like that wholly. We just have to live with it and go on."

"Yes," Bea said, "and that's the same conclusion I reached. I never knew most of my grandparents, Hal. They remained in Italy and died there. I only learned to love them at a distance by looking at their pictures. And in my lifetime at least, we've never had another death in the family, so this was my first, and I won't deny that it has hit me hard. We all know about death early on: we read about it in books, we see it in the movies, hear about it on the radio, and know when people in our neighborhoods pass away, but knowing about a thing intellectually is a far cry from knowing it experientially."

"I won't deny that," Hal said.

"I guess what I'm trying to say," Bea continued, "is that Connie's death struck me like a bolt of lightning. I told you before we left the house that I couldn't have gotten through this week without you. You probably thought that I was just repeating something I'd heard or giving in to my pain and letting my misery speak for me, but that isn't the case. Whether we like it or not, bolts of lightning change things. Call it a residual effect if you like, but Connie taught me a lot of things before she died, and now she's taught me one more, and that may be the most important lesson she's ever given me. Life is short, and therefore we'd better make the best of it while we have it because none of us knows how long it is going to last. Eleven days ago when I stumbled into you, I'd never heard of you or even imagined you. I didn't ask for you to appear so suddenly out of nowhere, and if I'd been asked before you did if I wanted someone like you to come into my life, I would have said *no*. I'm just starting grad school, and I've miles to travel before I get where I'm going, but without warning, here you are. Taking this in, are you?" she said, turning and facing him.

"You have my attention," Hal said, showing her a straight face.

"Well," Bea said, "my point is this. Life is for the living. Five days might not count as much for most people, but the five days we spent together—even the snatched lunches at Pren's, before I went down to Herrin for Connie's funeral—were enough for me. I love you, Hal Goff, and I want you to know it right now. I don't know where this war is going to take you, but wherever it does, when it's over, I want you coming right back here to me so that I can hold you and never let you go."

Hal smiled. "Let's call it a bargain," he said, once more opening his arms so as to provide her with the warmth and safe harbor she sought.

Over yet another supper at Skaggs the following evening, sharing a bottle of Cabernet with a Calvados to follow the *fruits de mer*, they talked about marriage. Both of them wanted to marry—and the sooner the better. At the same time, they recognized that probably the last thing that Bea's family could tolerate at the moment—her parents, aunts, uncles, brothers, and cousins—was an upheaval of the kind that a marriage based upon only six days of acquaintance would produce for them.

"It pains me to say so," Hal said, "but we'd best wait. Your family has experienced all of the heart issues it can stand for one year, and I'm sorry to touch the subject, Bea, but the announcement of a sudden marriage like the one we're talking about might lead to another for which we'd have to bear the responsibility, and that really would be hell."

"I know," she said. "I know, and I wish it weren't so, but it is what it is, isn't it?"

"I'm afraid so," Hal said, looking deep into her eyes and squeezing her hand.

"So *when*, do you think?" Bea asked.

"First things first, and steady as we go," Hal said. "I'll have to get down to Norfolk and find out what the Navy has in store for me, and before I go, there is no way of knowing. At the top of the list, they could send me as an instructor to some place like Great Lakes or to some training facility right here in the States. Next down the line would be some shore assignment on one of the coasts. Next down the line from that might be sea duty on one of the coasts, and after that, we have to face the fact that the most probable assignment would be some billet at sea somewhere abroad in one of the war zones. There is no way of knowing, and I am so far down the totem pole as an ensign that my only recourse is to go where they send me and do it with a smile on my face. If I knew someone who had influence—and I do not—even a mild request might just as well land me in Greenland or the tip of Tierra del Fuego. According to the Navy, they don't issue wives and make very few allowances for them. Truth told, we have a job to do, and the last thing the Navy will tolerate, and something I couldn't tolerate in myself, is a slacker."

"I think I understand that," Bea said, "and from what I already know about you, you couldn't stand yourself if you held back in any way, so I wouldn't expect you to. And that brings me back to my original question: *when*?"

"Break the news to your family when you think the time is right," Hal said, "and then, I'll marry you the moment I get a leave or come ashore from wherever it is that they've decided to send me. Is that fair enough?"

"Let's call it a bargain," Bea said.

After that, their days passed all too swiftly. Out of necessity, Bea studied in the mornings, often rising at 4:00 am in order to complete everything that she had to prepare before her afternoon classes, but her evenings she reserved for Hal, regardless of the time it might set her back. Twice more they dined at Skaggs, twice more they attended concerts at the music school, and early in the evening they twice took in relatively new movies at the CO-ED. Without turning the *web* into an actual bordello, they did turn it into a sort of necking pit where, with restraint, they couldn't get enough of each other. Then, all too suddenly, it was over, Hal's leave, and they found themselves standing on the platform of the train station in Champaign, less than a minute before Hal was to board for his journey to Norfolk.

"I love you. Come back to me," Bea said, holding him tightly.

"It's a promise," Hal said.

And then, following a hug and a lingering kiss, he hoisted his B-four bag, turned, and disappeared up the steps into a Pullman coach for the long ride.

3

Norfolk, when Hal stepped off the train, seemed to be socked in by a thick winter fog of the kind that chilled to the bone while dripping condensation everywhere. In some ways, Hal thought, Virginia humidity felt colder and more penetrating than the freezing temperatures thrown off by Illinois' ice and snow, although in making that assumption he left off the icy winds that blew through Chicago from the depths of Lake Michigan.

"Always like this, is it?" Hal quizzed the cabbie who drove him to Naval Headquarters.

"Winters is like to freeze your balls off," the cabbie said, "worse than North Dakota."

About that Hal harbored some doubts, but when the cab drew up before the massive personnel headquarters to which the Marine gate guard had directed him, Hal paid the driver what he owed him, snatched up his B-four bag, and made a beeline for the entrance. Inside, after checking in and handing over his travel orders to one of the yeomen manning what amounted to a long reception desk, he found himself directed upstairs to the office of a Lieutenant Peale with an additional warning from the yeoman that amounted to "Mums the word, Sir, but be careful that he don't peel the hide off you 'cause he can be a nasty bit of work, Mr. Peale, an' he ain't on his best behavior today. His wife dumped him last week, an' he's been on a tear e'er since."

Oh great, Hal thought. "Thanks for the warning," he said to the sailor. "I'll try to keep my mouth shut."

Upstairs, Hal knocked once on a frosted glass door which carried Peale's nameplate. Hal knocked once, entered, and announced himself by saying, "Ensign Harold Goff USNR, reporting for reassignment, Sir."

"And expecting that Purple Heart you're wearing to get you some kind of cushy assignment?" the man behind the desk barked, without rising, without extending his hand, without a smile of welcome, and without a response any less sharp than his tongue.

"No Sir," Hal said, remaining braced up but taking in the man before him—small, with darting weasel eyes that barely glanced in Hal's direction while showing him nothing more than a sneer of distaste.

"Right," Peale snapped, nearly hurling a manila envelope at Hal across the top of his desk. "Pretty ribbons don't mean a goddamn thing around here. *Well*, aren't you even going to pick 'em up? Those are your orders!"

"Yes Sir," Hal said, reaching forward and taking up the envelope, wondering if he was supposed to examine it or merely hold it until Peale gave him yet another order.

"Oh, for *Christ's sake*," Peale snapped again before Hal even had time to glance at the envelope in his hand. "Don't you even want to know where you're going, you dimwit? But save it, because I'll tell you. You're going straight back to sea in a heartbeat, straight back down to Pier 3 where you are going to report aboard *LST-198*, and on that miserable son-of-a-bitch, you're going to cross the Atlantic, thread the Straits of Gibraltar, and show up eventually—if one of those German or Italian bastards doesn't sink you—in Tunisia where the Navy Department, in an obvious moment of complete idiocy, is making the mistake of sending you aboard a rescue tug, *ATR-3X*, as the executive officer. What the dunderheads at the Navy Department must be thinking by doing so defies imagination, so get your ass in gear, get the fuck down to the *198*, and I hope the roll on that bastard keeps all of you sick all the way to Sfax. Now, Mister, get the fuck out of my office!"

Without altering the expression on his face, Hal saluted, did an about face, and left Peale's office.

"You were right," Hal grinned at the yeoman as he walked past the reception desk. "I'd have to think he was the most perfect asshole I've ever met."

"Yes Sir," the yeoman laughed. "Same conclusion the rest of us have reached."

☙

It was another sixteen days before *LST-198* got underway, and not until a substantial convoy had formed. With the zigzag and one major course change to elude a potential Nazi wolf pack that was rumored to be forming north of their track, the 4,700-mile transit from Norfolk to Sfax required nearly eighteen days while steaming at what Hal considered to be the moderate speed of 12 knots. In truth, the *198*, according to her specs, wasn't capable of a great deal more, her top speed hovering around 16 knots. With some of the merchant carriers in the convoy doing well to make 14 knots going all out, the convoy's commodore, a retired Navy captain dragooned back into service, set 12 knots as a reasonable cruising speed. And so, it turned out to be the middle of March before the sixty-three-ship convoy reached and began to disperse into their various destinations along the North African coast.

In looking back, and regardless of the constant roll that the *198* experienced, Hal hadn't found the trip trying. The captain of the LST—a lieutenant named Alberts, another reserve officer and a graduate of Rutgers—had been congenial enough, and owing to Hal's former experience had shown no hesitation about integrating him into the watch bill for the voyage. So for eight hours a day, by standing one in three, Hal honed his skills as a watch stander on the bridge, enjoyed lively conversation with the other ship's officers during meals in the wardroom, and when not on watch, either wrote long letters to Bea or read Churchill and came to the conclusion that aside from all of the British prime minister's other apparent talents, he seemed to be a fairly fine historian with a powerful command of the English language.

The cargo that *LST-198* carried to North Africa seemed to consist mostly of Sherman tanks and a bevy of Diamond T 6 × 6 trucks, all of them pre-loaded with either dry rations or non-perishable medical supplies that, sooner or later, would be needed somewhere in the European theater of war. Where that might be turned into a matter of considerable speculation in the wardroom of the LST. The *198*'s chief engineer, a lieutenant junior grade named Driscoll, thought it would be Southern France, whereas the communications officer seemed convinced that the next invasion would go in across the beaches of either Sardinia or Corsica, and the operations officer opted for some place like Corfu in Greece. Wisely, the captain and the executive officer refused to speculate, and as far as Hal was concerned, he imagined that the most direct route into Europe would take them either through Sicily or some point on the Italian boot. Discussion of the subject proved endless and went so far that an anchor pool was arranged, each man putting down a dollar against which geographical location would be selected and another dollar to cover the date speculated for whatever invasion eventually took place.

"What about a third pool?" the first lieutenant ventured. "We could each put a dollar down against how many German POW's we'll carry back to the States once whatever invasion we're going to make comes to an end."

"I think," Driscoll laughed, "that you might be stretching your greed a mite too far. We may just as easily be carrying back wounded, and I don't think we ought to place bets on that."

"No," said the first lieutenant. "Point taken."

Eventually, around March 25, in company with no more of the convoy than the fourteen ships that had continued to steam together past Algiers, Oran, Bizerte, and Cape Bon, the remains of the convoy reached Sousse, entered the small but packed port, and dispersed to a variety of berths. There, finally, no more than one hundred yards up the sea wall, Hal spotted his new ship, *ATR-3X*, tied up outboard in a nest with two other rescue tugs, both of them moored alongside a much larger fleet tug—a steel-rather than wooden-hulled ATF which he imagined to be carrying the senior officer in the group. After thanking the *198*'s captain for his hospitality and saying a swift goodbye to the other officers with whom he'd shared his meals, Hal once more picked up his B-four bag, left the ship, and went forward to greet his fate.

Second class petty officers happened to be standing in port officer of the deck watches aboard the ATF and the two ATRs that Hal crossed to reach the *3X*. On *ATR-3X*, a bona fide first class quartermaster who named himself Keller seemed to be standing the deck; it was to Keller that Hal handed his orders following an obligatory exchange of salutes and names.

"I'll send 'em straight to the ship's yeoman," Keller said, taking the packet of orders and travel vouchers that Hal handed him, "and welcome aboard, Sir. She ain't large, the *3X*, but she's home. Vega," he said, speaking quickly to his messenger, "show Mr. Goff straight up to the captain, and then drop his orders in the ship's office."

Vega, a runt of a sailor who nevertheless made up for what he lacked in size with the immensity of his mustache, seized Hal's orders and virtually leapt, and in the following second,

Hal started to move with speed as the kid darted through a hatch and started up a ladder toward the compartments above the main deck.

When Hal first met Lieutenant Joseph Bender, captain of the 3X, he reasoned that he couldn't have been a lieutenant very long. The gold lace on the sleeves of his uniform blues, hanging suspended from a hook on the bulkhead beside him, looked brand new, as though his stripes had been sewn on mere days or, at the most, weeks before. Unlike Peale, Jos Bender greeted Hal with a smile, rose from the chair in which he'd been sitting, shook Hal's hand vigorously, and barely avoided cracking his head against an overhead light fixture when he did so. If Bender didn't stand six inches over six feet, Hal reasoned, he stood five and a half, and Hal couldn't remember ever seeing an officer so tall anywhere during the previous year of his service. In addition to the man's height, his face appeared both long and thin, the dark eyes close set, the nose sharp, the thin lips covering a set of choppers that must have rivaled a beaver's. Taken whole, Bender seemed about as homely a man as Hal had ever faced, but when the man spoke, he spoke with warmth in a way that heralded a gregarious nature and had the effect of making Hal feel immediately at home with the man who would be commanding him.

"Seat yourself and take a load off your feet," Bender said, sitting back down in his chair while indicating that Hal should sit on the fold-down couch that stretched fore and aft beside his desk. "Good voyage over?"

"Yes Sir," Hal said.

"Roll a bit, did she, that LST?"

"Rolled a lot, Sir," Hal said with a smile, "day and night one might almost say."

Bender laughed. "Rode one myself, once," he said, "from Boston to Norfolk, and once was enough. At any minute, I about half expected her to go right on over and dump us all in the brine."

"Yes Sir," Hal laughed, "that was my expectation as well. We hit rough water west of Gibraltar, and for a while there, it seemed touch and go. Does the *3X* roll like that?"

"She rolls, sure enough," Bender laughed, "but within reason."

"A reasonable animal is always the best kind," Hal ventured, showing the man a grin.

"Right," Bender said, responding in kind before turning his attention to a message resting on his desk. "The Navy was good enough to send me a spot of advanced information about you, so let's touch base on it."

"Yes Sir," Hal said, becoming serious.

"Graduate of the University of Illinois in history, graduate of the midshipman school in New York with reasonably high marks, assigned duty as exec on *YP74A* in the Pacific, sunk owing to enemy action off Tulagi, recovery and convalescence at Balboa in San Diego, award of Purple Heart for wound in action, three weeks' convalescent leave … somewhere. That about right?"

"Yes Sir," Hal said.

"Good leave, was it? Feeling fit now?"

"Yes Sir," Hal said again.

"Good," Bender said, looking up from the message and once more studying Hal's face. "You're going to be my exec, as I expect you know, so here are my old shoulder boards and a pair of my old silver bars to go with them. You can get yourself over to the tender and have the sleeves of your blues re-striped as well. This tug rates a lieutenant, junior grade as an exec, so you're being spot promoted to fill the billet, with the appropriate rise in pay to go with the promotion.

Hal raised his eyebrows. He'd seen no reason to expect anything of the kind.

"Yes, well," Bender smiled. "Sounds good when you first hear it. Once you see the workload that goes with it, you may think twice about it. The man who preceded you and left only two days ago is going to a destroyer as a department head. And he thinks he's getting shuck of a load. He isn't, but we'll let him find out the truth when he gets there."

"Yes Sir," Hal grinned.

"So," Bender said, "if you've done duty on a YP, even the converted kind that your *74A* must have been, you already know something about tug duty. That right?"

"Yes Sir," Hal said, "as well as pushing ships in any number of places, the *74A* pulled plenty of barges and lighters from Tulagi to Guadalcanal and back."

"Right," Bender said. "That's what I'd imagined. We're bigger than your last tug, I'd wager, so let me give you a quick rundown of our specs: 852 tons, 165 feet in length, 33 feet in the beam, 15 feet 6 inches in draft, max speed at around 12 knots, and we're armed with a 3"/50 forward and two 20 mm Oerlikons behind the stack. We ain't a destroyer, but we can sting if we have to."

"If you don't mind me asking, Sir," Hal said, "where does the *X* come into it?"

"Yes, well," Bender said with a chuckle, "if you can believe it, the Navy in its wisdom installed a sonar on this one, as an experiment, and two K-guns back aft that I neglected to mention in my little run through of our weapons. As far as I'm concerned, the possibility that we should detect and run down a German U-boat or an Italian sub seems remote. Nevertheless, we're equipped for that kind of action, and if the occasion occurs, I intend to see it through. The other tugs with which we've operated don't have anything of the sort, so with regard to the sonar, we're different from the rest, hence the *X*, for *experimental*."

"My only experience with organizing an attack on a sub occurred during the dry runs we practiced at midshipman's school," Hal said.

"Not to worry," Bender said. "That's been my only experience as well, so if we ever do run into a U-boat, we'll do the best we can and hope that it's enough. Take my point?"

"Yes Sir," Hal nodded.

"Right," Bender said, instantly switching subjects. "Now, we're carrying a crew of forty-one men, one or two of whom have to be watched. They aren't criminals, mind you, but they do like to gamble. That Vega who brought you up here likes to run a crap game whenever he thinks he can get away with it, and if Vega's busy or on watch, we've got a slick seaman from Perth Amboy named Prince who thinks himself an ace poker player. So, if you come across either of those two running either of those pastimes, put a stop to them. As far as the rest of the crew, they're pretty straight and fairly well trained. We had high marks in refresher training before we came over here, and thus far, we've only had two men from the original crew transferred off the ship after promotions. Show 'em you know your stuff, and I don't think you'll have any trouble out of them."

Hal couldn't help wondering if he had what Bender had called "the stuff."

"With regard to officers," Bender went on, "there are five of us. Ensign Yaakov, Boris, is our third officer, and technically, for the billet, he's the designated gunnery officer. And beyond that, let the heavens be praised, we have two highly qualified warrant officers—Lewis, the chief boatswain who will be in charge of towing and everything else above the main deck, and Garcia, our chief machinist, who will cover everything below. Both of them have twenty years' service behind them, and as far as I'm concerned, they're worth their weight in gold. You, Yaakov, and I will handle bridge watches, navigation, operations, supply, and personnel, but with regard to just about everything else having to do with the *3X* itself, a word to one or the other of the chiefs ought to take care of it."

"That makes the two of them worth their weight in gold to be sure," Hal said.

"Right," Bender said. "Your squat is just across the passageway, so dump your gear in there, figure out how you're going to turn around in such a confined space, and then go out and acquaint yourself with the layout. Once you've done that, you can come back here, and the two of us will get to work."

"Yes Sir," Hal said, rising from his chair. "One question, Sir, if you don't mind?"

"Speak," Bender said.

"We're preparing for an invasion, are we?"

"Aside from the normal work we're assigned, yes," Bender said quickly, "but where we're to invade is a total unknown. We haven't heard a word about it yet, and if you make the mistake of listening to the rumors, you're liable to hear that we're going to invade everywhere from the coast of Portugal to the Beirut waterfront."

"Understood," Hal laughed. "They were already running anchor pools about it on the LST."

"And if Vega or Prince aren't trying to run one here," Bender said, "I'd be much surprised. From what I hear, they each made a packet off the pools they ran wagering when Eisenhower would declare the North African campaign secured."

ATR-3X, when Hal went out to look the ship over, held few surprises for him. Just above his and the captain's cabins he found the pilot house with all of the standard fittings, the quartermaster's shack, and the signalman's flag bag and signal light. Directly below but aft behind his own stateroom, he looked into the officer's bunk room, found it even more confining than his own cubbyhole, and rejoiced to think that he wouldn't be sleeping there. Below, starting forward, he walked back from the chain locker, the crew's head, the wardroom, and the galley, passing by the tiny sickbay before glancing into the crew's mess. Then he returned forward and descended below the main deck to take a look at the even more confined crew's quarters where the space between the closely hung tiers of aluminum and canvas bunks might have given a lesser man claustrophobia. A miniscule sonar compartment seemed to be installed just aft of the crew's quarters with both water and general storage compartments below those, and farther back aft, he found the boiler room, a machine shop, and the 1600 horsepower engine which propelled the tug. Finally, astern of the engine spaces, he came upon the magazine as well as a much larger compartment for storing an immense quantity of salvage and towing equipment. From the ubiquitous smell of fuel oil seeming to permeate everything, he knew the fuel tanks to be located beneath both.

In each space Hal entered he found men working, nodded by way of recognition, but didn't stop to talk with any of them. In the beginning, he thought, it would be best to maintain a degree of distance, give them a good look at him, let them adjust to a new face, and allow them some time to wonder what he might be like. Too much familiarity too soon wouldn't do any of them any good, not the crew and not him. Better in the beginning to let the men be a trifle wary of him and then ease up later when the adjustment had been achieved.

Curiously, his apparent underlings, Ensign Yaakov, Lewis, and Garcia, didn't appear to be aboard. Hal asked Bender about them when he finished his tour and returned to the captain's stateroom.

"Oh right," Bender said, with a shake of his head. "I should have mentioned it. They're off at the incinerator burning six months' worth of superseded classified material. You've done it yourself, I reckon, so you know the drill."

Hal knew the drill all right: list every single page to be destroyed on an interminably long burn report, crumple each page, throw it in a brown paper burn bag, seal the bag, arm one's self, collect a second armed individual to accompany you to the incinerator so as to verify in writing what the two of you have done, load the bags in a truck, drive them to the site, set them on fire, watch them burn, and then rake the ash so that not so much as a single shred of what had been on the pages remained intact. The degree of security involved nearly defied the imagination, and the job itself was something that a good cub scout could have accomplished, but which, in the Navy, fell to the lot of junior officers who hated its tedium with a passion. Hal himself had to do it at least four times during the time he'd spent on *YP74A*.

"They'll be hungry when they get back," Hal quipped.

"And thirsty," Bender said, "for the beer that we have no means to provide for them."

"To be sure," Hal said.

"Right," Bender said. "Ready to get to work? I've got three reports here for which you're going to have to prepare drafts. Two of them don't amount to much, but a semi-annual report on our ammunition storage means that you and Yaakov are going to have to inventory what we have on board."

Yaakov, Lewis, and Garcia—"The Happy Wanderers" as Bender referred to them when they got back—returned in time for lunch. It was over this lunch that Hal met his fellow officers and recognized that while the five of them ate in the wardroom, they also drew their food from the crew's mess, carrying their meals into the wardroom from the galley on stainless steel trays before sitting down around the table.

"We pay for our own rations in the same way that officers on larger ships do," Bender said, "but with our food pro-rated according to a formula that has been developed for smaller ships like ours, we're still getting off with lighter mess bills than we would pay on a destroyer or something bigger, and if you were wondering about having to double as the ship's supply officer, discard the notion. That falls under my supervision, regardless of my inclination."

Hal felt relieved but nevertheless imagined that more of it would fall under his own supervision than Bender was telling him.

Ensign Boris Yaakov—"Yak" to the others at the table—apparently came from the area around Scranton in eastern Pennsylvania where his father had mined coal for a living and where, prior to his acceptance into Penn State, Yak had also spent a year underground.

"Nothing for it," he said to Hal as the two exchanged words over the day's meatloaf. "I knew that if I wanted to get out of there I had to go to college, and if I intended going, I had to pay my own way because the folks didn't have the money to put me through. So, I went into the mine, and frankly, I hated it and hated being underground, but I made enough that way to get me through my first year. After that I managed to get a walk-on scholarship for football and worked summers above ground to pay my room and board."

"My grandfather mined coal in Illinois," Hal said. "And he was adamant about my father not having to do it, so Dad, when the time came, managed to get himself through two years in a commercial college and went into business. A millionaire he was not, but he made a living in insurance, and when my folks were killed, the policy he'd taken out left me with enough to finish my own degree. Your folks immigrated from Russia, did they?"

"They did," Yak said. "My father was apparently conscripted for the Russian army in World War I, fought and was wounded at Tannenberg, and then, somehow, managed to get himself and my mother on a ship out of Finland. He came here, settled around Scranton, and with no education beyond some kind of primary school and very little English to speak of, managed to wrangle the lowest job in the mine and worked his way up. A year after they got here, I was born in 1918, at about the same time as the Revolution occurred in Russia. Damn glad to have missed that, I don't mind telling you."

"Speak Russian, do you?" Hal asked.

"Yes," Yak said. "Grew up in a Russian neighborhood where everyone spoke the language. Didn't pick up English until I started school."

"How is it that you missed having an accent?" Hal asked.

"The older folks," Yak said. "They didn't have much English themselves, but they knew how the language was supposed to sound, and they'd get all over me if they heard a mistake."

Large, darkly complected with a heavy shadow of beard by the middle of the day, Boris Yaakov didn't seem to have a trace of what Hal would have imagined as Slavic features. But then, beyond a writer or two and a minimal smattering of Russian history, Hal didn't know much about the environment from which Yak's family had apparently immigrated.

With regard to Chief Lewis, Hal was surprised to learn that the man had grown up in Albuquerque, New Mexico whereas Garcia, who Hal might have expected to have Southwestern roots, had actually been born and raised in Omaha, Nebraska.

"Miles of corn, and all of it unending," Garcia said. "I found it and still find it the most boring landscape I've ever seen, unless a guy were to mention Iowa."

Hal laughed. "And how is it your family settled there?" he asked.

"From what my ole man said, and I ain't sure that he really knew, he figured my grandpa had been a cowboy and had gotten up there while drivin' a herd north from somewheres in Texas. But don't try to hold me to it 'cause I ain't got the slightest idea whether it's true or not. The old man, after his pa died, got on with the railroad, so that's where he stayed."

"And you," Hal asked Lewis, "how is it that your family came to settle in New Mexico?"

"The Army," Lewis said, mildly reticent, his voice gravelly. "I guess he joined up for that Spanish-Merican War but got stationed down ta Fort Bliss, in Tex-ese. Took his discharge 'fore New Mexico even become a state. Didn't like Tex-ese much. Too dusty. Got hisself up to Albuquerque, liked that well enough, an' stuck. Got hisself a job with the city and stayed on. Met and married my ma there, and I come along quick in the offing. So,

Mr. Goff, now that you've heard what we've got to say, what's your excuse?"

"Not much to it, I'm afraid," Hal said, and in the two minutes which followed, he gave them the same details that Bender had been over with him that morning.

"But you didn't have no trouble with them Jap aircraft off Guadalcanal?" Garcia asked when Hal thought he had finished. "Rumors we heard said they was plentiful."

"They were," Hal said, "and we saw several of them, but at a distance usually and to the west. They were after the big boys, don't you see—the destroyers, cruisers, and transports. We had 'em overhead at Tulagi on a couple of nights, dropping bombs by means of flares, but they were never after us. *YP74A* was too small to interest them."

"I wish we could say that about the *3X*," Yaakov chuckled. We had a couple of Italian Macchis try to strafe us as we came around Cape Bon."

"On the whole," Bender said with a twinkle, "we found them bad for the digestion. Tended to upset the men's stomachs, if you see what I mean."

"Small wonder," Hal said. "Fast, were they?"

"Sure seemed like it," Yaakov said. "Bix, the gunner on the starboard 20 mm, only expended about ten rounds in their direction, once we'd spotted 'em, and in the next second, they were gone."

"But you weren't hit?" Hal asked.

"By the grace of God," Lewis said. "Captain pulled a tight turn on 'em, and that give 'em the flummox, rounds spittin' into the sea."

"I'm guessing it was a wake-up call," Bender said. "Portent of things to come. Once we move north and try to invade somewhere, I'd imagine we're going to see a lot more of Macchis, Messerschmitts, or whatever. Germans are supposed to have a load of them on the airfields in Sicily and farther up the boot, and don't let any rumors about the *Regia Aeronautica* fool you. The Italians are good fliers, and from all we know, they come right at you. They've apparently pounded the hell out of Malta, so whether we go to Southern France, Sicily, Italy, or Greece, we're going to have to be on our guard. I want our gunners and lookouts primed and ready on their aircraft recognition because I sure don't want to have to explain how we came to shoot down a P-40, a C-47, or a Spitfire by mistake. You drill the men, Yak, but Hal, you're going to have to oversee what he's doing to be sure our people are up to speed on the subject."

"Yes Sir," Hal said, knowing at once that he would need to study a whole new array of silhouettes in order to be up to speed on German and Italian aircraft recognition himself.

"And do it quick," Bender said, "because we're apparently scheduled to make a run up to Bizerte the day after tomorrow."

That news, coming so unexpectedly, made everyone in the wardroom sit upright.

"Exactly," Bender said, having achieved the effect that he'd intended. "Thought that might get your attention. Had a message just before lunch from COMSERVFLT. Because we have a sonar, I assume, we're the designated leader of a three-tug squadron which will be escorting eight LCIs and an empty tanker, all of them coming north from Sfax as they return from whatever it is that they've been doing south of here. To put you fully in the picture, Hal, Cape Bon is only about eighty miles off the Sicilian coast and within easy range of any Italian or German aircraft stationed there. And Bizerte is only a hop, skip, and jump farther. We'll remain well within the swept channel, so that ought to keep the mines off of us, but it will behoove us all to be alert for U-boats and aircraft both, and I don't want any slip-ups. Frankly, Hal, how you made your own trip over here without running into anything along that stretch is beyond my comprehension."

"I think," Hal said, "that we were so well escorted by the destroyers that came over with us that the Krauts stayed away and the matter never came up. And we had some air cover too."

46

"Well," Bender continued, "for this run, we're about as close to a destroyer as the convoy is going to get, so best, I think, if we all play our parts up to the hilt and keep a sharp eye out for trouble. Brief your people, get 'em ready, and we're going to take in all lines and get underway at 0400."

⌒

Two days later, exactly as Bender had specified, they took in all lines, each of the three ATRs in the nest, and departed Sousse, swiftly picking up the oiler and the eight LCIs outside the breakwater. Hal—standing the first watch so that Bender could take a look at his ship-handling in the event that he didn't prove capable—took the *3X* out, demonstrating at once both to himself and to his new captain that he would have no trouble acting as a competent officer of the deck aboard a tug larger than the one upon which he'd formerly stood watches.

"Like the feel of her, do you?" Bender asked, the two of them standing side by side on the open bridge above the pilot house.

"Yes Sir, I do," Hal said flatly. "Less like a tuna boat and more like a ship, if you see what I mean."

"All in all, I think she handles pretty well," Bender said, showing more than a little pride in the vessel under his command. "I did a year on an armed trawler out of Boston before I got orders to the *3X*, and just between the two of us, I wouldn't trade the *3X* for that trawler in a million years. Bobbed like a cork and rolled like a barrel, the trawler. Damned glad to get off her, I was. Felt like a bit player or a fifth violin, if you see what I mean, and right out of the war altogether during that year, plodding back and forth, supposedly guarding the entrance to Boston harbor. Ships were being sunk all up and down the coast during that period, but we never saw anything more than channel buoys the whole time I remained aboard. This is different. For better or worse, the *3X* is in it. Our part may be small—I doubt very seriously that we're going to be called to take some shore target

47

under fire—but for what it's worth, we're going to contribute, and I think that's what it's all about. So, Mr. Goff, I can see that you're going to have no trouble handling our ship. How are you with communications, maneuvering boards, and celestial navigation?"

"I know you'll judge for yourself, Captain," Hal said deferentially, "but I managed to navigate the 74A from Hawaii to Port Moresby without getting us lost, and from Port Moresby to Guadalcanal. With regard to maneuvering boards, I think I know more than enough to work a solution for a station change that will keep us from being cut in half by a destroyer or a cruiser."

"I'll depend on it," Bender said. "And you think you can guard two radio circuits at once and still remember what each of them is sending out?"

"Done it many times," Hal said, showing Bender a smile.

"All right," Bender said. "Looks like we're in business. So, get on the horn and signal the other two tugs to take station port and starboard of the oiler. I'm going to hop down and make sure that sonar is manned, ready, and pinging. How the hell the Navy expects us to defend against a U-boat with the tacky equipment we're carrying is beyond me, but we'll give it our best shot and hope that's enough. What did you calculate in terms of time of arrival?"

"At 8 knots," Hal said, "with nearly 230 miles to go, I'd say that we ought to make Bizerte around 0900 tomorrow morning."

"As long as we don't run into trouble?"

"As long as we don't run into trouble," Hal said.

But they did run into trouble rounding Cape Bon. Not ten minutes after dawn the following morning, the starboard lookout spotted two Savoia-Marchetti bombers, nearly flat on the deck, coming straight at them from out of the northeast in the direction of Sicily. The lookout who spotted them and shouted the alarm had apparently looked at the silhouettes that Yak had drilled him on for long enough to make a positive identification. The gun crew on the 3″/50 moved heaven and hell to train their mount around in time to get off a round or two, the gunner's mate, and Bix—up early like everyone else to man the vessel's General Quarters' stations—responded exactly as he was supposed to do, instantly training his 20 mm on the incoming aircraft but waiting until Bender shouted "Batteries released" for the 20 mm to begin spitting out rounds.

Standing on the open bridge not three feet from Bender, and after having warned the little convoy by radio of an air attack to starboard, Hal had no choice but to wait and watch transfixed as the planes approached. It was instantly apparent to him that, having decided to make such an attack, they weren't aiming at the tugs but rather at the empty oiler, riding high not five hundred yards astern of the 3X. As a result, in the screen, given the angle of the Italian attack, only the 3X and the tug to starboard could bring their guns to bear. But if the Fascist pilots had expected something relatively easy that could give them a clear bomb run, they were in for a surprise. The Oerlikons and the 3″/50s on the LCIs astern of the oiler also opened fire on the two bombers, rounds and tracers going out to thwart them from a multitude of directions.

Much to Hal's surprise, nether of the Italian pilots sheared off as he had twice seen Jap bomber pilots do when they apparently thought themselves faced with too much anti-aircraft fire. Instead, both pilots simply dropped lower toward the sea and kept coming in hopes that the morning sun, flat on the horizon, would blind the gunners and permit them to carry out their attack. And to everyone's displeasure, it mostly did.

"*Shit!*" Bender barked. "That goddamn morning sun!"

Before the man could say anything else, the Italians were in among them, unloading two bombs each in a frantic attempt to skip them straight into the side of the tanker. The next second, as they shot up and roared over the target vessel, climbing for altitude, every 20 mm on the port side of the convoy did its best to pick them up and shoot

49

them down as they made their escape. The bombs—one of which Hal actually saw skip across the top of a wave and go flying out to port in the direction of the port side tug—exploded harmlessly no more than two hundred yards beyond the oiler's bow. The three others qualified as near misses, missing the ship but exploding within fifty yards of the vessel, huge plumes of water rising into the morning sunlight, each explosion ripping the air with a noise that sounded like a clap of doom. Given Hal's vantagepoint, it seemed like a near run thing, and it left him shaking and with a more than hollow feeling at the pit of his stomach.

"*Christ!*" he exclaimed when he found his voice.

"Yes," Bender said. "Too damn close for comfort by half, if you ask me. See what I mean about Italian pilots? And we didn't even get a piece of 'em, but all the same, be sure you commend the lookout and Bix for staying alert the way they did and giving it their best."

"Yes Sir," Hal nodded, trying to collect himself and stop his hands from shaking. "You don't think they'll come back?"

"That bomb that went skipping past the bow of the tanker looked pretty big to me," Bender said flatly. "I'd guess it was a thousand pounds or larger, and each of them dropped two, so I'd have to think they've shot their bolt for the morning. Two to one they'll go home and report that they sank a cruiser or a battleship."

Despite himself, Hal chuckled. "Good for a medal, do you think?"

"In the Italian air force, who knows?" Bender grinned.

But not all was well; the tanker didn't get off without damage, the force of the near misses popping welds somewhere. The captain of one of the leading LCIs astern of her called in to report that, while riding empty, the oiler had nevertheless started streaming a slight trail of oil behind her, and not long after that, the captain of the oiler also called and reported damage to two mostly empty fuel tanks below and behind her superstructure. The damage did not turn out to be extensive, and it didn't cut the oiler's speed by so much as a knot. Without hesitation, however, Bender ordered Hal to write a brief after-action report and radio ahead to Bizerte, alerting the salvage crews there to the fact that the oiler would need repairs upon arrival.

"One thing I'll have to say," Hal said, carrying the report he'd written for Bender's approval before he sent it off, "the Italians certainly employ the most original camouflage patterns I could ever have imagined. Do all of their planes look like those two?"

"No one ever said the Italians weren't the world's greatest artists," Bender laughed. "The stuff they've shown us in that regard has been absolutely stunning and totally original, and if they don't have a distant descendant of Michelangelo or Raphael designing those camouflage patterns for them, I'd be wholly surprised."

The 3X and her charges reached Bizerte without additional hindrance at almost precisely 0900 as expected, threaded their way up the narrow channel to the berths assigned them, and tied up well before 0930, the oiler and the LCI proceeding deeper into the harbor where repair crews awaited the tanker and where a nest had been designated alongside the sea wall for the LCIs.

"Know much about this place?" Yak said to Hal as the two of them sat down in the wardroom for a cup of coffee after securing the ship from sea.

"Not a lot," Hal said. "Read a short piece on it before we left Sousse. Settled by the Phoenicians sometime around 1100 BC, I think. Taken over by the Romans, and then the Vandals, and later by Islam, and eventually I think the Turks got hold of it. For a while, I think it was called something like Hippo Polis, or something like that."

"This the place where St. Augustine was Bishop of Hippo?" Yak asked.

"No," Hal said. "That Hippo was in Algeria, although I can't really say where."

"What I don't know about North Africa would fill volumes," Yak said. "Not exactly what we were given to study in school, if I'm not mistaken."

"No," Hal said, "not exactly. "Before I got to high school, I doubt that I could have spotted much beyond Egypt, the Congo, and South Africa on a map."

"Will we be allowed ashore, do you think?" Yak went on.

"According to the captain," Hal said, "yes. But every man that goes is to carry a French letter, if you take my meaning, and the men are going to have to show us that they have them before they leave the ship. The word is that VD is rampant here, or so the Navy supposes, and we sure don't want an epidemic of the clap or worse breaking out aboard, particularly without a doctor on board to treat it."

"Goes without saying," Yak laughed. "Court martial offense, if I'm not mistaken, although I don't think the powers that be take it that far very often. Wonder what the food's like ashore?"

"Probably not too bad," Hal mused. "I don't know much about Arab food, but I'm guessing that there must be plenty of French and Italian cooking available. As long as we don't drink the water and stick to beer or wine—if there isn't a prohibition against them around here, 'cause I don't think Moslems are supposed to drink—I'd say we'll be all right."

"Sounds good to me," Yak said, "but you're right about taking care. A case of amoebic dysentery wouldn't do any of us any good. Any word on how long we're to be here?"

"Apparently for a good long while," Bender said, having heard Yak's question while coming through the door with his own mug of coffee. "Message from COMSERVFLT, just came in. We won't be going back to Sousse. We're to stay here as a ready force to help any ship in that gets mugged between here and Oran."

"Shit," Yak said, "Oran's a far piece. That could expose us to every U-boat from here to Gibraltar, not to mention air attacks and whatever mines get loose and drift into the channel and are missed by the sweepers."

Bender laughed. "Yes," he said, "the troops are bound to be thrilled. Justification for earning combat pay, and all that. It'll give Bix and the rest of your gunners an opportunity to exercise their talents, perhaps."

"I don't suppose that we could convince Garcia to fabricate a major engineering casualty that would keep us in port?" Yak ventured.

"Not a chance." Bender laughed, pulling back a chair and seating himself at the head of the table. "And if you bother to take a look around, you might notice that we are surrounded by anti-aircraft emplacements because, just so you know, this place is getting plenty of nightly attention from both the *Luftwaffe* as well as the *Regia Aeronautica* flying out of Sicily.".

"*That*," Yak said, sitting bolt upright, "is a thoroughly revolting development! Perhaps I'll start sleeping in my helmet."

"Hopefully," Hal said, "they'll continue to think us too small to bother with."

"Keep that thought," Bender said. "By the way, Hal. Sack of mail came in. Mail clerk says there's a letter for you. In fact, he says there are several."

And with that announcement, Hal rose instantly to his feet.

4

In fact, when Hal finally cornered the mail clerk, he found three letters waiting for him, all of them from Bea, all of them written on pale blue stationery. How they had reached him so rapidly he couldn't possibly explain to himself but imagined that one or another mail bag had been put onto a bomber or air transport that was making its way east from the States, and indeed, when he opened the letters, he found that they had been written weeks before and failed to catch up with him before he left the States. As a result, although filled with love and devotion, none of Bea's letters, having been written within a week of his departure from Champaign, touched on anything so significant as informing her family about their intentions. Instead, Bea confined herself to professions of affection and, in one of the letters, regrets that they had not gone off together for the expressed purpose of spending a weekend in bed. The fault, she said, was hers for not sending him off to war properly. Hal smiled, knowing full well that the fault was no more Bea's than his own and intended to lay the matter to rest in the very next letter that he sent her. In looking back, things had simply moved too fast for the both of them. Falling in love had been the last thing that either of them had anticipated, and it was only after Bea's return from her cousin's funeral that the fact of it hit them. Hal ached for her, but at the same time, when he reflected upon what the two of them had experienced and the decision that they'd reached, he felt glad that he hadn't rushed their relationship and led Bea into a situation that she might later regret on nothing more than moral grounds. Hal had always assumed that Bea was Catholic, but in truth they had never talked about religion. How dedicated a Catholic she was, he really didn't know; that would be something for the two of them to determine later. But if or when she finally informed her parents about her intentions, he didn't want her to have to do so with anything like lingering guilt on her conscience. He knew, of course, that Bea's views might have lapsed as far as his own, but because neither of them had raised the subject, he felt content that they had restrained their hunger for one another until a time when it would not seem furtive, clandestine, or out of bounds.

"Want to go ashore and take a meal?" Bender said, sticking his head through Hal's door. "Everything all right at home?"

"Things at home are fine," Hal said, folding the letters and placing them on his bunk, "and a good meal ashore, if we can find one, sounds mighty fine."

"Garcia says he's content to stand the duty as command duty officer," Bender said, "so we'll drag Yak and Lewis along with us, if you don't mind."

"Not at all," Hal said. "When do we go?"

"1600, 1700?"

"You call the time, and I'll be ready," Hal said.

"And we'll leave Garcia to inspect the troops going over and see that they have their condoms," Bender laughed. "I'll give liberty to half the crew tonight, but with the proviso that all of them are back on board by 2300, which seems to be the witching hour here according to the Shore Patrol and the Army MPs who guard the waterfront. Word has it that our people don't go too far into town, so for most of them, I expect they'll stay pretty close to the quay and whatever bars they find there."

"That sounds not only reasonable but wise," Hal said. "Safety in numbers."

"Right," Bender said. "I would imagine that there are plenty of Italian, French, and Spanish whores working the bars, but from what I've heard, look at one of the Arab women in the wrong way, and a guy is liable to get his throat cut. Might be an exaggeration, but the Arabs are supposed to be touchy in that regard."

"The surprise is that their women don't seem to be, otherwise I can't imagine how they could live in peace with three other wives in the house," Hal quipped.

"According to rumor," Bender laughed, "from what my friends tell me, living with one wife in the house is difficult enough. Makes me think you'd expect more patience out of an Arab male. But apparently not, so warn the troops to stay clear of Arab women, and we ought to be home free."

Three blocks into Bizerte and up a narrow, winding street outside the gate from where the *3X* happened to be tied up, Hal, Bender, and the others stumbled onto *La Botella Azul*, The Blue Bottle, not an Italian or French but a Spanish restaurant which seemed to be sandwiched between two of the city's massive white-walled enclosures. The narrow entrance where the bar happened to be located proved deceptive, for beyond it, deeper inside by twenty yards, they found themselves inside a fairly noisy and busy dining room with a small stage at one end where two guitar players alternated playing what Hal imagined to be an attempt at Flamenco music. The room was crowded with a plethora of sailors, soldiers, and officers of the lower ranks, but not so much that the waiter who met them couldn't find them a table. They wound up in a corner not twenty paces from where the guitar players were attacking the strings, and it was there, once they'd seated themselves and called for beer, that they found it necessary to repel any number of B-girls who immediately descended upon them in the expectation of finding easy marks.

"Not what I need tonight," Bender said, showing the others a smile.

"Not none of us," Lewis humphed. "More like some good chow with enough beer to wash it down."

The beer served in The Blue Bottle turned out to be both French and Italian, most of it, Hal imagined, acquired from large stocks warehoused somewhere after being left over from the occupation. The food, on the other hand, was Spanish to the core, the four of them splitting two dishes of tapas before Bender and Yak dug into a cast iron pot of rabbit stew while Chief Lewis and Hal contented themselves with servings of a seafood paella that they found no less than satisfying.

"Not bad," Bender said, when he finally put down his fork. "Heavy on the garlic, maybe, but who could complain?"

"Not me," Yak said. "If this represents what's available here, we're liable to get fat eating on the beach."

"Long as the money holds out," Lewis grunted.

"You mean we actually have to pay for this?" Hal joked. "I would have thought that a generous Navy would want to underwrite the entire meal."

"Dream on," Bender laughed.

"I won't complain," Hal said. "Beats the hell out of a daily ration of Spam, I can tell you."

"Served Spam in the Pacific, did they?" Yak asked.

"Continuously," Hal said, his displeasure about the memory spreading everywhere across his face.

"Hate to tell youse," Lewis put in, "but that meatloaf the cooks served us aboard for the last couple days is what you might call an aberration. We got us enough Spam comin' to feed a division."

"Then it behooves us to eat ashore at every opportunity," Hal laughed. "I've already had enough Spam to last me a lifetime."

"Just wait until you sample our chipped beef on a shingle," Bender said. "I'm sure you'll find it pure delight."

"Oh," Hal said, "you mean the ship serves that too? I seem to have fallen into a gourmet's paradise."

"We'll check with you again in a couple of weeks to see if that assumption holds," Yak laughed.

"So," Hal said, seeking to change the subject, "what was the trip over like, for the *3X*? Did you make the invasion or come later?"

"Later," Lewis said.

"Much," Yak said.

"We were still in the States and still in the shipyard building when the invasion hit North Africa," Bender said. "Commissioned one week after, put to sea, and went straight to training in the Chesapeake. We didn't get over here until the week before the Africa Corps surrendered, but rather than tie us up around Tunis, they sent us straight down to Sousse towing barges; the only action we saw was when those two Macchis attempted to strafe us."

"Aside from huntin' for mines," Yak said, "and tryin' to watch out for U-boats, you really couldn't say we've had much of a war yet."

"An' far as that's concern'," Lewis piped up, "things has been jus' fine, and I won't be put out none if they stay that way."

"Dream on, Chief," Bender said, "but I doubt you're going to get your wish. Not now, not up here. I can't read the future any better than anyone else, but now that we're in Bizerte, I'm guessing that we're going to have to be on our toes. I reckon we're gonna have more than our share of work, and this close to Sicily, I'd guess that the Krauts are going to try to interfere with it."

"Oh, aye," Lewis said. "And damn their rotten hides for the effort."

They talked on, the four, drinking a couple more beers each before finally rising to their feet and retracing their steps to the ship.

Once there, as though Bender's assumption had suddenly made itself manifest, they found a message waiting for them ordering them to get underway as soon as the crew's liberty ended. They were to proceed to a position forty miles northwest of Bizerte to find and take in tow a subchaser which had been disabled by an engine casualty.

"Your beer buzz worn off enough so that you think you can take us out without running us aground?" Bender asked as the two stood together on the open bridge at midnight, readying the *3X* to get her underway.

Hal chuckled. "Three cups of mess deck coffee seems to have done the trick," Hal said. "I'm sure I'll be tired by morning, but at the moment, I'm wide-eyed and bushy tailed."

"All the troops get back on time?" Bender continued.

"That kid Vega looked a little worse for wear," Hal said, "but yes, they're all back and rarin' to go."

"Good," Bender said. "Once we hit the breakwater and secure from the Special Sea and Anchor Detail, I want to set Condition II. Until we find out what this duty up here is going to be like, we'll run the watches port and starboard with both of the 20 mm manned and only go to General Quarters if we detect a threat. Somewhere down the road, if we find that things can run smoothly out here, I'll think about setting Condition III so that we can go over to a more restful watch schedule."

"Understood," Hal said.

"All right," Bender said. "Call down to the engine room and tell them to stand by to answer all bells, and once they reply, you can get us underway and take us out."

According to what Hal remembered, the voyage up from Sousse—save for their encounter with the Savoia-Marchettis—had been relatively tranquil, with the sea state never exceeding what he imagined to be a State 3. But during the few hours they'd spent in port, things had changed. Something in the way of weather had blown in, and what they found immediately outside the breakwater was a sea state that ran to 5 or more and a chop that instantly upset everyone's stomach. Men did not actually become seasick, but nearly everyone moved in that direction. Given the circumstances, regardless of the fact that his watch would last from midnight until Yak relieved him at 0600 in the morning, Hal found himself glad to be up on the bridge. Despite the cold spray shooting back over the bow, he had a dim view of what lay ahead and could compensate for both the pitch and roll that the ship found itself experiencing.

"Wouldn't you know," Bender said by way of an observation on the sea state.

"In for a penny, in for a pound," Hal said, "and this sure isn't going to make hooking up to that subchaser any easier when we find it."

"No, it isn't," Bender said. "Rather than send a boat over, Lewis is going to have to shoot them a line, either with a bolo or with a shot gun; we can only hope that the boatswain on the subchaser knows enough to properly make fast our towline once they've pulled it over."

"Planning to use the wire rope?" Hal asked.

"Not if it stays like this," Bender said. "Manila will provide us with some give and take, I think, and a subchaser should be a light load. That, however, is something I'm going to leave strictly to Chief Lewis to decide because what he doesn't know about the best thing to use and about towing in general probably wouldn't amount to enough to fill a shot glass."

"Bank vault worth of experience?" Hal said.

"Bank vault worth of experience," Bender said, "and the two of us can count ourselves lucky to be able to rely on it."

Using Hal's morning fix, which he shot with a sextant even before he went off watch—Bender standing by and taking the con while he took his readings and then worked out the ship's position—they reached the supposed location of the subchaser at around 0630 that morning and didn't see it anywhere.

Throwing over a wood chip in order to try to judge which way the currents were running according to nothing more than seaman's eye, both Hal and Bender concluded that they were running south toward North Africa, inaugurated a search pattern that would gradually take them south, and began searching the seas for the disabled vessel. Within an hour, they found it, the subchaser having drifted more than ten miles south from its last reported position. They managed to send over their messenger followed by their towline and hooked up with the grateful chaser by 0830, at which time, gently taking up the slack and with the seas moderating only slightly, they started back toward Bizerte.

The two Fiat G.50 Freccia fighter aircraft that found them before they retraced their path to Bizerte by as much as ten miles were planes which both the lookouts who first spotted them as well as Hal, Yak, and Bender were able to precisely identify by their slightly bulbous bodies. This time, fortunately, the planes were flying high when the men on the *3X* first spotted them. For a minute or two at least, neither Hal nor Bender believed that the Italians had seen them, at least not from an altitude where they seemed to be flying. Indeed, both planes passed distantly overhead to the northwest, and for a few more minutes—and regardless of the fact that Bender had ordered the ship to General Quarters the minute the aircraft were first spotted—everyone on the bridge experienced a moment of relief as they imagined that the planes might pass them by without detecting them. But their hope in that regard proved to be too much to be true; minutes later, the starboard lookout shouted a warning that the two planes had circled all the way around, dived for the deck, and were coming straight toward them from the North African coast.

As Bender gave a batteries released order to the gunners aboard the *3X*, Hal was on the horn, alerting the chaser to air action starboard. The lookouts on the chaser had already seen the danger they were all in, trained their own guns around to meet the threat, and made Hal's warning no more than obligatory. As the Fiats came at the vessels, making a speed which closed in on 300 miles per hour, their four machine guns blazing, both the chaser and the *3X* opened up on them with everything they had, a collection of two 3"/50s and three 20 mm combined.

All told, once the engagement started, Hal didn't imagine that it lasted more than fifteen seconds, both planes hurling themselves at the two ships from an altitude so low down that Hal didn't believe they were more than fifty feet above the sea. As far as Hal could tell, the 3"/50 rounds failed utterly to connect. But judging from the tracers going out, at least one of Bix's 20 mm rounds struck the easternmost of the Fiats. A scattering of fragments flew from its wing and unsettled the pilot's aim so that the rounds he was throwing out were off target in the critical moment, two rounds only chipping splinters from the starboard rail forward of the pilot house but wounding no one.

Back behind them, the chaser did not fare as well. The westernmost attacker had gotten a total of thirteen rounds into the subchaser, wooden splinters kicked up by the rounds wounding three of her crew. One of the solids that the Fiat threw out connected with the breach of one of the subchaser's Oerlikons, wounding no one but putting the gun out of action.

As the two fighters roared overhead and sped away, the air splitting with the sound of their engines, the two 20 mm on the port side, instantly unmasked, picked them up and did their best to blow the tails off both planes. They failed to connect before the Fiats flew out of range, and everyone readied for what they imagined would be a second attack. But the attack failed to develop.

"I think we may have escaped the bullet," Bender said. "If the bastards had had bombs, they might have done for us."

"I think Bix got a piece of the one on the left," Hal said, "so perhaps that explains why they've cut for home before the pilot goes into the drink. Didn't look too bad from my viewpoint, but maybe it was worse than it looked."

"Let's hope," Bender said. "No reports of wounds?"

"None," Hal said. "We got splintered, that's all."

"Leaves you shaking, doesn't it?" Bender said.

"Yes," Hal said, "it does."

"What about the chaser?" Bender asked. "Give them a check and see how they fared."

And Hal did.

Once arrived back in Bizerte, after having thrown a bevy of fenders over the side to cushion the impact, Chief Lewis quickly took in the towline while Bender eased the *3X* alongside the subchaser, made the two vessels fast to one another, and worked the vessel over against the seawall in the area where the Navy had set up a growing repair facility. Just as soon as the chaser put over her brow, two stretcher bearers instantly removed one sailor with a long splinter protruding from his leg, while two other men with their shoulders bandaged walked ashore under their own power, all three disappearing into an ambulance which hurtled down the quay and around a corner at something just short, Hal thought, of light speed.

"That there splinter in the leg looks to me like a 'get home early' wound," Lewis said, walking up beside where Bender and Hal were standing as they watched the chaser's captain see his wounded away.

"Looks to me like a sure ticket to ride," Bender observed.

"And some compensation for the pain," Hal said. And then he turned to Bender. "Will we be staying here or moving back to our former berth, Captain?"

"Moving back," Bender said, turning away from the direction in which he'd been watching what had been going on aboard the subchaser. "There may be something else coming in beside this one, given all the work these repair types have going, and CONSERVEFLT wants all three tugs moored together, probably where he can quickly find them if he intends to shoot a rocket up one or another of us."

They moved then, taking in their lines from the chaser after receiving a word of thanks from the subchaser's captain, and within thirty minutes found themselves once more tied up outboard in the nest of three tugs from which they'd started the night before.

"Outboard like this," Yak observed, "I'm not sure that a night or two at rest is going to follow. Looks to me like this position is the one most likely to be called out for the next emergency as well. You'd like to think they would put the three of us on some kind of rotation for this sort of thing."

"Yes," Bender said, "but they haven't, and I think it's a sure bet that we'll be going again, just as soon as something unfolds."

And they did, only the second time they were called out, two days later, the tug next to them went with them. Two LCTs had collided and disabled themselves during a landing exercise not ten miles east of Bizerte where the Army had taken to conducting a training operation in advance of whatever invasion might be coming in the future.

When the 3X set off in company with the second tug to retrieve the two LCTs that had collided, Hal expected both of them to be well off the beach and somewhere in the open sea, drifting, unable to get underway owing to whatever casualty each had suffered. But when the 3X finally came in sight of the beach where the landing exercise was going on, Hal and Bender were surprised to find the two LCTs carried by whatever current was running offshore, pushed ashore by the surf, and broached on the beach.

"Shit," Bender said, surveying the situation through his binoculars. "They ought to have Mike boats configured for retrievals like this. With our draft it's going to be dangerous for us to get within a hundred yards of the beach."

Hal looked at the situation as they found it, knew what was coming, and kept his silence.

"All right, Hal," Bender said flatly, "looks like this one is going to be on you. I'll get us in as close as I dare and anchor. The minute I do, you get the boat in the water, work around astern, and take our towline in tow as Lewis pays it out. You're going to have to judge conditions for yourself once you get in there, but don't go any closer than thirty yards to the beach 'cause you sure as hell don't want the surf carrying you all the way in. Turn and run parallel to the beach once you're in there and have your bow hook fire a shot gun with the messenger right over the stern of that LCT on the right. Those birds on the LCT are going to have to turn to with a vengeance in order to haul the towline in by themselves because that's as much as I intend to risk in order to get them tied up. If I could take us in closer, I would, but I can't; we'd run aground."

"They will probably damage their rudders and their screws as we try to haul them off," Hal said.

"Yes, but there's nothing for it," Bender said, "and rudders and screws are easy for the repair facility to replace. If we want to get these birds off, and we do, we're going to have to do it this way without counting the cost."

Once anchored and with the *3X* in position, Lewis and his deck crew lowered the ship's whaleboat in record time. Hal and the boat crew, wearing helmets and life preservers, held the monkey lines as the boat descended into the sea. Given the chop, all four of them were nearly thrown off their feet by the sudden motion of the waves. Recovering swiftly, the bow hook and the stern hook tripped the pelican hooks holding the boat to the blocks. The next moment, Click, the coxswain—the short, ape-shaped boatswain upon whom Lewis invariably relied—had the boat away, cresting one wave before dropping into the trough, and taking them back around toward the stern where Lewis and his crew swiftly passed them both the messenger and the eye of the towline. Then, with the boat laboring, they began to move toward the beach, Lewis's deck crew paying out the towline with enough speed so as not to impede them.

"No closer than thirty yards," Hal said to Click, standing behind him as they neared their objective.

"An' then we'se to shoot 'em the goose and turn beam on?" Click questioned.

"That's the idea," Hal said, before calling forward to Morris who would handle the shot gun with the messenger line attached to see if both the gun and the man were ready.

With the surf running both stronger and higher than Hal would have liked, the evolution when it came time to make it didn't go off exactly as planned. Morris, on Hal's order, fired the shot gun on cue and sent the messenger line hurling forward, but with Click turning a second too soon, Morris' aim was slightly off. The messenger line did not fall directly across the LCT's stern as Hal hoped but instead fell directly behind the LCT's stern. Fortunately, one of the stranded sailors happened to be down on the beach, hiding from the shot behind the landing craft's hull. The minute the rod attached to the messenger struck the beach, the man was able to come out from behind, pull it from the sand into which it had partially embedded itself, and toss it straight up to the sailors who had come out from behind their own cover on the fantail of the LCT. And in the offing, with only slight delay, several of those men struggling together began to haul in the messenger and the heavy towline that Lewis had attached to it. Within ten laborious minutes, they had the eye aboard and thrown over the towing bits welded to the stern of the LCT. When they did, by means of two semaphore flags, Hal signaled the ship that the LCT was ready to tow. Swiftly, he gave Click an order to return to the ship.

Given the chop, hooking back up to the two hoisting blocks that would lift the whaleboat from the water to the rail proved no easy task, the heavy blocks rising and falling with the ship's roll before the bow and stern hooks could get complete control of them and secure the boat by means of its lifting eyes. Finally, the hook up was made, the davits engaged, and then with a jerk followed by a slow rise, the heavy boat came loose from the sea. It rose gradually until the boat crew cut off the engine and stepped across the rail onto the deck. The deck crew then reengaged the davits so as to lift the boat back into its chocks where it could be fully secured for sea.

"Our LCT is all hooked up," Hal reported to Bender, once he arrived back on the bridge.

"No trouble?"

"No," Hal replied.

"All right," Bender said. "Word to the fantail," he said to his sound-powered phone talker. "Stand by *to* tow. Signalman, word to the LCT, standby *for* tow."

And with that and enough time lapse for both entities to reply that they were ready, Bender ordered the slack taken out of the towline, the anchor raised, and the engine room to begin moving the tug forward with minimal revolutions, doing his best by means of both the capstan and the ship's slow motion to gently ease the LCT back off the beach and into the sea.

Bender and Lewis had been wise, Hal thought, to use the wire rope for the operation because the tension the line went under would be less than if one of the fiber towlines had been used. The fiber lines might have expanded and contracted much more, causing the stern of the LCT to jerk and snap in response to rapid changes in the line's tension. The wire rope, relying on the firmness of its twisted wire cables, would be less likely to cause the same kinds of reaction as the LCT moved a little at a time and would therefore involve less stress on the towline—*if* in fact the LCT came free, if it hadn't hung up so firmly on the beach that two tugs operating together would be required to move it off the sand.

After some careful maneuvering by both Lewis on the capstan and Bender on the con, the LCT with several screeches that could be heard even on the bridge of the *3X* gradually came free from where she rested. First she slid her stern around so that it pointed in the direction of the ship's fantail; then with several more screeching sounds, she slid free from the beach, gouging a deep groove through the sand where the corner formed by her steel bottom and her starboard side moved toward the sea. Even standing beside Bender on the bridge, Hal could feel the sudden release from tension beneath his feet when the LCT pulled loose and was once more afloat.

"Bingo!" Bender laughed. "Well, that's the worst part of the job. Now all we have to do is get her back to Bizerte without once more being attacked from the air."

Hal didn't think they would be attacked from the air. Considering the two attack transports, several LCIs and even more LCTs participating in the landing exercise, not to mention the number of destroyers sent in to escort them and the air cover that seemed to be about, Hal imagined that if the Germans or the Italians did tip to what they were doing and throw in a raid, they would have much bigger fish to fry than to go after a lone tug and its tow.

"Somehow," he said skeptically, "I would imagine that their attention will be directed elsewhere, as long as this lot is still out here."

"And so I will continue to hope," Bender said, clapping Hal once on the shoulder by way of agreement. Glancing back toward where the LCT that they were towing had come fully one hundred yards off the beach, he spoke again, and this time without pleasure. "Oh Christ," Bender said, a wholly different tone sounding in his voice. "That doesn't look good at all."

Hal looked, and what he saw did not look good. The second tug, attempting to repeat the evolution which the *3X* had only moments before performed so successfully, had run into trouble when its whaleboat had gone in too close to the beach, been caught by the surf, and as a result of the coxswain not being able to control it, had ridden straight in and been pitched up the beach by a wave.

"Rats," Bender said quickly. "That means we're going to have to stick around to render assistance if needed."

Fortunately, this was not the case. The coxswain of the other tug's whaleboat may have made a mistake, but the man keeping control of their messenger had not, having held on to the tug's messenger line for dear life. He'd never lost hold on the tug's towing eye, so within short order, he hooked the towing eye up to the whaleboat, the distant tug engaging its own capstan so as to pull its own whaleboat gently back into the sea. The coxswain, somehow exercising a degree of control over the boat, steadied her enough so that the bow hook was able to shoot the messenger back across the stern of the second LCT. With the towing eye properly secured by the bits, the tug was able to pull the second LCT from the beach in much the same way that the *3X* had done, the tug's own whaleboat with a damaged screw or rudder tying up to the side of the LCT so that both vessels, one large and the other very small, could be towed back to Bizerte.

"And that added how much time to what should otherwise have been a less lengthy operation?" Yak asked, joining Bender and Hal on the bridge.

"Right on an hour and twenty minutes," Hal said, glancing at his watch.

"What with the things we'll have to do getting these birds back and seeing them down to the repair facility," Yak said, "I'd guess that puts us right out of the running for a trip to The Blue Bottle for tonight."

"Spam it is, then?" Hal asked, half sarcastically.

"Spam it is," Bender said, "a surprise development designed to make our crew a far sight less happy."

"From time to time," Yak said, "their combined perception can be acute."

Across the weeks that followed, the 3X and the two other tugs associated with her found themselves kept more than busy. Almost daily, one or another or all three were called upon to help move ships in and out of the harbor, help them change berths, help them to moor, and help them to replenish by moving fuel barges, water barges, or stores barges alongside them and then moving the same lighters away once the jobs they were doing had been accomplished. The work seemed endless and generally went on from early morning to well after dark. Owing to nothing more than pure exhaustion, the officers in the wardroom only managed three meals at The Blue Bottle across a period of four weeks.

Had the work been the only thing that any of them had to worry about, it would have been enough, but in addition to the work, either the Germans or the Italians or both put in air raids at regular intervals. Most of them happened at night, forcing the officers and crew to race from their bunks in order to take up their General Quarters stations so that the guns would be manned in the event that they had the opportunity to shoot at the interlopers. While they put up rounds like most of the other ships in the harbor, the searchlights generally seemed so slow or so inept that they seldom felt that they had done any good beyond merely breaking the monotony of what had become a routine.

In the middle of June, as if to interrupt what had become a standard treadmill of operations for them and directly on the heels of a long day's work, they were once more dispatched down the coast some seventy miles in order to find and take in tow a Liberty ship which had been torpedoed and dropped out of her convoy. Steaming under the cover of darkness at Condition II and with Hal navigating, they required a little over six hours to reach the supposed position of the stricken Liberty ship. They finally located her on the edge of the channel some fourteen miles from the coast and got a heaving line with the messenger over her bow and their wire rope made fast in less than a half hour. By dawn they were towing, moving slowly ahead in their attempt to return to Bizerte.

Miraculously, Hal thought, the Liberty ship seemed in no danger of sinking. An aerial torpedo dropped from a Heinkel 111 had hit the ship late on the previous afternoon, apparently blowing away a part or the whole of her rudder and severely damaging her screw; she had gone dead in the water and dropped out of her convoy. An escorting destroyer had shot the Heinkel down, but with a multitude of other ships to shepherd, no one had remained behind in order to take the Liberty ship in tow. The ship herself, having isolated the damage, was in no danger of sinking, so her crew was not taken off. Instead, with whatever patience and fortitude merchant sailors mustered, she radioed for help and waited alone for the kind of assistance that the 3X had been designed to provide.

"Big tow," Bender said, once he and Hal began to feel the pull at the end of their wire rope.

"Just about as big as the pull of my eyelids trying to shut," Hal quipped.

"Not feeling tired are you?" Bender laughed.

"Oh no," Hal grunted, "at least not more than your standard zombie, I don't think."

72

"So what's our estimated time of arrival?" Bender asked as the dawn began to break.

"Once we see how she's going to run," Hal said, "and if we're able to make the speed we hope, I'm guessing we ought to make port before dark, or a little thereafter."

"As long as we're not held up," Bender said.

"And as long as we make that jog around the corner of the minefield without any difficulty," Hal said. "I've got it well plotted, but a lot is going to depend on what kind of a fix I'm able to get at sunrise this morning."

"Well, make damn sure you get a good one," Bender cautioned. "Don't want any slip-ups on that point."

And Hal did get a good one—a fix that proved almost pinpoint. But when the time for their turn did finally come up, their fix hadn't helped as much as they'd hoped because well out in front of them by several hundred yards, the lookout on the flying bridge spotted a mine floating over the crest of a wave, causing consternation to break out on the bridge.

"You're sure of your fix?" Bender barked at Hal, worried, angry, looking for someone to blame.

"I'm sure of it," Hal said. "We're at least five miles north of the edge of the minefield on the plot, and the current's running north. This one must have broken loose and drifted up toward us."

Bender took no more than a few seconds to make his decision. Without hesitation, he moved heaven and hell, called the crew to General Quarters, helped the gunners to find the target which had by that time closed to within three hundred yards just about a point off the starboard bow, and ordered them to cut loose with everything they had. Very rapidly the rounds began to go out from both the 3"/50 and the starboard 20 mm. At a range of no more than two hundred yards, amid the cacophony of the guns and the horrendous spread of shrapnel that they were exploding out in front of them, a round or fragment connected with one of the horns on the mine. It blew, shaking the 3X like a leaf and throwing a column of water so high into the sky that it momentarily blotted out the morning sun before it collapsed back into the sea.

"*Shit!*" both Bender and Hal said at once and they were showered with spray flowing back from the blow.

"Ha," Yak said brightly, flying up onto the bridge just in time to catch some of the spray for himself. "Regular Fourth of July, wasn't it? Kudos to my gunners, dead-eye Dicks, the lot of 'em. More fun than a weenie roast, wouldn't you say?"

For a moment, Hal wondered if Bender might not turn and try to strangle Yak, but then, very quickly, he saw that Bender had gotten control of himself and adjusted to the sudden release of tension that he felt.

"I'll tell you what," Bender said to Yak, "in case you missed the fact, it's damn lucky your gunners got onto this one, otherwise it would have been our weenie that got roasted."

Yak sensed he'd overstepped. "We were that close?" he questioned, his tone altering appreciably.

"Yak," Bender said, taking a deep breath and doing his best to bring down his blood pressure, "you seem to have forgotten that we're made of wood. If we'd gotten another fifty or seventy-five yards closer to that explosion, it might have split us right down the middle. As it was, it shook the daylights out of us, so Hal, you, Yak, and Garcia are to inspect every corner of this ship, right now, and get your damage reports up to the bridge ASAP. Move!"

Neither Hal nor Yak hesitated. Both of them were down off the bridge and running within seconds, collecting Garcia and going into every accessible compartment on the ship to check seams and fittings to make sure that everything had remained secure. As it turned out, the 3X had remained together and watertight, none of her seams having worked loose. In the engine room, however, two pipe fittings had sprung leaks owing to the vibrations she'd experienced in the explosion, and those, one of the shipfitters quickly repaired using nothing more than a few turns with a pipe wrench.

Even Hal felt a sense of relief once he'd finished their tour of inspection, and when the two of them returned to the bridge on the heels of the reports they'd already sent up by means of the sound-powered phone talkers, Bender had moved a long way toward recovering his equanimity.

"Apparently she's been pretty well built," Bender said with a smile, "because I thought the vibrations from that mine were going to shake my teeth loose. The captain of the Liberty ship flashed us a message thanking us for saving their bacon, and Hal, I want you to draft a letter to Bettison and Sons, the builders, thanking them in general terms for a well-built ship, and put something in about superior craftsmanship. No specific details about what we just went through, mind, but something short which expresses our satisfaction in serving aboard the *3X*. Take my point, do you?"

"Yes Sir," Hal said.

As far as Hal was concerned, the mine had provided them with enough excitement to last them for a week, if not a month. Not an hour later, however, as though they were encountering one thing after another, the lookouts alerted them to the fact that they were about to come under air attack. Even as his blood raced, Hal took comfort in the fact that Bender had not secured the ship from General Quarters and that all of their guns were still manned and ready.

When they finally picked it up, the attacker turned out to be a single twin-engine Dornier Do 17, coming in both low and fast from the Liberty ship's port quarter in an apparent attempt to finish off the partial kill that the Germans had made the afternoon before.

Whether the German had known what he was going after or was merely out hunting for a target of opportunity was something that none of them could have known, but when the attack developed, it didn't matter. The German clearly intended to bomb the Liberty ship and put paid to it with all of its valuable cargo. As it closed to within what Bender judged to be an acceptable range, he made a slight turn to port to unmask the 3"/50, and the gunners cut loose. Right from the start, the Dornier was well beyond the range of the port 20 mm, but as far as the gunner felt concerned, it didn't matter, the 20 mm spitting out rounds by the dozen and filling the sky with as much lead as it could throw, while the gunners on the 3"/50 threw out rounds of frag as fast as they could load them, clouds of smoke and the sharp odor of cordite engulfing the men on the bridge.

And to everyone's shock, whether by chance or intention, one of those rounds actually did the job that it had been designed to do. Exploding near enough to the tail section of the Dornier, it totally blew the after half of the plane away before whatever bomb the plane happened to be carrying blew up in a rapidly expanding ball of fire and smoke which threw debris in every direction.

The roar which went up from the ship seemed almost as loud as the sound of the not-too-far-distant explosion. Before the gunners on the *3X* connected, the Dornier had closed to within a thousand yards of the big Liberty ship; unless the bombardier on the Dornier were an incompetent, Hal didn't see how the German could have missed. Something—he wondered possibly angels—had looked after them that morning, first with the mine and then with the Kraut, and Hal had no intention of questioning either the powers that be or the luck that pulled them through. The relief he felt in that moment nearly brought him to his knees, and when he saw the expression on Bender's face, he knew that the feeling was mutual.

"*Christ*," Bender said quietly, "I don't know how steady I can be after that one. Talk about luck. I thought we were going to come a cropper for sure."

"Same here," Hal said, removing his helmet and wiping the sweat from his brow. "Once that bastard started in, I wouldn't have given two cents for our chances, not at the speed we're towing, not with the incompetence of the 5″/38 on that Liberty ship. I don't think they even got out a round."

"They didn't," Bender said. "Either their gun crew's asleep over there, or something is wrong with their gun."

The difficulty was explained later in the morning when, after thanking the 3X for saving their bacon a second time, the captain of the Liberty ship reported an amplidyne on their single 5″/38 gun burned out which meant, in a nutshell, that the gun couldn't be trained on any target that might come against it.

"I wonder what caused that casualty?" Hal said, when he heard the news.

"Overuse in training possibly," Bender said, "but it's just as likely that the yard, when they built the thing, gave them something defective, and it failed. Don't suppose we'll ever know."

"Captain," Yak said, once things had settled down and both the 3X and her tow were finally approaching Bizerte, "what about extra liberty for the gun crew?"

"Done," Bender said with a smile. "And that will mean a hot time in The Blue Bottle tonight. And Hal, after you've drafted our after-action report, I think you ought to tell Lewis to have one of his seamen, someone with some artistic talent, to paint a small Nazi flag on each of the bridge wings. Fighter pilots do it, and I don't see why we shouldn't follow suit. It ought to give the troops a lift by showing clear evidence that we haven't been twiddling our thumbs."

"Done," Hal said, showing Bender a smile.

5

Three days after the Fourth of July 1943, carrying a sizable manila packet under his arm, Bender rushed back aboard from a visit to COMSERVFLT and met Hal on the quarterdeck.

"All liberty and shore leave are canceled immediately," he said, his tone deadly serious. "I don't want anyone so much as even stepping onto the pier. Assemble the officers in the wardroom, Hal. We've got things to go over and damn little time in which to do it."

Orders were given, the men were warned, and not five minutes later, with coffee mugs before them, Hal, Yak, Garcia, and Lewis sat around the wardroom table as Bender dropped the massive operations order for *HUSKY* in front of them.

"Shit," Garcia exclaimed. "We gotta read all that?"

"No," Bender said. "Fortunately for you, I just sat through two hours of a Top Secret briefing covering the most salient points, so for you guys, at least, all you need to read are the parts of this that pertain to your own individual areas of concern. For the whole of it, I'm about to give you a briefing on particulars, and without intending a pun, it will also be brief because we're due to get underway three hours from now."

Eyebrows were raised, and everyone took note.

"It's Sicily," Bender said when he knew he had their attention, "Operation *HUSKY*. And you aren't to breathe a word about it to the crew, not before we put to sea. Admiral Hewitt who's in command of what is being called the Western Naval Task Force doesn't want a word of this getting out because, as far as we know, the Germans and the Italians think we're going to hit either Sardinia or Greece, and our masters don't want them thinking anything else. So silence is not only golden, it's imperative."

Everyone got the idea.

"The Brits," Bender continued, "will run an Eastern Naval Task Force out of Alexandria, and the general intention seems to be for both of us to go at Sicily from two directions. The Royal Navy has mustered in excess of eight hundred ships for this one, all of them for the purpose of putting Montgomery's Eighth Army ashore in the Gulf of Noto so that they can capture Syracuse and sweep up Sicily's east coast, east of Mount Etna, capture Messina, and slam the door on the retreating Italians and Germans."

Hal assumed that the retreating Germans and Italians would be driven toward Messina by American forces landed somewhere further to the west, and what Bender next said confirmed him in that view.

"We've managed to assemble something in excess of five hundred ships to take Patton's Seventh Army in to the west," Bender continued, "with the intention of forcing three major landings in the Gulf of Gela. Code names are being used, so JOSS Force—that's to carry General Truscott's 3rd Infantry Division—will go in farthest to the west at Licata. DIME force will carry Terry Allen's 1st Infantry Division up to Gela, and that's the bunch we'll be assigned to, and General Middleton's 45th Infantry Division, CENT Force, will go in farthest to the east at Scoglitti with the expectation that they'll eventually link up with the Brits. All told, both the Brits and ourselves included, the invasion front will stretch nearly a hundred miles across the enemy's front. It is by far the biggest invasion ever to be launched."

To Hal, it sounded big. In fact, it sounded enormous, and he couldn't begin to imagine how the entire thing might eventually mesh and be controlled.

"We have plenty of carriers going with us?" Yak asked. "For air cover?"

Bender's face darkened. "No," he said. "I think there'll be paratroops going in the night before, to attempt to seal off the beaches, but our carriers are apparently busy in the Pacific, and while the Royal Navy has a couple to lend support, they aren't nearly as big as ours and don't pack the same punch. And I picked up another rumor or two at the briefing that didn't sound encouraging."

"Like to pour acid on us, them rumors?" Lewis asked, starting to fume.

"That seems to be about the size of it," Bender said. "From what I heard, but this is only scuttlebutt, the RAF and the Air Corps think that they can seal off the beaches by means of strategic bombing behind them, by knocking out airfields, roads, and bridges, so there's no clear plan for air support over us or on the beaches themselves."

"*Shit*," Lewis said, "that'll leave us all wide open to whatever the Krauts throw at us!"

"No one else was happy about it either," Bender said. "Sorta looks to me like we'll be going in without air cover, and I for one can't be the least bit happy about it."

"Mr. Yaakov," Lewis growled, "youse betta be damn sure them guns of yours is up to workin', 'cause youse gonna be all we got ta keep our asses from bein' shot off!"

"You'll remember when we took on three hundred rounds of three-inch ammo two days ago," Yak said. "Well, those rounds are carrying VT fuses, you'll be glad to hear. Proximity fuses, fuses that will blow once they sense that they are even close to an incoming target. Make you feel any better, hearing that?"

"A mite," Lewis said, "but the proof'll be in the puddin'. Start gettin' hits and make a believer outa me."

"Just watch us," Yak said.

"Hal, you got anything to say?" Bender asked.

Hal had been glancing at the op-order. More specifically, he'd been looking at the pages concerning the routes the various forces would be taking in order to reach their objectives.

"The Sicilian Channel between Cape Bon and the westernmost point on Sicily is barely a hundred miles wide," Hal said, "but apparently, we won't be going over that way. According to what I'm seeing here, we're going to round Cape Bon, steam south for a good piece, turn, and then move up toward Malta from the distant south. I'm guessing, but my guess tells me that we're after deception, that we're doing it in order to leave any Kraut reconnaissance planes that spot us with the impression we're headed for Greece. That the way you see it?"

"I haven't looked at that part of the op-order yet," Bender said, "but off the top of my head, that sounds about right. This is the 7th of July, and maybe that explains why we're leaving tonight, because H-hour is supposed to be at some as yet unspecified time on the 10th."

"So," Garcia said, "we've got a long haul ahead in order to cover a short span."

"So it would seem," Bender said. "Get it laid out on the chart, Hal, but keep that chart in your stateroom, locked up, because I don't want anyone getting a look at it until we've taken in all lines and cleared the harbor. All right, gentlemen, that's about the size of it, so let's get this tug secured for sea and get ready to go."

And with that, everyone rose and dispersed.

Getting underway two hours before sundown, the 3X and the two tugs with which she normally operated made an easy transit south. By sunrise the following morning, they were just off of Sousse where they joined an escort screen that had gathered to shepherd a flock of LSTs and LCIs, all of them filled to overflowing with both infantry and equipment, all of them destined eventually to join DIME Force in the Gulf of Gela. As far as Hal could later remember, he thought that the screen commander might have been riding a destroyer, possibly the *Maddox*, possibly the *Bently*, but in fact, he took little note of the specific ships in company. When not actually standing watch or catching, here and there, an hour of much needed sleep, Bender had him glued to the chart, tending to the ship's navigation.

Theirs was by no means a swift convoy. Given the slow speeds of both the LSTs and the LCIs, each of the watch standers sometimes felt like they were moving at no more than a crawl, but blissfully, the seas remained fairly calm. Then, suddenly, on July 9 in the vicinity of Malta, a Mediterranean gale of nearly hurricane proportions kicked up, showing Hal the worst weather he had ever seen at sea anywhere. By that time the large attack transports had joined with them, and even those with their high bows began taking green water all the way back to their breaks.

"*Jesus Christ!*" Bender protested, seizing one of the stirrups hanging from the overhead to keep himself from being thrown off his feet, "I ain't never seen nothin' like this in my entire life!"

"Nor I," Hal replied, gripping both sides of the chart table in an effort to keep himself from going down. "If this ain't a State 8 sea, it's a 9! How the hell we're ever going to land troops in seas like these is something I don't even want to think about."

"They'll have to call it off, sure," Bender said. "This would swamp the LCVPs in a heartbeat and drown every man in Allen's division, and that's if they could even get down the sides of the transports and into the boats at all. Seas like these would probably pitch them right off the sides of the landing nets."

"You really think they would call it off?" Hal asked. "Don't you suppose they'd just delay it and wait the storm out?"

"To tell you the truth," Bender said, once more nearly thrown off his feet as a big wave crashed down on the ship's bow, forcing the 3X to plunge, "I don't have the slightest idea. I hate to ask, Hal, but you'd better go down and have a look around. See if we're holding together and take a look at the crew. I'd guess about half of them must be barfing up their guts."

Hal went down, and Bender had been right. About half of the men, those not on duty, were seasick, but Lewis and Garcia were putting up with no malingering. Sick or not, those who had barfed were cleaning up their own messes, swabs in hand, with both warrant officers inspecting afterward to see that the job had been done right. The others, those not immediately employed on watch, had taken to their bunks, and the 3X seemed to be weathering the storm in the way she'd been designed to do, a fact that gave Hal a degree of satisfaction that he imagined Bender would share.

Bender, when Hal returned to the pilot house, looked slightly green around the gills himself, but he continued to bend to the work, conning the ship through the gale in a way that minimized, as far as possible, the worst that the storm could throw at them.

By 1400 that afternoon, the gale had worn everyone to a frazzle without showing the slightest sign that it might be letting up. Things really became serious when one of the LCIs in the flock experienced an engineering casualty that barely left her able to make headway and the Task Group commander sent the 3X an order to drop back and take the LCI in tow.

"Well," Hal said, when Bender handed him the message, "if this doesn't throw us into the soup, I don't know what will."

"Right," Bender said, his jaw setting. "I guess it's what we've been designed to do, so here's where we really begin earning our pay. Give me a maneuvering board solution to exit the screen without getting tangled up and I'll bring us around, and as soon as you do that, get Lewis on the sound-powered phones, tell him what we're about, and have him get lifelines on every man back there with him. They got into life jackets the minute this started, but I don't want any of them going overboard while we're trying to hook up. And tell Lewis to use the wire rope for this one because I don't want us popping a fiber line and losing a man owing to a snap-back."

Minutes later, with Bender on the con, the *3X* successfully exited the screen to port and doubled back, the waves immediately causing her to yaw and almost surf from the crests of the swells in front of her. Moving down the outside of the group formation, she passed the transports, the LSTs, and finally the LCIs as they struggled forward, spotted the stricken LCI a couple of miles to the south, passed her to port, came up around her stern, once more pitching and rolling, and worked her way forward until she was roughly alongside but still a good thirty yards from the laboring troop carrier.

As far as Hal could see from his observation point on the port side of the pilot house, the captain of the LCI, probably a junior grade lieutenant, had only allowed two men out onto the foc'sle of the LCI, and those two, hanging on for dear life, were being endangered by every wave that broke over the bow. How they were going to seize the heaving line when Lewis shot it over, pull in the messenger, and then haul over the towline amid those high seas mystified Hal. After a manner of speaking, it seemed a do or die operation, so without hesitation, everyone aboard both vessels put it in motion. To Hal and Bender's relief, it went off considerably better than anyone had had a right to expect.

Blissfully, by firing high, the gunner back beside Lewis on the fantail managed to loop the nylon shot line connected to the messenger directly over the heads of the two men on the foc'sle of the LCI. Once those men rose to their feet and got their hands on the line to haul over the messenger, more men emerged from behind the LCI's brakes. So, as soon as the foremost man on the foc'sle managed to thread the line through the vessel's bullhead, the enlarged working party on the LCI hauled over first the messenger and then the towline with uncommon speed, quickly dropping the towing eye over whatever towing bit seemed most handy.

A quick glance at the seas made Hal think it had been almost too easy, too unanticipated, and too successful to last. But it wasn't, and by moving slowly straight out ahead and with Lewis on the capstan back aft, the *3X* quickly took up the slack in the line and began to tow—not without difficulty, not without occasional stops and starts as one or the other of the ships crested a wave, either creating momentary slack in the line or putting it under increased tension, but with enough steady motion so that the tow eventually seemed to regulate itself into a fairly routine evolution.

"I don't think I could have imagined it," Yak said when he finally came up to the pilot house to relieve Hal for supper. "I thought we might be hours trying to hook up."

"Neither could the two of us," Bender said, from where he stood, holding onto a stirrup and leaning his weight against the pelorus. "Hal and I figured that if we didn't lose one man over the side, we'd lose two, and I worried about collision every second while we were alongside. I don't know that I could call myself a believer, but someone up there must be watching over us. As it turned out, hooking up to that Liberty ship we pulled in turned out to be almost more difficult."

Remembering the moment, Hal could only smile and nod in agreement. "The question now," he said, "is what happens when we get into the Gulf of Gela, particularly if this bird can't get her engines going again."

"I guess we'll cross that bridge when we get to it," Bender said. "In the meantime, what's it like below?" he asked, turning once more to Yak.

Yak laughed. "Well," he said, "they were pretty sick for a while. Hell, I was sick myself, but I think most of us are better now, and if you can believe it, I actually stopped Vega trying to skin two of Garcia's snipes in a crap game back in the salvage locker."

Hal could not believe it. How the dice could even remain level in the seas around them, he couldn't imagine.

"If that doesn't border on a gambling disease, I don't know what does," Bender said. "If this were peacetime, I think I'd try to send that kid to a Navy shrink. As is, I doubt that the Navy has a shrink out here anywhere."

"And if they do," Hal joked, "let's hope they're in consultation with whoever thought up running an operation like this in the midst of a gale."

"I can see," Bender grinned, "that you weren't born yesterday."

At some point in the middle of the night, Hal sensed that the gale had spent most of its force. That did not mean that the invasion force, DIME force, could run free and clear by any means. While the seas had moderated, they'd moderated only slightly, taking the sea state down to a level that Hal imagined to be somewhere in the range of a State 5 to a State 6, with waves and swells that still remained high enough to create an untold number of difficulties when H-hour arrived and it came time to load and dispatch the landing craft.

The Army, thinking to surprise the enemy, had demanded and succeeded in arranging for a night landing under the assumption that they would catch the Italians napping. In fact, by the time the vast array of ships got within five miles of the beach, the Italians had turned on their massive search lights, the sound of anchor chains sliding through the hawse pipes leaving no one ashore in doubt about the trouble that seemed to be coming their way from the sea. And to make matters worse for the landing force, the Army in its supposed wisdom had also made the decision to forgo a preliminary shore bombardment owing to their mistrust of naval gunnery and their misguided attempt to surprise the enemy in the still dark hours of the morning. Always, Hal thought, in the Pacific, many hours of shore bombardment preceded whatever invasion force happened to be going in, and then, to help matters along, that invasion force landed after sunrise so that the troops had a clear view of what they were up against. How the Army's ploy for *HUSKY* would come off, Hal didn't know, but right from the start, it didn't look promising.

In fact, right from the start, it wasn't. Miles to sea, the transports experienced a fearful time attempting to unload into their landing craft given the continual turbulence of the seas. The men going ashore, having been tossed like bean bags for hours and hours before they were sent to the landing nets in order to climb down into their landing craft, were seasick beyond measure. To make matters worse, advanced landing scouts and reconnaissance parties had discovered underwater sand bars within one hundred yards of the beach, built up over the years by runoff from inland streams and rivers. The sand bars were going to impede the LSTs in particular, making it extremely difficult for them to get in to the beach so that their massive bow doors could open and they could disgorge their loads of precious men, trucks, tanks, and equipment. Already over the circuits, Hal could hear talk of locking together pontoons to create makeshift piers to which the LSTs could tie up and send their cargoes ashore. What that meant, Hal thought, was that the tugs would be forced to go in and help some of those vessels to their berths—and the *3X* would be getting closer to the invasion beach than any of them had ever imagined.

Well before dawn, the fighting in support of the landing had already commenced. Without regard to the Army's strictures about bombardment, at least one destroyer had taken one of the Italian search lights under fire to extinguish it, and there were reports of another having fired directly into a pillbox that had shown the temerity to open fire on the fleet from a distance.

Twelve miles out from the beach, having towed the LCI which they'd picked up the previous afternoon alongside the remainder of the LCIs which were waiting to go forward, Bender received an order from the commander of those ships. While the LCI in question found herself still unable to use her engines, control of the vessel was to be turned over to yet another LCI, the 3X relinquishing responsibility for the little ship so that the two LCIs could tie up together, the first propelling both toward the same beach under a single ship's power.

Given the high chop of the swells, the transfer proved ticklish. The 3X put over every fender she could find to absorb the shock of the two vessels coming together and then, as gently as possible, eased the stricken LCI over against her healthy sister ship so that the two of them could make up as a single unit in order to proceed on into the beach.

"This is the kind of thing that could give an able man gray hair," Bender said, as the exchange was effected and the two ships finally broke away from one another. "And doing it in the dark has made it twice as bad. Why we aren't nothing more than a pile of floating splinters after this is anyone's guess."

"War is hell," Hal grinned.

"Boy, isn't that the truth," Bender said. "What time is sunrise?"

"In about five minutes," Hal said.

Not five minutes later, just as the sun began to rise, DIME force came under a vicious air attack. Stukas descended on them like a cloud of eagles diving straight down from the north, one, almost before the ships could start their guns firing, unloading directly over a destroyer, the *Maddox*, which had been patrolling for submarine defense not four miles behind the 3X. Hal could not see the bomb as it fell, but much to his horror, both he and Bender had a clear view of the massive explosion that resulted when the bomb hit, the entire stern of the destroyer disappearing at once in a blazing pillar of fire and smoke.

"*Holy shit!*" Bender roared, momentarily paralyzed by the sight.

"*Jesus,*" Hal gasped. "That bastard hit the magazine."

"Bring us around! Bring us around!" Bender shouted at Hal. "We've gotta get over there and try to find survivors!"

Even before Hal had reversed course and fully brought the ship around, he knew that finding survivors was going to be difficult, for as everyone on the bridge looked on with horror at the awful spectacle in front of them, the remains of the *Maddox* went straight down before as much as two minutes elapsed, taking with her, Hal imagined, most of her officers and crew.

By that time, both of the *3X*'s 20 mm were firing such a staccato of rounds that the sound they were making rivaled a string of Chinese firecrackers. Interspersed in between, the thunder of the 3″/50 alerted Hal to the fact that they were also under attack, bombs falling from the Stukas in an ever exploding array all over the seas around them as one or another of the Kraut pilots tried to do for yet another of DIME force's ships. As the helmsman steered erratically toward one splash after another under the imagined assumption that two bombs would never fall in the same place, Hal saw at least one of the enemy planes take a hit as it attempted to recover from its dive. The Stuka's starboard wing was blown off by either a three- or five-inch gun from one of the surrounding ships, the fuselage instantly whirling halfway around in the air before the remains rolled fully over and drove straight into the sea.

"At least that's something," Hal said, to no one in particular.

"But not much of an exchange for the *Maddox,*" Bender said.

"No," Hal said. "It's not."

Near where the *Maddox* herself had gone down when they finally reached the point, they found no one. Farther to the east, after widening their search and joining with another tug looking for survivors, they did pick up two men, badly burned and in need of urgent treatment. With little delay, they managed to transfer them onto an APA Attack Transport which, they'd been informed, carried a doctor. But before they could return to the site and continue their search, they received orders to move in toward the beach for the purpose of doing what they'd imagined they might be called upon to do—assisting one of the LSTs while it tried to make up to one of the pontoon piers that had been bolted together and snaked out from the beach.

Twice more that morning, they came under air attack, and once, according to Yak, Bix had actually gotten some 20 mm rounds into a Macchi that had tried to strafe the LST that they were pushing, causing the Italian fighter to pancake in the sea some two thousand yards from where they were working. With the much bigger ship to shield them, none of them had been aware of the strafe, so Bix had only connected with the fighter on its way out, blowing off a part of the plane's tail section which instantly caused it to dip onto the sea. And had Yak not reported the case to them, none of them would have noticed. Regardless of the fact that masses of infantry were already ashore and moving inland, they had come under fire from the beach, from some kind of machine gun which had apparently been well hidden and gone utterly unnoticed by the troops storming ashore. None of the men in the pilot house ever spotted the gun; they only knew that it had opened up on them because three of the machine gun's rounds had pierced the starboard bulkhead immediately above their heads, sending splinters flying against their helmets, one of them sticking into Hal's shoulder without going very deep, another lancing into Bender's bicep and drawing a trickle of blood.

"*Ow!*" Bender winced. "What the hell was that?"

Hal's response had been a loud grunt as he snatched the splinter and drew it from his shoulder.

"Machine gun?" he said. "Somewhere."

"Friendly fire, more like," Bender said. "Think this will qualify us for Purple Hearts?"

"I've had enough of Purple Hearts," Hal said. "But thanks very much, all the same."

"You're bleeding, you know?" Bender said.

"But thankfully, not enough to matter," Hal said. "We've got this big boy tied up to the pontoon now. Reckon we can take in our lines and get the hell out of here?"

"Do it," Bender said. "And the sooner the better."

Reports from the beach concerning the 1st Division's progress were sketchy throughout the morning and the afternoon. Given the numbers of ships going in and unloading supplies, and given the number of times the 3X found herself called in to help one or another of them to maneuver near the assault beaches, both Bender and Hal concluded that General Allen's troops were moving inland, establishing a perimeter, and reaching their objectives. By the afternoon, already, large numbers of Italian prisoners were appearing on the beach to be loaded into retracting LSTs for removal to North Africa. Here and there, while in close enough to see what happened to be going on, Hal spotted a German in the mix. Late afternoon put them under yet another air attack, and twice during the night, working beneath flares that the enemy planes dropped, this or that German bomber tried to get at the larger transports with a torpedo and failed, one or two destroyers having to withdraw from action owing to damage caused by near misses from bombs that were also dropped.

On the following day, to everyone's surprise, the cruiser *Boise* and a couple of destroyers suddenly opened up at about 0900 in the morning and began throwing a bombardment inland with such a massive roar that Hal imagined it would wake the dead in Sicilian cemeteries. Only later and well after the fact did they learn that both the Italians and the Germans had tried to throw a massive tank attack against the 1st Division that morning. Although much had been getting ashore from the LSTs that were able to make it up to the pontoons, the tanks, anti-tank weapons, and anything else that might have been used to repel armor remained in short supply on the beach. As a result, and in the absence of any air support whatever, the Army finally took a chance, called upon naval gunfire support, and found themselves astonished by how effective it turned out to be, direct hits doing for any number of the enemy's tanks while breaking up and repelling the Nazi assault just in the critical moment when it was about to penetrate toward Gela and split the Seventh Army in half.

But aside from the roar of the guns and the flash from their broadsides, Bender, Hal, Yak, and the remainder of the crew aboard the 3X remained blissfully unaware of what was going on. All of their attention was focused on taking a damaged LST in tow, a near miss from yet another German bomb having so damaged the ship's screw that she'd gone dead in the water not two miles off the beach.

By the time the 3X got a towline over to the LST, the gale that had bedeviled them across the preceding days had dissipated, making the hook up a matter of almost textbook routine. To Hal's relief and the relief of not a few others, including both Bender and Yak, they were suddenly out of it and moving south toward Malta with the larger ship floating behind them at the end of their wire rope.

"You reckon they'll send us back once we've dropped this bird off?" Yak asked, as he prepared to relieve Hal from the morning watch.

"Probably," Hal said. "But not before we get a break from things."

"But you think we're out of it for a space?"

"If one of those bastards doesn't find us and attack from the air on our way down," Hal said, "and as long as some lingering Italian sub or U-boat doesn't try to take us out."

"Really," Yak laughed, "you're almost too reassuring."

"So where's Bender?" Hal asked.

"Trying to catch a couple hours of sleep," Yak said.

"Good," Hal said, "by my count he's been up and on the bridge for forty-eight hours straight, maybe more."

"He said pretty much the same thing about you," Yak said. "Said that you'd better get down there and try to catch a few *zzzzs* yourself while the getting is good. You can rest assured that I'll sound the general alarm the minute one of those dive-bombing Stukas shows up. I checked sonar just before I came up to relieve, and they don't have a thing going down there save for the pings we're sending out."

"And let's hope it stays that way," Hal said. "All right, Yak. I'm going straight to my rack, but don't forget to raise the roof if something unpleasant develops."

To everyone's relief, nothing unpleasant did develop. After managing to catch three full hours of sleep, Hal was back on the bridge with Bender by the time they reached Malta that night, caught up with the pilot boat, and managed to tow the LST into the harbor at Valletta where the Royal Navy's salvage crews were prepared to put her in a floating dry dock to replace the ship's propeller.

According to what they saw in Valletta, the city had been bombed and bombed and bombed again, leaving piles of debris everywhere. No one went ashore because, given the activity they'd passed through the three previous days, it was vital that the crew of the 3X catch up on some well-earned rest. So what they saw of Valetta limited itself mostly to the harbor, and what they saw wasn't pretty.

Breakfast went down late that morning, Bender permitting a delayed reveille so that each man could snatch an extra hour from the ship's routine, and when it did go down, it consisted mostly of powdered eggs, canned bacon, and hard cheese. About the only thing fresh turned out to be the coffee, but no one complained because across the three days before—tossed hither and yon by the gale and the invasion—meals had largely consisted of Spam sandwiches made with stale bread.

What the men hoped for but what they didn't get was a day in port. Even as the ship's five officers gulped down their breakfast, Bender received a message through radio which ordered them to take on fuel and get underway by 1000 that morning with the purpose of making the beaches in front of Licata where at least two LCIs, both of them seriously damaged during the landings, had also broached and needed to be retrieved.

"This is bound to be a fucking shit detail if there ever was one," Bender observed, passing the message to Hal as soon as he'd read it.

"And that's if we can even get close enough to the beach to pass either of those birds a towline," Hal said, swiftly reading what Bender had handed to him.

"You suppose their crews are still onboard?" Yak asked.

"Sorta depends on how much fire they were taking," Bender said. "If they were getting plastered the way the message indicates, the CO might have put his people ashore where they could find better cover huddling with whatever infantry had dug in around the beach. And for all I know, they may still be there, or they may not. I guess we'll find out when we get up there."

The *3X* got back up there to the waters off Licata at around 1700 that afternoon. The minute they closed to within half a mile of the beach, they came under air attack, a single Reggiane Falco II sweeping in on them at 300 mph from directly over what the charts had called Telegraph Hill, attempting to put the sun behind its attack as the ship made its approach to what the op-order had designated Red Beach. Even before the air attack commenced, Hal and Bender had already spotted the two broached LCIs ashore, so that they were making straight for them when the Italian fighter descended upon them. From what Hal could see, they had been fortunate in doing so; having made a 20-degree port turn in order to approach the LCIs from the base course they followed on their way up to Malta, they had unwittingly succeeded in pointing the bow almost precisely in the direction from which the air attack came at them. All three of their guns, the 3″/50 and both 20 mm, happened to be unmasked at the time.

The gunners, operating on Bender's standing instructions, didn't wait for his command to open fire. Instead, the moment all three of them identified the incoming threat, they closed their firing keys and began to throw out everything they had. Even from where he stood, taking as much cover as the forward bulkhead of the pilot house afforded him, Hal could see the fighter's machine-gun rounds striking the water and walking toward the ship perhaps three hundred yards out in front of them. But with bright 20 mm tracers going out, along with everything else that the ship had started firing back, by the time their splashes had closed to within 100 yards, those machine-gun rounds showed a pronounced turn to starboard. That's when Hal knew that the umbrella of fire that the ship had started putting up had proved too much for the nerves of the Italian pilot and that he had altered course, veering away from his attack a moment too soon for his rounds to do them any damage.

"*Shit!*" Bender hissed. "That was too damn close for comfort. Kudos to the gunners, Hal. If we hadn't been in position for all three of them to open up on him, I think he would have come straight in on us."

"Agreed," Hal said, feeling his body shaking slightly as he made his response, "but that's no guarantee that he isn't going to try it from another direction in another second or two."

But to everyone's relief and probably to the relief of the Italian pilot who had attempted the strafe, he was gone, already out of sight to the east. The only sign of his continued presence in the area was the distant AA rounds that the ships down around Gela were putting up, the tiny black puffs of flak they were throwing into the sky barely visible in the air above them as the Falco II passed over their heads.

"All right," Bender said, once more turning his attention to the LCIs on the beach, "how close can we go without getting ourselves into trouble?"

"There's supposed to be one of those sand bars in there about forty yards off the beach," Hal said, "submerged beneath this tide, so according to what the chart's showing, I don't think we ought to approach closer than 100 yards, at least 125 yards to stay on the safe side."

"That's going to be a long haul on the towline for you," Bender said.

"Come again?" Hal said, his eyes opening wide.

"This hook up has got to be done right," Bender said flatly, "and that means you're going to have to go in and see that it is. Sorry about that, but that's the way it has to be."

Hal felt a lump in his throat. He knew Bender was right, of course, but that didn't mean that he and the others taking the towline in to make the connection wouldn't be taking a risk.

"Reckon we ought to take side arms?" Hal asked, once more getting control of himself after a stab of fear and a momentary lapse.

"My guess is that the beach has been fully cleared," Bender said, "but in this war, a man can't be too careful. If I were you, I'd carry a .45, and I think you ought to break out rifles for the remainder of the boat crew. I doubt that they could hit anything with them, not after the long months since they were last on the rifle range, but if push came to shove, they might at least force a sniper to keep his head down and not risk firing at you."

Something would prove better than nothing, and on that assumption and on Bender's orders, Hal hurried below, called out the boat crew, issued them with small arms, consulted with Lewis whose crew would pay out the towline back aft, and made himself as ready as he could to head for the beach.

☙

Hauling the wire rope all the way to the beach proved a trying experience for everyone in the boat. Lewis and his people had provided an able assist by tying floats to the heavy rope at twenty-yard distances in an attempt to keep the line from sinking and dragging on the bottom; nevertheless, given the weight of the line, Hal found things hard going in the boat. And to make matters worse, a German or Italian round, fired from the direction of Port Empedocle to the west, landed inland by three or four hundred yards, throwing up a cloud of dirt and dust that they had no trouble seeing from where they all sat in the whaleboat.

"*Shit!*" exclaimed Kawalski who happened to be acting as stern hook, "as if we didn't have enough to worry about!"

No one else said a word. All of them, Hal knew, including himself, were simply too stunned by the blast and too scared to make a sound, each of them as the boat went in merely hunching down lower as though the effort might save them.

Ashore, the captains of the two LCIs, both junior lieutenants, had called their crews back to their ships following a night spent in nearby foxholes and bunkers. In order to aid whatever tug or tugs came after them, they'd broken out every shovel carried aboard both vessels and put their men to work digging the beach sand away from the areas they could reach around their rudders and screws in the hopes of avoiding more damage than necessary when they were once hooked up to a tug and the tug began to try to retract each of them from the beach.

Bender had been smart, Hal thought, in timing their arrival on Red Beach to coincide with a high tide. As a result, given the channels that the shoveling sailors had managed to cleave from the sand, rudders and screws promised to be almost awash by the time each vessel accomplished its hook up. Whether or not that would prevent enough damage for each LCI to once more make turns and get underway when it came off the beach, Hal didn't know. If it did, fine, but if it didn't, the *3X* would take one, or the other, or both, in tow and haul them back down to the repair yards in Valletta.

With the ape-like Click once more at the helm of the whaleboat and given the light surf that happened to be running as the tide came up, and without running the danger of broaching the whaleboat, he worked in close enough to the beach so that Hal could leap over the side into waist-deep water. Carrying a loop of the towline's messenger with him as he went, Hal handed it straight over to one the LCI's boatswain's mates who stood waiting to take it from him at the water's edge. After Hal showed the man exactly the chock he wanted, with the messenger and the wire rope threaded through upon on the LCI's stern, Hal went forward, climbed a chain boarding ladder onto the deck, and found himself met by the ship's captain. The two of them then made for the stern to examine the hook up.

As the LCI had been designed to do, she'd dropped her own huge Danforth anchor approximately one hundred yards before she'd beached, expecting to use both her own winch and the anchor to allow her to retract when the time came. When she'd broached, she'd beached so hard that her own winch simply didn't have the power to pull her loose and back into the sea. Nevertheless, with her retracting cable still intact, Hal knew that its strength combined with the pull that the *3X* would be able to exert would probably be more than enough to free the vessel and haul her back into the water.

"Not that one," Hal said to a seaman on the LCI's fantail who had just received the messenger from the boatswain on the beach and was about to thread it through the same chock that held the cable to the Danforth. "I don't want your winch cable chafing my wire rope. Thread it through that chock off to the starboard side."

As soon as the sailors assembled on the fantail of the LCI hauled the towline up through the chock intended and brought the eye aboard, Hal himself took the eye and placed it over precisely the pair of bits that he believed would give the *3X* the best opportunity for exerting the kind of strain on the ship that it would haul if off the sand and back into the sea.

Less than a minute later, by giving commands to the LCI's winch operator and by speaking to Bender on the bridge of the *3X* by means of a walkie talkie that actually performed as it was supposed to, slack was taken out of both the wire rope and the cable to the Danforth. As both sources of power exerted more and more tension on their lines, the LCI moved, jerking at least one foot, and then another, and then two or three feet more until her stern slipped straight into the channel her crew had dug from the sand. With a final prolonged screeching sound, she found herself again floated and off the beach, the *3X* continuing to haul her back over the sandbar to the point where she could recover her immense Danforth anchor before the *3X* towed her into open waters. There she freed herself from the tow while the whaleboat came once more alongside and took Hal off as he climbed down the sea ladder and leapt from the bottom rung into the well of the whaleboat. Once again heading back for the beach, once again hauling the towline, they went in to attempt to retrieve the second of the LCIs.

"Shit, Mr. Goff," Morris, acting as bow hook, said to Hal as they started back for the beach. "You see the way that bastard had been shot up? They was holes everywhere 'long her port side!"

Hal hadn't noticed. So intent had he been on what he'd been doing that he hadn't so much as seen the damage to the LCI or bothered to ask the ship's captain about it. With regard to the second LCI as they approached it, he counted two blackened holes that looked like they'd been made by something in the neighborhood of a 37 mm anti-tank round, and not a few others that looked like 20 mm holes, all of them high enough up on the side to have endangered the crew, a few even up around the pilot house. They left a bitter testament, he concluded, to the ordeal the LCI had experienced during the invasion, and how many, he wondered, had been wounded in the process?

Hauling the second LCI off the beach proved a far more difficult evolution than retrieving the first because the cable connecting the ship with her Danforth anchor had been severed, probably by a Kraut round; their ability to retract the ship from where she'd ridden up on the sand rested solely with whatever force the *3X* would be able to exert on her. As a result, the extraction of the second ship took nearly three times as long as the recovery of the first. The *3X* managed to do it, but by the time the exercise reached completion, every man engaged felt sweated through and utterly exhausted. To make matters worse, whatever gun the Krauts had off to the west had landed two more rounds within three hundred yards of them which merely increased both the tension and the fear that everyone had worked under.

Once the second LCI had been floated and hauled across the bar, her captain quickly discovered that a casualty to her engineering plant—a casualty caused on the previous day by one of the Italian rounds that had hit her—wasn't going to permit her diesels to start. The *3X* would indeed have to tow her all the way back down to Malta where the repair yards could take her in hand.

About going back to Malta, no one complained. What they did complain about, and loudly, was the air attack that they underwent not fifteen miles from the coast. With no warning of any kind, a flare burst overhead. Less than a minute later, a German or Italian bomber which they could not identify in the darkness threw enough rounds at them in a swift overhead pass to hole and splinter the peak of the bow in several places, the ship's 20 mm gunners only having time to throw out a few rounds as the plane made a hasty exit after passing almost directly overhead.

"*Christ!*" Bender growled. "If that bastard hadn't expended its bombs somewhere before it caught us, we'd have been toast!"

"Thank the Lord for small favors," Hal said, once more feeling himself shake. "I'll get down there quick march and make sure that no one has been hit."

And with that, racing below, Hal made a swift inspection of the spaces up forward. Fortunately, no one had been wounded, regardless of the fact that at least one of the machine-gun rounds had passed through the berthing compartment before lodging in a stanchion directly beneath the main deck forward. More rounds had passed into the chain locker at approximately the same elevation, the peak rails catching several as well.

"No one has been hurt," Hal said to Bender and Yak upon his return, "but we have damage. Looks like 7.7 mm machine gun rounds to me because one of them is lodged in a stanchion down there."

"Must have caught us with the machine gun in his nose bubble," Yak said.

"And we're damned lucky that was all," Bender said. "Get up both an after-action report and a damage report," he then said to Hal, "and we'll see if the repair folks at Valletta can do anything for us when we get in."

They didn't reach Valletta before the sun came up the following morning. There, after working the LCI into the confines of the repair yard, three of the facility's fitters who had experience with wooden ships swiftly came aboard and went straight to work on the damage that had been done to the 3X. By 1900 that night, she looked as good as new and was once more readying for sea. To everyone's relief, the ship received an order that allowed her to stand down for twelve full hours before she was once more to be dispatched north to the beaches around Scoglitti where any number of broached LCVPs were waiting to be retrieved from the invasion beaches.

6

By July 16, according to the reports that the radiomen peeled off their nets and sent up for them to read, the 3rd Infantry Division had taken Port Empedocle and, with Patton driving them hard, seemed to be working rapidly north in the direction of Palermo. Somewhere out there, at last, they had finally run into an Italian formation—a regiment, brigade, or division—that showed itself willing to fight, so their advance while rapid seemed nevertheless to go forward against some stiff resistance. On the east coast where it had been assumed that Montgomery's Eighth Army would move rapidly north, the fact proved otherwise. North of Syracuse, the Eighth Army had been stopped cold, and to Patton's consternation, Montgomery had worked a fiddle with higher command so as to jog west onto roads that were supposed to have provided Middleton's 45th Division with several routes north. He edged them even farther to the west and took over the routes for himself, infuriating Patton and the remainder of the Americans as Montgomery tried to edge his way around the western slopes of Mt. Etna.

During this period, after retrieving no fewer than sixteen broached LCVPs, an LCT or two, and yet another stranded LCI from the beaches in the vicinity of Scoglitti, with Port Empedocle finally taken so as to provide an actual harbor for Allied ships, the

3X found herself dispatched there. Once arrived, she spent the next several days helping supply ships to move in and out of the port until, finally, on July 22, Truscott's 3rd Division punched its way into Palermo and drove the Germans out.

"What do you want to bet that Patton turns east and makes a run on Messina from Palermo?" Bender said.

"Sounds to me like a sure bet," Garcia said over lunch in the hour before they left Port Empedocle to round the cape and start north to Palermo where their most recent orders had directed them to report.

"From what we've seen and heard out of him," Yak laughed, "I think it's a sure bet that he'll move like a lion in an attempt to beat Montgomery into Messina. Those two, I'm told, don't like each other."

"The question I have," Hal said, speaking thoughtfully, "is whether or not the Germans will try to pour more troops into Sicily from the boot. Positioned as we appear to be, with Montgomery having given up his drive to the north and edged his way around Etna to the west, I don't see how we're going to trap the Krauts if they want to try to escape. Looks to me like they could give us a hell of a fighting withdrawal, all the time narrowing their front while extracting a bunch of their people across the Straits of Messina as we try to catch up with them."

"Fortunately," Bender said, "unless we get pulled in to do something in direct support of whatever Patton throws east, we don't have to worry about that. Looks to me like our worry is going to be fending off air attacks while we try to move transports and supply ships in and out of Palermo, not to mention the occasional cruiser."

"I wonder what Palermo will be like?" Yak mused.

"I'm guessin' them Fascists will be gone," Lewis laughed, "but I doubt the Mafia will be. Far as I knows, Palermo's somethin' like Mafia headquarters in Sicily."

"Thanks for the thought," Bender said with a smirk.

"Them's usually got bigger fish ta fry than no accounts like us," Lewis grunted, "but a word to the wise: best to leave their women alone, save for the ones they's sellin."

"And how the hell is anyone to know the difference?" Yak replied, eyes wide with disbelief.

"By what they charge," Lewis retorted. "I'd be bettin' the Mafia molls come at a high price."

"And, one hopes, with recent VD inspection cards to prove it." Hal grinned. "Reckon we ought to warn the troops to steer clear?"

"Ha," Bender said, "I'd guess that we could warn them until the cows come home, but when you start to consider a couple like Prince and Crisp, I'd imagine that even written warnings would fall on dead ears. Eat up, everyone," Bender said, glancing at his watch, "we've got to get this tub underway."

Hal had no idea what Palermo had been like before the war, but Palermo as the men of the *3X* found it did not look like a garden spot. The occasional palm tree had escaped destruction, and some of the buildings that Hal could see from the flying bridge as they entered port and tied up beside the quay did look formerly regal, but while the port hadn't been pounded in the same way as Valletta, it looked grim, bomb damaged to a considerable extent, and dirty with swirls of dust emerging from one narrow street after another. Surrounded by mountains and flanked by the rocky face of Mount Pellegrino, Hal found the physical terrain imposing and wondered how much the surrounding ranges cut off easy transit into other parts of Sicily.

"Might have been a beautiful spot once," Bender said, as the two secured the ship from the Special Sea and Anchor Detail.

"And might be again," Hal said, "just not at the moment."

"No," Bender said. "Looks like we pretty well beat the hell out of the harbor."

"With the salvage crews already trying to raise whatever ships the Germans have sunk before clearing out," Hal said.

"And we're going to have to be mindful of them, going in and out," Bender said. "Get over to the harbor master and see if we can't get a chart that shows where they're located. Better take our chart in case they don't have one and you have to annotate the one we've just used."

"Right," Hal said.

The harbor master, when Hal found his office, turned out to be a genial lieutenant commander named Revel, a swarthy man with a head of unruly black hair who immediately showed Hal the chart that he'd been keeping, to allow him to annotate his own.

"Port Empedocle operating up to speed now?" he asked, as Hal finished the job he'd been sent to do.

"Yes Sir," Hal said. "The salvage crews seem to have gotten rid of most of the mines and raised whatever hulks the Italians left behind in their attempt to block the harbor, but with the truth told, I think they went out of there so fast when Truscott pushed them that they didn't have time to do much damage. We started moving ships in and out of there almost from the moment we took the place."

"Wish I could say we'd had it that easy here," Revel said, speaking with a slight shake of his head but a twinkle in his eyes. "We had to clear more mines than we would have liked and one or two hulks which the Krauts sank near the entrance, but we got that job done and are well started on the inner harbor now. My hope is that we'll be operating close to full tilt within a week, at least with enough berths to support Patton to his satisfaction."

"When do you imagine he'll start moving east?" Hal asked.

"Oh, he's already started," Revel said with a smile. "The man himself, you'll understand, is putting up in some Sicilian palace hereabout, but Truscott no more than entered the city before Patton ordered him to turn right and push east for Messina as fast as his men could go."

"And how fast would that be, if you have any idea, Sir?" Hal asked, genuinely interested.

"I imagine that the Krauts are going to put up a pretty strong defense," Revel said, "so I'd expect that it's going to be a fighting grind all the way. And to make matters worse, that coast road they'll have to take will present a multitude of obstacles to Truscott's people. The way that thing's been built, if you ask me, the Germans will be able to cut it at will, by blowing bridges and stretches of road for nearly the entire length. The road's built high up on the sides of hills almost all the way, and some of those hills are damned steep from what I've been told. Knock out a piece of it here and there, and Patton's engineers are liable to be building bridges during every hour they're awake. Between the two of us, I wouldn't like to be Truscott because Patton's liable to be on his back like stink on a skunk for as long as it takes, and knowing Patton by reputation, he won't be happy if it takes any more than record time, and probably, not even with that."

Hal grinned. "I hear they're calling him 'blood and guts.'"

"You have good ears," Revel said with a chuckle. "The man's a pip, no doubt about it. Look, Mr. Goff, from what my messages show me, I think your ship probably won't be required to work tonight because everything that's supposed to be coming up from Malta is already in port and tied up. Anyone give you any gouge yet on places to eat or drink?"

"No Sir," Hal said, "we only pulled in and tied up right before I came over here. We haven't been in port a full hour yet."

"All right," Revel said. "I'll give you the names of a couple of places that are safe and where your people will be treated right. The Belladonna is two streets over and one street back, and its sign is intact—green background with red lettering. It's a tavern of sorts that serves wine and beer, and there are plenty of B-girls working the joint, but I can't recommend the food. The MPs watch the place pretty closely, so thus far, it's remained reasonably tame, and if your crew puts in there, I doubt that they can get themselves into much trouble. Mama Galdoni's is one street farther down and two streets back. You can buy wine, beer, and grappa there, and the pasta is excellent. What with the war and all, I'm doubtful you can find much in the way of meat dishes, and I don't know that you'd want to try them if you did, but from time to time, she has rabbit that some hunter has delivered, and that's not bad. No girls in that place; it's a trattoria only but worth a visit."

"Thanks," Hal said, "I'll put out the word to the crew.

"Better be sure to send 'em with protection," Revel said. "Boys may be boys, but the VD rate here is high enough to worry about."

"Understood," Hal said. "We inspect to see that each of them is carrying before we allow them ashore, and I'm doubtful that it could be any worse than Bizerte."

"Right," Revel said, "and don't hesitate to come back if you find anything I might be able to help you with regarding harbor facilities."

One more question," Hal said.

"Speak."

"Air raids," Hal asked. "How much of a problem are they likely to be?"

"To be on the safe side, I'd keep at least one of your 20 mm manned day and night. We get fair warning from radar here, something I don't suppose your ship carries, so you'll hear the sirens go up well in advance of anything coming in, but a ship can't be too careful. According to what we know, most of the raids we get are coming straight down from Sardinia. Now that the Air Corps has finally got its head out of its ass, we do have some air cover in the form of a combat air patrol, but we don't have night fighters yet, and the

Germans seem to know it, so that's when the most of their raids have been hitting us."

"Understood, and thanks," Hal said, "And thank you, Sir, for the word about where to eat. After the rations we've been getting, I'd imagine that our entire crew will want to descend on Mama Galdoni's before, that is, the white hats swarm over to The Belladonna." And with that, Hal took his leave.

Mama Galdoni's, when Hal, Bender, Yak, and Lewis found it, Garcia standing as command duty officer for the night, didn't look to be anything that any of them would want to write home about, and neither did Mama Galdoni when they finally got a look at her where she stood cooking in the kitchen. Furnished with straightforward wooden tables and wire chairs, Hal didn't imagine that the tables had seen a coat of paint in forty years, and the surrounding walls looked to be of the same vintage. The pasta dishes, however, cooked with nothing more than garlic, mushrooms, and tomato sauce, came as a welcome alternative to the spare fare that the galley on the 3X had been serving them, particularly while they'd remained at sea, and the beer that Hal had ordered and the grappa with which he followed the meal both proved to be strong.

"That stuff carries a kick to beat hell," Bender said, taking a sip of the grappa before setting his own glass back on the table.

"'Taint lemon water, that's for sure," Lewis said.

Yak, when he first took a taste of the grappa, fell to coughing so hard that Hal worried he might choke.

"Christ!" Yak managed to splutter when he'd recovered himself. "Whose idea was it to order this stuff? Tastes to me like you could start a good-sized forest fire with less than a thimble of this brew."

Bender laughed. "I went to college with an Italian roommate named Moretti," he said. "I gather that his grandfather distilled grappa every year, and according to what he told me, when winter set in and it came time to start a fire in their coal furnace, they threw in a shot of grappa and followed it with a match. And that was all that it took."

"Makes sense to me," Yak said, trying another sip. "This is far and away the strongest stuff that has ever touched my lips."

"Beats your family's vodka?" Hal asked.

"By a mile," Yak wheezed.

"You got any word' bout what's on for tomorra, Cap'n?" Lewis asked, changing the subject.

"Can't be sure," Bender said, "but I think a convoy from Bizerte or Tunis may be coming up, and if so, we'll be called out to help them into port."

"Navy ships mostly, do you think?" Lewis asked.

"Probably not," Bender said. "The escorts, yes, but I'd imagine that the others will be Liberty ships, carrying ammo and supplies for this drive east that Patton's supposed to be preparing."

"According to the harbor master," Hal said, "it's already started."

"Well," Bender said, "there you have it. And what I'd guess is that from now on the entire Seventh Army will be drawing its supplies from this port, which probably means that we're going to work our tails off all day long, if not all day and all night. Better enjoy the grappa while you've got the chance because who knows when we'll be able to get back over here for another night like this."

As nights on the town went, Hal laughed to himself, a plate of pasta, a beer, and a grappa to follow didn't amount to much, and he wondered how Bea would respond when he finally wrote and told her about their big night out on Palermo. Fifteen minutes of looking into Bea's eyes, seated in nothing more than one of Pren's booths, would have been preferable, but both Bea and Pren's were a long way away, Hal's only connection with them coming from Bea's letters which, he was pleased to think, hadn't flagged in the least for the whole time he'd been in the Med.

Apparently, according to the last letter he'd received from her, when the summer session concluded, she intended to go home for the weekend. If she did, Hal wondered if she would finally mention him to her family, reveal the plans they had made, and the fact that she intended to marry him as soon as she saw him again. Those were questions she hadn't addressed yet, and over the fumes that he could draw from the grappa, he found himself wondering about them. Then, he stopped. There was no point, he realized, in attempting to foresee how Bea's family would react, and any time he spent worrying about it would be nothing more than time wasted. Eventually, he knew, as long as Bea didn't alter her attitude toward him or allow her feelings to cool, the confrontation would come, and they would proceed from whatever results it would produce.

"Penny for your thoughts," Yak said to Hal, forcing him to once more focus on the three men at the table.

"Sorry," Hal said, "I was thinking about something."

"I hope she proved worth the effort," Bender laughed.

"Oh, she's well worth the effort," Hal said.

"Say *what*?" Yak exclaimed. "You've got a girl, and you've been holding out on us, for how many months now?"

"Why, it never occurred to me that anyone would be remotely interested," Hal said smoothly, "assuming that the rest of you have irons in the fire yourselves, as I'm sure you do."

"Why we ain't had no such thoughts at all," Lewis jibed. "Irons in the fire, my ass. We been wonderin' when you was gonna read us one of them letters you keep receivin."

"Oh *those*," Hal grinned. "You mean the letters from my draft board, from my insurance company, and from my old college dormitory asking me why I haven't yet fully paid for my room and board for my last semester there?"

Bender once more broke out laughing. "Right," he said, "and just as soon as another of those letters from your draft board arrives, one that's written on yet another sheet of pale pink onion skin paper, I do hope that you'll want to share it with the rest of us."

"Dream on," Hal said. "Communications between me and my draft board are strictly confidential."

"That's good," Yak said acidly, "that bit about your draft board. And will your draft board answer to that name when we finally get the chance to meet her?"

"If you think I'd ever risk exposing my draft board to a collection of snakes like you three," Hal laughed, "you must be standing in line to buy the Brooklyn Bridge."

By July 27, Admiral Hewitt, who had been in overall charge of things for the Sicilian operation, had apparently combined the ships left supporting the invasion into something called Task Force 88, the *3X* and the other tugs on the north coast adding what Hal imagined to be their two bits' worth of value to the larger treasury of the whole. Mostly, they assisted the big supply ships going in and out of the harbor, but twice they were called out to help retrieve PT boats which had run aground. As Patton's Seventh Army pushed farther east along the coast in its attempt to capture the Italians and Germans retreating ahead of it, they were called out as well to retrieve LCVPs which had broached on beaches behind the German lines when Patton had landed battalion units behind the Krauts' retreating rear guards in an attempt to capture them.

During one of those missions they'd come under heavy machine-gun fire from a distance, splashes in the water alerting them to their danger, but a quick reaction from one of the ship's 20 mm gunners had discouraged the enemy and silenced the offending gun when the enemy realized that it had drawn return fire and sought to avoid it.

On a third occasion, in which Patton seemed to be sending up an entire regiment to try to outflank the enemy by landing behind them, the *3X* had found itself assigned to escort duty. Its sonar and the submarine detection that it was supposed capable of effecting placed it in the outer screen in company with a couple of PCs and a truncated squadron of submarine chasers. All of them were pinging like there was no tomorrow; all of them were giving way to the accompanying destroyers which patrolled closer in, shepherding the landing craft while remaining close by to lend fire support to the troops once they went ashore.

That fight, when it did take place, turned out to be bitter. The Krauts stood their ground for much longer than anyone had anticipated, giving the assaulting regiment little more than a bloody nose until, finally, additional attacking troops broke through to them from the west, forcing the Germans to withdraw through the hills.

But at the time of the engagement, no one aboard the *3X* had the slightest idea what happened to be taking place ashore. Instead, at least twice during that day, their attention was riveted on the skies, the Italians and the Germans both throwing in small but determined air attacks against them. The first consisted of three Macchis and a single two-engine Breda "Lynx" which attacked from the direction of Sardinia, while later in the day, coming straight at them from the east, two Messerschmitt 109s accompanied by two Ju 88s tried to strafe and bomb them. During the early attack, one of the Macchis connected with and did considerable damage to one of the subchasers in the screen, the small ship momentarily catching fire before her crew managed to extinguish the flames. But the chaser's engines appeared to remain intact, and somewhat to Bender's and Hal's surprise, her captain did not call for a tow and managed to continue with his patrol, regardless of the fact that three of his crew had been lightly wounded. Given the antiquated nature of the Breda "Lynx," Hal rather expected the plane to be shot out of the sky as it made its single pass over them and unloaded its stick of bombs. Much to everyone's disbelief, aside from dropping bombs wide of the mark and doing no damage, the Breda sailed through the formation and flew off toward Sardinia utterly untouched by the array of guns attempting to bring the plane down.

With the Germans, later that afternoon, things had gone differently. The strafe they conducted—bobbing and weaving like a pair of contortionists—they managed to bring off successfully. One of the planes got some rounds into the *PC* but without doing it any serious damage, and following their strafe, both disappeared at high speed as though they had never come. The Ju 88s, coming in only moments later, were none so successful.

At first, neither Bender nor Hal so much as saw them; then, alerted by Yak who was standing down behind the crew manning the 3"/50, both men saw one of the Ju 88s coming straight for them. It was in that moment that every gun on the *3X*, as well as a host of 20 mm mounts on the two nearest subchasers, cut loose on the offending bomber. This time the enemy's attack did not achieve success, fire from all three ships converging on the nose cone of the bomber before it could approach to within eight hundred yards of the screen and blowing the plane to the skies in a ball of fire.

Given the suddenness of the explosion in front of them, both Bender and Hal nearly sank to their knees. For several seconds, as each tried to regain his composure, neither said a word.

"I thought that one had us for sure," Hal said, his heart still pounding as he finally caught his breath.

"So did I," Bender said after another second's hesitation. "I don't know which one of us got that bastard, and I don't care, but thank God for the 20 millimeters."

"Yes," Hal said. "Think any of those Krauts survived?"

"Not a chance," Bender said, "and good riddance."

"Yes," Hal said, "and what I'd most like now, aside from a stiff grappa, is for someone up the chain to send us an order and get us the hell out of here."

"Agreed," Bender said, picking up his binoculars and glancing swiftly toward where the plane had gone down.

As though in answer to their prayers, not an hour after dark, the Force commander, operating they assumed from one of the destroyers, did send them an order. The quick result was that they approached the beach, picked up an LCI that had taken aboard wounded from the fighting ashore, and put on turns to make its best possible speed back to Palermo and the ambulances which would be waiting to carry the injured to the hospital. Bender and Hal concluded that the 3X had been selected because its sonar and depth charges offered protection, however minimal, from any submarine attack that might be made on the LCI.

"Piece of cake, do you think?" Yak asked, coming up to the bridge as the two ships started back.

"Let's hope," Bender said, as Hal, who happened to have the con at the moment, gave a course change to the helmsmen, "but to stay on the safe side, you and Lewis get back down there on the fantail and check to be sure that our K-guns are ready, just in case we should get a contact and have to throw a depth charge or two. And incidentally, my man, I damn sure hope you commended our gunners for what they pulled off this afternoon. That was some right fine shooting they gave us!"

"Not only did I commend them once, twice, and thrice," Yak said, "I also told them I would request extra liberty for them when or if we ever get back to Palermo."

"You can tell them that they've got it," Bender said, "and you can also tell them that if there were a medal for what they brought off, I'd be putting them in for it. Once Hal and I saw that bastard coming straight for us the way he was, we thought we'd had it. Your gunners saved us all."

"I'll pass along the good word," Yak said.

To Hal and Bender's utter astonishment, not fifteen miles from Palermo and not long after exchanging recognition signals with a squadron of three PT boats that were out patrolling the waters east of the port, sonar suddenly created consternation on the bridge by reporting a firm contact 1,100 yards distant on a bearing of 330 which put the contact nearly three points forward of the starboard beam.

"*Holy shit!*" Bender shouted. "Come around Hal, and attack! That's bound to be an Eyetie or Kraut U-boat. There ain't nothin' of ours up in this area!" Then, speaking swiftly to the sound-powered phone talker, Bender shouted more orders alerting the Yak and the K-gun crews on both sides of the ship to be ready to launch their depth charges.

Reacting swiftly, Hal not only turned but put on flank speed, shouting down the voice tube to Garcia in the engine room to give them everything he had. The danger, aside from a possible torpedo from whatever sub they might have gotten onto, turned on picking up enough speed so that they wouldn't blow themselves out of the water with any concussion produced by their own depth charges when they dropped them. Possibly, Hal quickly imagined, that was why the Navy had installed K-guns which would throw their depth charges out to the sides of the ship rather than over the stern where the explosions would come closer to endangering not only their hull but their rudder and screw. Unlike the little subchasers, they were simply too slow to outrun the thunder they would unleash if they ever rolled a depth charge over their stern.

Following the bearing on the contact sent up to them from sonar, Hal found himself steering 310 by the time he turned in on the supposed sub to meet its line of advance. Then, with much less time than he'd imagined when he and Bender started their attack run, sonar reported them to be within one hundred yards of the supposed sub. From that moment, after counting off five or six more seconds, Bender shouted *"Fire!"* and everyone aboard heard the loud *krumph* sounds from back aft as the K-gun's cartridges were fired and the two ashcans took flight.

From where he stood behind the Pelorus and given the darkness of the night, Hal couldn't see either of the depth charges in flight. Moments later, when both charges exploded behind them, he did catch sight of the high white plume of water that the charge to port had set off. By that time, in hopes that sonar might once again gain contact, he'd turned slightly more to the south in order to give their operator the best chance for picking up a sound return.

Seconds passed, then minutes, and aside from screw beats from the LCI which had continued to steam toward Palermo, the sonar operator aboard the *3X* didn't hear a thing.

"Think we got it?" Hal asked, speaking to Bender, the helmsman and the lee helmsman hanging on his every word.

"No," Bender said, "if that wasn't a submerged wreck that hasn't been marked on the chart and if there was actually a sub out there, I think we missed him and that he's gone silent, escaped, or was never there in the first place. If we'd done damage, I think Riggs would have heard something on passive, and he didn't. What matters is that we've kept whatever was down there from getting at the LCI, and considering the slow speed a sub would be reduced to underwater, the LCI is out of danger. So let's make whatever tracks Garcia can give us and see if we can't catch up with her."

With the LCI having gained about two thousand yards on them while they'd been making their attack on the supposed sub and with both ships making approximately the same speed, the *3X* never did catch up with her. But with barely an hour more to go before they reached Palermo, it didn't matter. Quietly and without fuss, everyone aboard the *3X* imagined that they'd done what they'd been sent to do, safely escorted the LCI and her wounded to Palermo, and fulfilled the mission that had been set for them. Once they arrived and tied up for what remained of the night, Hal went straight to work at his desk drafting an after-action report that Bender would undoubtedly read over, sign in the morning, and submit. And after all had been written and typed, he finally dropped into his bunk around 0230 that morning and fell immediately asleep.

෭

The following day, much to everyone's relief, whoever happened to be running the show for Task Force 88 gave them a day off for rest and upkeep. Word from whatever Patton happened to be calling "the Front" along the northern coast suggested that the regiment they'd put ashore on the preceding day, after a grueling fight and after a relief force had broken through to them, had been left in possession of the field, so there had been a victory of sorts—although a costly one with too many men wounded. Elsewhere, the remainder of the Seventh Army and Montgomery's Eighth seemed to be making slow but steady progress, the steep and hilly nature of the terrain giving the Germans an untold number of places from which to hold up their advance before they once more picked up their equipment and continued to withdraw toward Messina.

"Well," Hal said over lunch, after all five officers had spent a long morning struggling with the administrative paperwork that went with their jobs, "I'd guess the generals will finally get to Messina within the next couple of weeks, but whether there will be any Germans or Italians left there when we arrive is the big unknown."

"Youse think them Krauts is gonna pull all their people back across them straits of Messiner?" Lewis asked. "Don't see how's they could do it, not with that Army Air Corps poundin' 'em."

"From what I hear," Bender said, "that's the problem. Our Army Air Corps isn't poundin' 'em. Our Army Air Corps appears to be pounding the Italian mainland with what they call strategic bombing, hitting rail lines, roads, and factories on the mainland

118

but leaving the Straits pretty much untouched. The scuttlebutt is that they think they're going to win the war that way. What's called tactical air support—the kind that the infantry needs—is low on their list."

"If we had some of those carriers that are out in the Pacific," Garcia said, "I'm guessing it would be a different story. Without their air groups to protect our surface ships, I don't guess either the Royal Navy or any of our masters are going to risk sending destroyers and cruisers into the Straits where they could cut off a German retreat and do us the most good."

"What the hell?" Yak said. "What about all those fighter bases we were supposed to be building after we took Gela and Licata? What about the fighters flying out of those bases?"

"I think most of them are escorting the bombers," Bender said. "That's speculation on my part, but from what one or two of our gunfire support observers have passed along, the Army is relying mostly on their own artillery and on naval gunfire support to help them on their way."

"At least," Hal said, "that's an improvement over the invasion, when they didn't believe we wouldn't wind up killing our own infantry. The way the Navy broke up that Panzer assault at Gela ought to have created a total revolution in their thinking. Ask an infantryman now what he thinks about naval gunnery, and he calls it the finest kind."

"It's a change, no doubt about it," Bender said. "At long last, the Army in our neck of the woods seems to have come to the realization that the Navy is good for something besides being a taxi and supply service from wherever they're based to wherever they intend to invade."

"Pity some of these birds weren't in the Pacific," Hal observed. "The Marines and the Army had one hell of a fight on Guadalcanal, but the simple fact is that the Navy did most of the dying. The goddamn naval battles that went on at sea out there were horrific."

"This is depressing," Yak said. "Why don't we turn our thoughts to grappa? Who's for going over tonight and giving Mama Galdoni's another visit?"

"You're on," Garcia said. "I haven't been there yet, and Lewis has been singing its praises."

"Count me in," Bender said.

"Can't go," Lewis said, reaching for his coffee, "this bein' my night for the duty, wouldn't you know."

"And you, Hal?" Yak asked.

"Wouldn't miss it for the world." Hal grinned.

"Not even for a date with your draft board?" Yak laughed.

"For that," Hal said, "I would make special arrangements."

Mama Galdoni's, when the four officers off the *3X* finally reached the trattoria that evening, had apparently received a windfall. From some source—Hal couldn't stop himself from wondering if it were not the Mafia—Mama Galdoni had apparently inherited a considerable portion of frozen U.S. Army chicken, all of it coming in boxes that still bore the G.I. stamp to herald its origin. As a result, rather than settle for mere pasta that evening, all four were able to begin with pasta before going on to a generous and incredibly tasty serving of chicken cacciatore before finally polishing off their meal with yet another nearly overflowing grappa.

"If you don't mind me saying so," Garcia said, shaking his head with pleasure while leaning back in his chair, "this is what I call living high on the hog."

"You haven't found the fare in our galley quite up to your standards?" Bender grinned.

"The fare in our galley sustains life," Garcia said, "but not much else. As far as I know, that Grunder who's cooking for us flipped hamburgers before the war at some drug store in Oklahoma City, and flipping burgers is about all he's good for. When I'm home, with the wife, I'm not a bad cook myself, so I know what it takes to put out the food Grunder is serving us, and it ain't much. Open a gallon can of carrots and steam 'em, open a gallon can of beans and boil 'em, and open prepared cans of Spam, ham, and stew meat and serve 'em, and you don't have what anyone would mistake for haute cuisine."

"He has a point," Hal said. "There have been times when I've almost thought I could do better myself."

"And how do you recommend that we get out of our predicament?" Bender said.

"As far as I know," Garcia said, "and I looked at Grunder's service record, he never went anywhere near cooking school. He simply put down that he'd been a cook when he enlisted, and they put him to doing it, pretty much sending him straight to us out of boot camp. It's not that I don't like him, you understand—he's a nice enough kid and all that—but he can't cook worth spit. The fact is, he's got a terrific interest in engines, so about half the time we're out, when he doesn't actually have to be in the galley, he's down in the hole having coffee with my boys. Suppose I try to interest him in striking for machinist mate, and then, if he's game, maybe I can lure him down into the hole and you can request a replacement and preferably someone who has been to cook and baker's school."

"Give it a try," Bender said at once, his long face breaking into a smile. "And if you can bring it off, I'll concede there's more than one way to skin a cat."

As the four of them stepped back aboard later that evening, Lewis emerged from the wardroom beneath a waning moon and drew Hal aside.

"At quarters in the mornin', Mr. Goff, youse gonna notice a change in that man Prince. Him's got hisself a hell of a shiner, right bright an' purple."

Hal exhaled, knowing that if it wasn't Vega, it would always be Prince. "What happened?" he asked, expecting the worst.

"Seems like him and a couple a them others got themselves mix up in a card game over on the beach somewheres," Lewis said. "Ways they tole it when they got back here, Morris and Click, Prince made a bad move of some kind, and some big gunner's mate off the cruiser turn the table over and knocked him flat. Morris and Click pretty much carry 'im back here, dazed, but awake."

"Corpsman check him for concussion?" Hal asked.

"Yes Sir," Lewis said. "He ain't got one, but that eye a his ain't gonna look pretty any time soon."

"I wonder if that might make him change his ways," Hal mused.

"Doubtful," Lewis grinned. "Seems to have poker in his blood, that one."

"Yes," Hal said. "All right, thanks Chief. I'll inform the captain. Anything else come up while we were over?"

"No Sir," Lewis said. "Duty section's turned in, save for those on watch, and the liberty men is startin' to come back from whatever it is that they've been doin'."

"Good enough," Hal said. "I think I'll turn in too, and don't hesitate to wake me if anything happens that I need to know about."

"Right Sir," Lewis said.

"Probably serves him right," Bender said, when Hal passed along the word about Prince. "At least Click and Morris got him back here in one piece. Lucky, the lot of them, that the MPs or the Shore Patrol didn't lock onto them. I'd like to think that Prince might take a lesson from this, but knowing that man's habits, he'll probably take the wrong one and redouble his efforts."

Hal chuckled. "Unfortunately," he said, "you're probably right. I'd be surprised to hear that Prince wasn't dealing cards at the age of three."

"If not at the age of two," Bender said. "I'd be surprised to hear that he wasn't born at a blackjack table somewhere."

Hal laughed. "Nothing required in the way of paperwork, I don't suppose. Corpsman will list him in the morning medical report, and that's about the limit?"

"Yes," Bender said. "For the moment, you and I can turn in without having to worry about it and, hopefully, sleep well."

"Aces," Hal said. "Good night."

Moving Grunder from the galley down into the engine room turned out to be easier than anyone had expected. In fact, when offered the opportunity, Grunder—short, squat, and overweight—simply leapt at the chance, telling Garcia that he'd never wanted to be a cook in the first place and had only been forced into the job by the personnel people who had written his orders following his time in boot camp. Bender, once Grunder put in a request, acted with haste regarding a request for the transfer of a new cook from somewhere, but it was Garcia who walked the request onto the tender where Task Force 88's personnel staff had taken up temporary residence. By means of whatever under-the-table connections a warrant officer had at his fingertips, he emerged with precisely the set of transfer orders that he'd gone there to obtain.

"Shay," Garcia said, standing in front of Hal in Hal's tiny stateroom, "Amos Shay. A black man. Went through cook and baker's school in '35 up at Great Lakes and has been cookin' on one ship or another ever since. He's been on the *Eversole* for the past year, but they're headed back down to Bizerte for an overhaul, and given the sudden 'emergency' we've developed, a guy I know on the staff over there showed himself only too willing to let us have him."

Already aware of the fact that nearly every negro in the U.S. Navy was either a steward or a cook and baker, Hal did not find himself surprised to hear that Shay was black. How well the man might mesh with the remainder of the crew remained to be seen, but knowing that they would all cross that road when they came to it, Hal didn't find himself in any way disconcerted by Garcia's announcement.

"How soon will he join us?" Hal asked quickly.

"Quick," Garcia said. "Order went straight over by messenger to get him off the *Eversole* 'fore she pulls out this afternoon. I'd guess he must be packin' his sea bag right about now."

"Good," Hal said. "If he's here in time to do the evening meal, he can't come too soon."

In fact, Amos Shay, a rated third class cook by the Navy, came aboard the *3X* fully an hour before Grunder once more served the crew Spam sandwiches for lunch. Garcia, having kept an eye out for the man's arrival, then brought him straight up to Hal's stateroom to introduce him to the ship's executive officer.

After a single look at Shay, Hal decided that if the man had been a white man, the Navy would have put his image on a recruiting poster. Tall, straight as a stick, a broad one, Shay must have weighed in at something over two hundred pounds, all of it incredibly well proportioned, all of it as rock solid as granite. And with that single first look at the man, any reservations Hal might have had about how Shay would mesh with the crew disappeared. With this man, he thought, no one on board, even the most ardent Southern redneck, would dare to make a crack.

"Tell me a little about yourself," Hal said as Shay stood at attention before him, "and you can stand easy while you do it."

"Yes Sir," Shay said, relaxing his stance. "Not much to tell Sir. I grew up in Washington, D.C., graduated from high school there, worked part time in a factory kitchen alongside my father, did a year at Howard, and joined the Navy when the money ran out. Last year, I advanced to PO3, but I've passed all the Navy's exams for cooks and bakers all the way up to the level of chief, and I hope to be advanced again as soon as a rating for PO2 comes open."

Hal knew at once what Shay was talking about. The rating for cooks and bakers happened to be one of the Navy's closed

124

enlisted rates, which meant that before a man could advance, an opening resulting from a retirement or a death had to take place. Shay, regardless of whatever talents he possessed, had remained a rated seaman for years according to his records, but whatever had recently happened to a cook somewhere else had finally opened a slot for him and, hence, his promotion to third class petty officer.

"You had a year at Howard University?" Hal questioned.

"I did, Sir. Yes," Shay said.

For Hal, that revelation attested to Shay's obvious intelligence and explained as well why he spoke straightforward English without a trace of Stepin Fetchit mannerisms. If he had dared, Hal thought, he might almost take the risk of putting Lewis to work with the man so that Shay could straighten out Lewis' own hopeless language usage, not to mention his pronunciation.

"But you left Howard owing to money issues?" Hal questioned.

"Yes Sir," Shay said. "When the Depression shut down the factory in '34, my father and I both lost our jobs, so that was the end of the money. In order not to be a burden on my parents, I joined up. I can't say that the pay has been gracious, but like the work, it's come steady, and I've been helping to support my folks with what I can spare."

"And you can cook something other than Span?" Hal asked with a smile.

"The ships I've been riding seem to think so, Sir." Shay grinned.

"Good." Hal grinned back. "Glad to have you aboard. Think you and your mess cooks can get up something other than more grilled Spam and spuds for our supper this evening?"

"You can bet on it, Sir," the man said, showing Hal a straight face.

"If you can bring that off," Hal said, "you won't be able to hear yourself think for the applause you'll receive."

Five hours later, not long after evening chow went down, if the crew and the officers didn't exactly applaud the efforts Shay made on their behalf that evening, they certainly roared their appreciation with enough volume to make the man smile. In the wardroom, eating the same meal as the crew, each man tied into crisp fried chicken, golden corn, and a hot baked potato accompanied by peach cobbler for dessert. Garcia positively beamed as everyone, starting with Bender, congratulated him for his find.

"Looks to me," Yak said, "like this guy is going to improve our morale about seven-fold."

"Youse betta believe it," Lewis agreed. "Ain't tasted me a meal this good since I wave goodbye to the ole lady on the pier when we'se pulled out."

"Garcia," Hal said, "you've done us proud."

With a hearty "Amen," Bender confirmed the remark.

7

By the end of the second week of August 1943, everyone, including the Germans, knew that the Battle for Sicily was approaching its end and the Allies were not going to capture the remnants of the retreating Italian and German divisions intact. The American and British forces were going to take prisoners, but owing to excellent German staff work, advance preparations, and brilliant execution, the wily Krauts had managed to whisk the large body of their troops away from encirclement and across the Straits of Messina with something of the same spirit and style the British had shown in rescuing their own army from the snapping jaws of the German Panzer forces at Dunkirk. According to an intelligence report that Hal and Bender read, by August 17—the day the campaign was declared officially ended—the Germans had managed to retrieve and remove more than 110,000 Axis troops beyond those who'd already been either killed or captured in the fighting. Tens of thousands of others, most of them Italians, it was thought, had simply discarded their uniforms and disappeared into the local population, making a peace, individual and timely, that perfectly suited each of them.

"So," Yak said, as the wardroom sat down that evening to a savory serving of Shay's pork pot pie, "what, I wonder, has taking Sicily cost us?"

"You are not, of course, speaking of dollars, are you?" Hal said. "For if you are, I wouldn't have a clue how to answer you."

"No," Yak said, "I was thinking more in human terms."

"Well," Bender said, putting a forkful of the pork pie in his mouth and chewing it before going on, "according to the intelligence reports we've received, at least to make a start, Mussolini has been deposed and apparently sent to prison somewhere, and that is one hell of an improvement in my estimation. My guess is that Italy is right on the verge of switching sides and coming over to us."

"If that turns out to be the case," Garcia said, "we'd better damn well get our hands on the Italian fleet before the Krauts do, otherwise we're gonna be in a world of hurt. If the Italians had been willing to risk those ships the way the Germans are sure to, they could have blown us to kingdom come with nothing more than that fast battleship *Roma* they've kept parked somewhere up there around Sardinia."

"Not to mention the cruisers and old battleships parked down at Taranto," Yak said.

"Krauts will try to sink 'em 'fore they can get loose," Lewis offered. "If the Eyeties won't scuttle, I'd guess the Jerries will try ta bomb the hell outa 'em."

"Looks to me," Bender said, "like we've been damn lucky as far as the Italian fleet goes. From every intelligence report I've read, their ships are a good bit faster than ours, and if they'd had a carrier to give them air cover, they could have played hell with us at nearly every turn."

"From what I've heared," Lewis said, "they ain't had radar backin' 'em up neither. Piss on 'em as we have, you sorta have to give 'em credit for guts when you think about the way they kept on runnin' destroyers an' convoys over to North Africa in an attempt to supply their troops. No matter what the odds against 'em, they gutted that one out, sure as shootin', no matter how big it cost 'em."

"Is it true," Yak asked, "that German U-boats carry Italian torpedoes?"

"Apparently," Bender said, "but what makes Italian torpedoes better than the ones the Germans build, I couldn't say." And then, spearing yet another piece of the pork pie with his fork, he gave his head a shake. "But if you ask me why American torpedoes seem to be the worst in the world and so much less effective than anything the Japs, the Eyeties, the Germans, or the British build, I couldn't tell you that either. The fact that ours are the worst seems to be as solid as rock, but with all our supposed scientific know-how, I can't begin to tell you why."

"You got any other figures on what I called 'the costs'?" Yak asked, shifting the table's focus back to his original question.

"The figures are strictly preliminary," Hal said, "according to what I read this morning, but in a nutshell, American and British losses seem to number close to 8,000 dead with 14,000 to 15,000 wounded and about 2,500 men missing. According to body counts, the Germans and Italians seem to have lost close to 10,000 dead, an estimated 40,000 wounded, and somewhere in excess of 120,000 captured or missing. I'd guess that the majority of those are from native Sicilian regiments and that they've simply thrown down their guns, changed their clothes, and gone home."

"That's what country folks call a 'passel," Yak quipped.

"You been reading *Li'l Abner* again?" Bender asked.

"Yessum, Sir," Yak said, showing the table a possum grin.

"Well, stop it!" Bender jibed. "The last thing we need on this ship is for everyone aboard to start talking like Mammy and Pappy Yokum."

"You wouldn't object, I don't suppose, if I invited Daisey Mae aboard?" Yak teased.

"Ha!" Hal chortled, "Daisey Mae, speaking Dogpatch with a Sicilian accent. This is something I can't wait to hear!"

"Ha," Bender replied, "Mind how you go Mr. Goff, or you're liable to receive a blistering letter from that draft board of yours."

"Not to worry," Hal laughed, "I only mean to look on from afar, watch Mr. Yaakov fall all over himself, and think back to more auspicious times."

"Which is what you're in hopes that we'll all report to your draft board when we get back to the States and finally meet her?" Garcia said.

"You've read my mind," Hal replied.

"So, Captain," Lewis said, forcing a total shift in the high jinks, "what's on for next, if youse got any idea?"

"Truth told, Chief," Bender said, "I don't have a clue. But I don't think the powers that be are going to leave us to sit on our hands, not with the way the supply traffic into Palermo seems to have picked up. Right now there are at least six Liberty ships out there in the roads waiting to get into port, and at least four destroyers burning up fuel oil trying to keep them from being potted by a U-boat if there happens to be one in the vicinity. Eventually, in what the admirals are bound to imagine to be 'due course,' we'll probably receive orders of some kind, but until then, I think we'd better squeeze the most we can out of Mama Galdoni's because where we go next is a mystery, and—no insult intended, Yak—I can only hope it doesn't include Borscht and a trip into the Black Sea."

Across the ten days that followed the Axis collapse on Sicily, the officers and crew of the *3X* experienced no let up with regard to the demands placed upon them. When they were not actually assisting Liberty ships, transports, oilers, refrigerator ships, and LSTs in and out of the port, to and from their berths, they were towing lighters loaded down with supplies. Once, they even towed an entire cargo of gasoline to a squadron of PT boats which were sheltering in a restricted cove some fifteen miles east of Palermo. That, according to Hal's memory, had been a nasty trip. Not halfway to their destination, a lone Macchi down from Sardinia on what must have been an independent hunt—a single fighter which had somehow eluded the combat air patrols that the Air Corps was supposed to have put up—made a strafing run on them. That run turned out to be something they only managed to deflect when one of Yak's 3"/50 rounds exploded close enough to the fighter to cause the pilot to flinch and instinctively touch his rudder in such a way that the machine-gun rounds he threw out fell mere feet behind the lighter they were towing and barely missed igniting a conflagration amid the fuel they were carrying.

Once again, high up on the flying bridge, breathless with relief, both Hal and Bender nearly sank to their knees with the sudden passing of the threat. Once again, having both turned white with fear, they could each hear the other sucking for air.

"If I live to be a hundred ..." Bender started to say and then didn't, not because he didn't mean it but because he didn't have enough air left to get it out.

"Yes," Hal said, "too close ... that one. We would have burned to a crisp."

"Fly boys shoulda handled it," Bender finally managed to say.

Hal said nothing and merely nodded his agreement. He imagined someone might have been getting plenty of air support, but he'd seen precious little of it and couldn't stop himself from wondering why. Things had seemed different around Guadalcanal. The "Cactus Air Force" out there—a hard-pressed collection of planes from every service under the sun—had been under constant attack by the Japs the entire time he'd been out there. Nevertheless, those fliers had seemed to be everywhere, lending every ounce of support that they could muster, both for the Navy as well as the Marines. Air support around Sicily, as far as Hal had found it, had seemed virtually nonexistent, and the longer the condition continued, the more it set his teeth on edge.

In the end, the *3X* resupplied the PT boats with the fuel they needed, returned to Palermo without the lighter in tow, and went straight back to the work they'd been doing in the harbor and the surrounding roads. As far as any of them felt concerned, the high points during that time coincided only with the chow they were served, Shay having so shaken up their expectations that there wasn't a man aboard who didn't look forward to every meal and race for the chow line the minute that the boatswain piped their summons.

There was, however, one additional high point to the period. On September 1 around 2200, fifteen minutes after the mail clerk returned from the tender with the mail bag, he dropped by Hal's stateroom and handed him not one but five letters from what the wardroom insisted on calling his draft board.

Feeling an instant warmth that had not been generated by the vagaries of the Sicilian summer, Hal threw himself immediately onto his chair and read every page Bea had written, twice and in order. Some of what the letters contained carried mundane, obligatory news—Bea seemed pleased that she had made A grades in all of the graduate courses that she had taken that summer; on her train ride down to her home in Herrin, she had seen a large fire burning in a coal mine near Mt. Vernon, and after having saved her ration coupons, she had treated herself to a new dress. But what most caught Hal's attention came in the last letter she had written. Bea had, finally, when she thought the time to be right, confronted her family, acquainted them with Hal's existence, and laid out their intentions in a way that they could not possibly misunderstand. Her mother, as Bea had expected, had accepted everything at once. Her father, showing less than his usual irascible response, had nevertheless suggested that he would like to meet Hal and have "a little talk" with him before "things" went "fully forward." Hal had already anticipated having to ask Mario Colombo's permission to marry his daughter, so Bea's news came as no revelation at all in that regard, and in order to help grease the wheels before he returned to the States, Hal resolved to write Bea's father a letter, both introducing himself and attesting to the sincerity of his intentions.

"Good news?" Bender said, sticking his head through the curtain that passed for a door into Hal's stateroom.

"Very," Hal said with a smile.

"Excellent," Bender said. "Enjoy it while you can because I've been called to a conference for tomorrow night, and I'd be willing to bet money that it's going to reveal where we're headed next."

"I can't claim the assistance of a crystal ball," Hal said, "but the only question I have is whether it's going to be south of Rome or north of Rome. My guess is that Sardinia's out, and I'd be totally shocked if they told us Southern France."

"Same here," Bender said, his long face turning serious. "I think we'll go to France, sure enough, eventually, but when we do, I'm betting on something crossing over to the north coast from England and then driving straight for Berlin."

"This year, do you think?" Hal asked.

Bender shrugged. "Could be," he said, "but without knowing what kinds of troops we're collecting in England, I wouldn't want to say. That was one hell of a big invasion fleet with which we went into Sicily, but as far as I can see, a lot of it still seems to be around. If we were going into Northern France, I'd sorta think we'd all be making tracks for the English Channel, and we aren't, and for my money, that spells something coming around here. Perhaps I'll find out something tomorrow night."

"I'll look forward to hearing," Hal said.

"And probably wish you hadn't," Bender grinned.

Jos Bender didn't return to the ship on the following night until nearly 2330, but once he arrived, he found all four of his officers gathered in the wardroom, nursing mugs of coffee.

"Well," he said, looking the four over, "want to hear it now, or wait until the morning?"

"Now," they all said in unison.

"Right," Bender said, tossing a thick operations order on the table in front of them before drawing a mug of coffee for himself and sitting down at the head of the table. "It's Salerno, at least for us. That's to be our part of Operation AVALANCHE. Montgomery is taking the British Eighth Army across the Strait of Messina starting on 3 September with the intention of driving north up the toe of the boot, but we're not going to be involved with that. We're set to go into Salerno on 9 September, under cover of darkness, with no preparatory bombardment, and personally, I find that a mistake."

Hal and the others also thought it a mistake.

"It seems to me that the Army should have learned its lesson on that one when we invaded Sicily," Garcia could not stop himself from saying.

"On that," Bender said, "I'd imagine that we're all agreed, but it is what it is, and no song and dance on our part is going to change a thing. So, here's the apparent order of battle." And immediately, drawing a chart from the op-order, he laid it out on the table before them. "What we call the Gulf of Salerno on the Tyrrhenian Sea curves south around from the island of Capri and the Amalfi coast—the mountains behind it separating Salerno from the Bay of Naples to the north—before moving on down past both Salerno and Paestum to Agrópoli at the foot of the gulf. You don't need me to tell you that the immediate Allied objective is the port of Naples, which enjoys the biggest harbor in Italy and is exactly what we need to keep our people supplied. General Mark Clark is commanding what's been designated the Fifth Army for this one, and what he intends to do is land at Salerno and drive north in order to capture Naples. With me so far?"

Heads nodded all around, indicating that they were.

"So," Bender continued, "here's what things look like at the moment. When we go in on the 9th, Darby with a battalion of Army Rangers and Laycock with two Commando units will land to the north and drive up into the passes overlooking Sorrento to prevent any Germans in Naples from using them to hit us on the flank. In the meantime, the British X Corps, consisting of their 46th and 56th Divisions, will go ashore over Salerno beachhead proper, extending their assault all the way down to somewhere below Battipaglia while the U.S. VI Corps, spearheaded by the 36th Division, goes in around Paestum, with the 45th Thunderbird Division probably following close behind and filtering in between the 56th and the 36th so as to present a four-division front."

"That 36th Division weren't in on Sicily," Lewis observed. "Reckon they's up to this?"

Garcia chuckled. "That 36th Division is a former Texas National Guard outfit. Whether they're actually up to it or not won't matter because all of them will nevertheless think that they are and then some. Based upon my past experience with Texans, those guys will be out there right now telling everyone that they'll have the Krauts tied up in a sack within twenty minutes of going ashore."

"Youse exaggeratin'," Lewis laughed, "but youse gotta point."

"And if you don't mind me asking," Yak threw in, "while this cakewalk is underway, what might the 3X be assigned to do?"

"Just about anything we're told," Bender said quickly, "although, more to the point, we're assigned to stand off during the landing but go in to render assistance to any of the landing craft which happen to hang up after the first waves have gone in."

"And that," Hal said, "is liable to put us right in the line of fire. I've been looking at the maps that are included in this op-order, and what they show is something that isn't on the chart. The Gulf of Salerno is ringed by hills and mountains, so if the Germans or any Italian Fascists who remain loyal to them have artillery back in those mountains or get artillery into them, our boys on the ground down there, Tiger-eating Texans or not, are going to get pounded to hell. And what occurs to me is that the closer we get to the beach, the more likely it is that we are liable to get pounded right along with them."

It was not a pleasant revelation that Hal gave them, and no one took the trouble to thank him for it, but he hadn't imagined that they would.

"Hal's right about that," Bender said, "and I wish he weren't, but there it is. So right from the get-go, we're going to have to stay battle ready and keep ourselves under the best cover that the *3X* can afford us."

And on that note, with each man picking up that section of the op-order that most pertained to his own duties—Hal finding himself sharing the largest collection of pages with Bender—everyone rose from the table and walked away. Each was desperate to get in a good night's sleep but knew that instead he would be reading and studying late so as not to be caught out when the invasion finally went forward.

The invasion fleet assembled to hit Salerno did not reach the immense size of the one that had invaded Sicily, but as far as Hal and everyone else felt concerned, it seemed large enough, stretching across the Tyrrhenian Sea in all directions. Making the transit in company with the designated support force, Hal and the others felt stunned by the tranquility of the seas. In contrast to what they'd all experienced before and during the invasion of Sicily, the perfect weather that accompanied them as they steamed the 180 miles that separated Palermo from the Gulf of Salerno was something that none of them could have imagined.

"You know how a lousy dress rehearsal is supposed to herald a perfect performance?" Hal said to Bender.

"At least that's the myth," Bender said.

"Yes, well, I can only hope that this smooth transit doesn't flip the tables on us and give us a nasty invasion by contrast," Hal said.

"I'll tell ya Hal," Bender said, "if we were already on the beach somewhere and trying to make a surprise attack on land during the middle of the night, I could see some sense to what the Army is doing by not launching a bombardment beforehand, but what makes them think that a fleet this size can approach the Italian coast without anyone ever knowing what we're about just strikes me as utter nonsense. If you want my opinion, I think all hell's gonna break loose the minute we hit the beach, and if the Krauts aren't sitting right there waiting for us, I'll be the first man to admit that I've been wrong."

"I don't think that's an admission you're going to have to make," Hal said bluntly. "And before this thing's over, I'd bet money that Yak and his boys are going to have targets on the beach for the three-inch and the 20s."

"I'd like to hope that we'd never have to go in that close," Bender said, "but the odds are against us."

"Sort of makes your bowels tighten, doesn't it?" Hal said.

"Into absolute knots," Bender said.

At 0330 the following morning, no sooner than the first assault waves started toward the beach, everyone afloat became instantly aware that Fifth Army's attempt at surprise had failed and that a preparatory bombardment, possibly lasting for hours if not days, would have been infinitely preferable to what finally developed. Rather than being caught off guard and unprepared for the assault, the Germans had prepared well by placing artillery in the surrounding hills and moving infantry, machine guns, and motorized troops right down to the beach in a committed attempt to meet the invasion head on and drive it straight back into the sea. As soon as the dawn began to break, giving their artillery observers a clear view of the beaches and Axis aircraft a clear view of where to strafe and bomb, all hell broke loose as both the British X Corps and the American VI Corps attempted to leave their landing craft and scramble ashore.

The 3X was largely withdrawn from the action on the beach, assisting a collection of subchasers, PCs, and two other tugs to screen and help shepherd supply ships—LSTs, LCIs, and LCTs—destined to go in with much later waves. The tug spent the early hours of the morning some eight miles out to sea, well out of range and danger from the machine-gun, rifle, and artillery fire the Germans seemed to be pouring onto the beaches but in danger, nevertheless, from the enemy air raids which seemed to be making incessant attacks on various parts of the invasion fleet. Twice that morning, standing on the flying bridge of the 3X with their binoculars glued to their eyes, Hal and Bender had a clear view of the air battles taking place high overhead—one in which two Spitfires shot two Heinkels out of the sky, while in another a Messerschmitt 109 got the better of a Thunderbolt. The pilot bailed out and pulled his rip cord several hundred feet above the sea in a fortunate train of events which permitted one of the subchasers in the outer ring not only to spot the pilot coming down, but gave the chaser plenty of time to leave the screen and race over to pluck the man from the sea. The actual recovery turned out to be something that both Hal and Bender missed seeing. No more than a minute before it could be effected, shouts from the lookouts alerted them that they were about to come under air attack themselves. As both men glanced swiftly to starboard, their guns began to thunder and rattle as they swiftly caught sight of a Fiat CR.32 racing toward them, machine guns blazing.

"God Almighty!" Bender exclaimed, as the little aircraft continued to race toward them, flashes from its machine guns showing brilliant against its cowling. "That must be the last biplane we'll ever see in a war!"

Hal imagined the same thing, but before he had time to think about it, rounds from the Fiat began to tear into the rail forward of the 3"/50 gun tub, throwing a cloud of splinters in all directions. Less than a second later, Bix on the starboard 20 mm finally connected with the tiny plane, rounds and tracers from the gun tearing off the Fiat's upper port wing, flipping it straight over onto its back and into the sea not forty yards off the ship's beam. It didn't explode but merely sank and disappeared before either Hal or Bender could say a word. Down around the gun mounts, the reaction seemed to be similar, for aside from the sound of the loader hoisting yet another canister of 20 mm rounds into position for loading, the men on the deck remained shocked to utter silence by what they'd seen.

Hal, when he came to himself enough to be aware of his reaction, found that he was shaking from head to foot. Bender, on the other hand, seemed utterly paralyzed for a moment or two.

"Damage reports," he finally whispered, barely finding his voice. And then, finding more strength with which to speak, added, "Get on it, Hal, and I want to know at once if we've had anyone injured."

Stimulated by the adrenaline that had suddenly started to flow, Hal was down from the flying bridge, into the pilot house, and on the horn with the sound-powered phone talkers around the ship within seconds. Moments later, he was able to shout up to Bender that no one was wounded before he set out on foot to inspect whatever damage the Fiat had done to the rail up forward. The gun shield, Yak told him when Hal got down to the gun tub, had saved them all.

"Splinters flying like hail," Yak said, his face white, "but the gun shield deflected 'em. We're all in one piece. Christ, that little bastard came straight at us! I couldn't believe it!"

"One of Mussolini's true believers," Hal said, still feeling himself shake. "Meanwhile, according to what the radioman just told me on my way down here, Italy's just surrendered."

"You're joking?" Yak said, a look of disbelief spreading across his face.

"Not according to the radioman," Hal said, "but I can't stop to talk about it now, and I guess we'll know more later. Hang in there, and keep your eyes peeled."

With that, and still on the run, Hal returned to the flying bridge and gave Bender a quick report.

"Nobody hurt," he said. "I gather the gun shield deflected the splinters. The rail forward of the gun tub is pretty chewed up. From the looks of things, that little shit got fifteen or twenty rounds into us."

"We've been lucky," Bender said. "If that pilot had so much as breathed on his rudder, he would have taken out the gun crew."

Bender was right, and Hal knew it.

"Yes," he said. "I guess luck is the word for it."

About their luck that morning, both men had cause for second thoughts. At 1102—Hal remembered the time precisely—the 3X received an emergency call to break away from the screen in which she'd been serving, head for Blue beach where one of the 36th Division's regiments had gone ashore, and take in tow an LST which had gone dead in the water while retracting from where she had been disgorging vehicles onto the beach. Somehow, the ship—which had been hit and holed by any number of German or Italian rounds in her haste to retract—had failed to raise her

Danforth in time, and had fouled her screw on her own anchor cable in her haste to get away. The man who commanded her had managed to drop one of his forward anchors in time to keep the ship from broaching onto the beach. But there could be no doubt that the LST was in considerable danger of being damaged beyond repair or even sunk by shore fire coming from German positions inland, and the Navy wanted her retrieved and removed from danger.

"This looks like one of those situations where we really begin earning our pay," Hal said, fighting down the urge to throw up which the order had generated.

"Right," Bender said, the quiver in his voice leaving Hal in no doubt that Bender felt exactly the same way. "Get down to Yak and tell him to have his gunners ready for anything," Bender said, "and then get back to Lewis and tell him the same thing. What we want to do here, for everyone's good, is get in there as quick as we can, hook up without a hitch, and get the hell out of there before the Germans blow us to smithereens."

Bender hadn't tried to sound funny or downplay what they faced by making light of it. He'd merely spoken the straight truth without embellishment, and Hal knew it. And thus, they started toward the shore.

The 3X approached to within two miles of the beach, threading her way between destroyers and cruisers doing rapid-fire shore bombardment in support of the troops and moving between transports waiting to unload troops or go forward with more supplies. The beach, what they could see of it, looked like a continually exploding cloud of fire, smoke, and dust, punctuated by periodic clearings where absolutely nothing appeared to be moving. Closer in, having spotted the stricken LST below what Bender and Hal had marked on their chart as the limit of Blue beach and within sight of Agrópoli south of Paestum, shellfire from the beach—German or Italian—began falling into the sea around them, some of it distant, some of it no farther away than fifty or sixty yards from where they continued to move.

"Keep your fingers crossed," Bender said. "Right now, I'm guessing that whatever spotters the Krauts have back in the hills can see right over those clouds of dust in front of us, so until we can get in there close enough where they won't be able to see us directly, where the dust and the smoke will cut off their line of sight, they're liable to start throwing rounds at us."

One quick glance at the assembly of much larger ships which the Allies had marshaled for the invasion made Hal skeptical about Bender's warning. Like as not, he thought, the German artillery observers would be concentrating their attention on the cruisers and destroyers lending the invasion force their fire support. Any shells which fell in the vicinity of the 3X would most likely be random mistakes, overs or unders or rounds thrown completely askew for some unaccountable reason. That did not, however, change the fact that any one of those rounds—whether fired by mistake or not—might have the capacity to kill them in an instant and sink them out of sight. It was with that thought that Hal fought to concentrate his mind on the job at hand in hopes that they could bring it off and get the hell out of the danger zone in record time.

Closer in, when they were less than a mile from the beach and only a few hundred yards from the LST, buzzing sounds alerted both Hal and Bender to the possibility that they had come under sporadic fire from a heavy machine gun somewhere on the beach. Neither imagined that the machine gunner had decided to concentrate on them, and they wondered whether they were imagining things. Then, with a shock, Hal spotted something with his binoculars—something far off to the right, beyond where the LST happened to be anchored. Topping a hill in the direction of Agrópoli and at least three thousand yards distant, coming straight down an inland road toward the flank of whatever troops the 36th

Division had ashore in the area, was the unmistakable silhouette of a German armored vehicle. Above all the other noise that could be heard, Hal stirred up a whirlwind.

Without taking time to inform Bender, who had moved to the opposite side of the bridge, his attention wholly focused on the dangerous maneuver of hooking up to the LST, Hal roared orders down to the gun tub as fast as he could get them out. "Target, *Yak!* Kraut *Flakpanzer!* Two points off the starboard bow! Range three thousand yards! Open fire! *Open fire on it!*"

Through his own binoculars, Yaakov didn't need more than five or ten seconds to spot the Kraut vehicle. The minute he did, he moved heaven and hell to direct the 3"/50's pointer and trainer onto it. Then, within only a few more seconds, and with the gun crew moving like whirling dervishes, the 3"/50 slammed out a single high-capacity round that sounded to their ears like the crack of doom.

Their round, when the smoke issuing from the muzzle cleared enough for everyone to see the target, had clearly struck somewhere to the side of the road down which the *Flakpanzer* happened to be moving, and a good forty yards in front of it. Their second round, going out only moments later and after correction for direction and distance, landed dead center in the middle of the road only about twenty-five yards in front of the attacking vehicle, its rapid-fire gun, the relative equivalent of a 20 mm, still spitting rounds toward the 36th Division with a row of tracers that Hal could easily follow. That fire, however, quit in a hurry the moment the *3X*'s second round dropped in front of the *Flakpanzer*. After coming to a dead stop, the miniscule greenish-colored freak of armor reversed the motion on its treads. The enemy vehicle then resumed fire forward while backing away at an ever-increasing speed as it made a desperate attempt to recover the sixty or seventy yards that separated the nasty bug from the cover of the hill over which it had, only moments before, first launched its attack.

In the meantime, because Bender was totally focused on making a safe approach to the LST, Hal had done no more than shout the word "tank" in Bender's direction when the man had turned to inquire what the *3X* had taken under fire. With a mere nod of his head to indicate that he'd heard, Bender once more directed his entire attention to getting safely alongside the bigger ship and getting the messenger line over to the LST so that the deck crew aboard could begin hauling over the towline. As a result, Bender had no choice but to leave what Hal had called a "tank" to the attention of his subordinates. Finally, after a fourth, fifth, and sixth shot at the enemy vehicle, and just as it was cresting the hill and about to disappear beyond it, Yak and the gun crew's seventh round caught the *Flakpanzer* on what Hal could only think of as its hind quarter. The shot spun it directly into a drainage ditch and flipped it onto its side. This time, every man aboard who had seen or participated in the action whooped and cheered; Yak was down in the gun tub jumping up and down like a kid who had just slid home after stealing the plate for a home run, while the rest of the gun crew were slapping each other on the back with all of the enthusiasm of championship winners.

Hal might have paid more attention to the celebrations below, but events didn't allow him the time. In that moment the deck crew on the LST finally hoisted the towline aboard and signaled to Bender that they'd secured the towing eye over the appropriate bits and were ready to move. Bender quickly slapped Hal on the shoulder and shouted to him to be ready to relay his orders to the helm and lee helm in the pilot house by means of the voice pipe. Immediately on Bender's first order, the *3X* began to back away from the big LST, which seemed to hover above it. As it did, something big plunged into the water not forty yards off the beam, exploding with enough of a concussion that everyone above decks felt it and found themselves drenched by the geyser of seawater that the explosion raised. Whether that geyser had been thrown up by a bomb or a shell, no one ever asked and no one ever cared; all of them were too busy with the work they were doing to question the matter further, the tug having distanced itself enough from the LST so that it could swing fully around and begin hauling the bigger ship away from the beach and out to sea. There they intended to turn the vessel over to one of the Fleet's much larger salvage tugs which could put a diver over, with a torch, so as to free the LST's screw. Then, if the vessel's power plant had not been damaged, it might finally get itself underway and withdraw from the battle under its own power.

For perhaps ten full minutes, the extraction went as planned—and then, it didn't. A single German shell holed and exploded somewhere inside the LST's stern, the part which happened to be closest to the shore, with the 3X towing her outbound by her bow. The compartment immediately caught fire, sending up plumes of black smoke which, after thirty tense minutes of firefighting by the LST's crew, were brought under control. Bender and Hal learned that rather than explode and blow up owing to a conflagration in the ship's magazine or a fuel tank, only the crew of the LST would be inconvenienced, their living compartment having been burned out and consumed by the fire but leaving the ship herself intact.

Regardless of the fact that shells from German artillery on the beach were still dropping into the water around them, both Hal and Bender felt a sense of relief upon hearing the location of the fire and the fact that it had been successfully put out.

"I don't know where the magazine on an LST is located," Bender said, "but that's one hit that gave me the willies. I had visions of the whole ship catching fire and blowing the both of us sky high."

"Not a pleasant thought," Hal said.

"So, tell me about the tank, the one you said that Yak and the boys knocked out with the three-inch."

145

Hal grinned. "Well," he said, "I stretched things a bit when I called it a tank, although technically, I suppose, it was one, or a kind of one. *Flakpanzer*, I think it was. The body of one of those things probably isn't much larger than one of the Whippet tanks used in World War I, but it carries an anti-aircraft gun about the size of a 20 mm, and it can move. If I hadn't seen a picture of one of the damn things in an intelligence report I wouldn't have known what it was."

"And you got it?"

"On the seventh round."

Bender grinned. "Reckon we ought to paint a tank on the wing, alongside the planes we've shot down?"

"Don't know why not," Hal smiled. "It'll give the lads something to crow about. After all, how many other ships can say that they've done for a tank?"

"Make it so," Bender said, "and when we do get into port, make sure that the three-inch gun crew gets some extra liberty to go with it."

Two hours later, well out from the beach and well out of range from German artillery, the *3X* found the big salvage tug she'd been directed toward, turned the LST over to that ship's ministrations, and once more located and joined the supply convoy from which she'd been called in order to make the rescue. When she was again summoned to retract an LCI that had been hit and half sunk near the beach, everyone aboard found themselves more than gratified to find that the infantry had advanced farther inland—possibly up to three or four miles—and with the German artillery concentrating on stopping them, far fewer guns were being directed toward the invasion fleet.

With the crew performing like the professionals that they'd become, hooking up to the listing LCI took them less than ten minutes. Soon Bender had them moving once more back toward the open sea, going as swiftly as they could without flooding the stricken landing ship. There, everyone hoped, the welders on the salvage tug would be able to throw a patch on the LCI which would allow her to pump enough seawater from her flooded compartments so that she could return to Palermo where the yards could restore her.

Later that night, after the sun had gone down and the *3X* had joined with the remainder of the fleet which had withdrawn miles to sea, Hal, Bender, Lewis, and Garcia gathered in the wardroom for a late supper and dined like the crew on Shay's meatloaf, all them praising it to the skies.

"Think the worst of it will be over by tomorrow?" Garcia asked, scooping up the last bite with his fork.

"I wish," Bender said, "but no. From what the captain of the salvage tug told me, this one isn't going to go like Sicily. I don't know where he got his information, but from what he said, things have been touch and go on the beach, and we're not moving forward the way we hoped to."

"Which means that those of us who ain't on watch better get us some sleep while the gettin' is good," Lewis said.

The man had a point, and Hal knew it.

8

When the messenger woke him and told him that Bender wanted him up on the bridge, Hal had managed only three hours of what he might have called hard sleep before the war once more interfered with his plans.

"Fresh as a daisy, are we?" Bender greeted him when Hal finally pulled himself up onto the flying bridge and found the *3X* steaming beneath a waxing moon down the port side of a collection of ships that seemed to be heading west.

"Punchy, more like," Hal groaned. "What's up?"

"This thing at Salerno's going to be tougher than we thought," Bender said, half his face shadowed by the moonlight. "And the Krauts have thrown something wholly new into the mix."

"Oh yeah, what?" Hal asked, still feeling groggy.

"Glide bombs, radio controlled," Bender said. "Apparently the bastards send over a high-flying bomber which sits up there at eight or ten thousand feet, drops a bomb, and then the son of a bitch on the controls guides it straight down by means of radio signals or some kind of guide wire. From what I understand, they already sank one empty Liberty ship this afternoon, and about the time you turned in, they did for the light cruiser *Amarillo*. Caught her on the fantail, as I understand it, deep, and mucked up her rudders and screws so that she can't move under her own power. We're going to pick her up and tow her back to Palermo in company with a few other damaged ships and with a destroyer as escort."

"That's just peachy," Hal said with a smirk, "but on the other hand, if it gets us out of the line of fire for the rest of tonight and maybe a part of tomorrow, you won't find me complaining."

"Exactly," Bender said.

And it did get them out of the line of fire for several hours—or almost. After finding and taking the *Amarillo* in tow and joining up with the LST and the LCI that they'd rescued the day before as well as six other badly damaged ships—but ships that could move forward under their own power—they made it to within twenty miles of Palermo the following morning, before a lone Heinkel 111 flying from the direction of Sardinia attempted to put a torpedo into the *Amarillo*. The attack appeared to be well executed, but owing to the fact that the destroyer escorting them had radar, it had picked up the German before the Heinkel had closed to within six miles of them. As the plane came straight at them, hugging the surface of the sea, the six 5"/38s carried by the destroyer and the multitude of guns on the cruiser threw out such a wall of steel that the Heinkel nosed straight into the sea before it had closed to within two miles of them or loosed its fish. Once alerted to their danger, Yak and the 3"/50 had managed to pump out perhaps two rounds before the plane disintegrated and hit the deck in a ball of fire.

"Ha!" Yak shouted up from the gun tube. "Does that give us the right to add another little Nazi flag to the side of the bridge wing for a kill?"

"Fat chance!" Bender shouted back as he broke out laughing. "If you guys had won a million-dollar lottery with a shot like that, your share, among all the others, wouldn't have amounted to fifty cents!"

The little convoy reached Palermo at around 1000 hours that morning. Once arrived, the *3X* was kept busy working with three other harbor tugs moving the damaged ships alongside repair facilities and, in the case of the cruiser, into a floating dry dock, until 1300 that afternoon. At that time, blissfully, they were granted six hours of stand down for rest and upkeep before the orders they received directed them to reverse course and return to Salerno.

"Upkeep?" Hal questioned when Bender read him the message he'd received.

"The only upkeep I intend to assign," Bender laughed, "is to send every man on this ship straight to his bunk. Our upkeep is going to be the human kind, and I want everyone not actually on watch sleeping the fatigue of the last two days and nights off with as much relief as they can muster. See to it, Hal."

And Hal did.

By the time they returned to Salerno in the early hours of the morning on September 13, message traffic and radio communications indicated to Bender, Hal, and everyone else in the wardroom that the battle for Salerno beachhead was not going well. By any measure, things ashore, if not at sea, had reached some kind of crisis, for there were indications, vague and unspecified, that "as a precaution," the fleet was to prepare for "a retrograde movement" in the event that higher authority declared an evacuation necessary. In the midst of that, all anti-aircraft fire over the fleet was ordered suspended as transports flew in a sizable portion of the 82nd Airborne Division to bolster the 45th and 36th Divisions which were being pressed hard by a German attack that had come straight down from the hills in an attempt to split the American front between them.

As everyone aboard later learned, the battle during those hours had been one of those things that Wellington had once called "a near run thing," the Germans and whatever Italian Fascists were left to them nearly splitting the front and driving to the sea. What Hal and

Bender concluded was that the outcome of the battle had depended upon three things, two of them seemingly minor, one of them major. Complete penetration of the American front apparently depended upon a German armored column being able to use a bridge over the Sele River; when the enemy column arrived, it found the bridge destroyed, which allowed prepared American battalions to attack it from both sides. German General Kesselring's staff work and preparations were also faulted in his failure, for at the critical moment in the fight, he had simply not committed enough reserves to continue with it. But the truly deciding factor turned out to be naval gunfire support which thoroughly pounded the Germans into defeat, knocking out their armor wholesale and decimating them to the point where they had no option other than to withdraw what happened to be left of their attacking column.

Throughout the day, while the battle raged, Hal, Bender, and the rest of the men on the *3X* knew very little about it. Instead, their attention remained wholly focused on the tasks they were assigned, and those seemed never ending and likely to drive them to exhaustion. They assisted two LSTs in linking up with pontoons that would permit them to disgorge their prepacked loads of vehicles and armor onto the beach; they helped even smaller tugs not only to move pontoons into the beach from offshore but position transports beside them so that they, too, could unload. When they were not doing that, they assisted three LCIs as well as five LCTs and a total of seven LCVPs in getting themselves off the beach where they'd either broached or ridden up so high on the sand that they'd lost the ability to retract.

German gunfire onto the beach from their artillery in the surrounding hills had slacked considerably during the operations the *3X* conducted that day, but it had by no means stopped entirely. Every time a round landed in the water nearby, Hal felt his heart leap, the overall effect leaving the men tense and jumpy as they went about doing what they had to do. With regard to hooking up and retracting the LCTs and the LCVPs, both Bender and Hal thought their own boatswain's mates competent to make the hook ups and left them to it, sending the ship's whaleboat forward to take the messenger ashore and effect the connection. But with the much larger LCIs, Hal himself, with Bender's approval, elected to go forward with the boat in order to gauge the force vectors that the tug's wire rope would exert on the LCI's chocks and bitts. Given the job to be done and the proximity to danger, no one could afford to make a mistake, and it became Hal's responsibility to see that they didn't.

Farther down the beach that afternoon, in the same hour that Hal once more found himself going forward to hook up their tow to the last of the LCIs that they were to retract that day, a German bomber that got through the Allies' air cover succeeded in dropping one of the ubiquitous glide bombs right down into the well deck of an LST that happened to be unloading onto a pontoon. Within seconds, given the jerry cans of gasoline that must have made up a part of her cargo, the entire ship blew up, showering burning fuel and debris in all directions. How many men were killed, Hal didn't know. That a number survived, he could see for himself, counting at least twelve, all of them blown straight off the ship, their heads bobbing in the water as far as he could see at the distance. As if that weren't enough action to half cripple everyone with fear, two shells suddenly dropped straight down not forty yards away from the whaleboat, one of them exploding with enough force to shower all of them with water as the geyser it threw up came back down. The other, possibly a 37 mm anti-tank round, exploded against a nearby pontoon, throwing out BBs of shrapnel. One of the tiny pellets caused Kawalski to yelp as it sliced across his forearm, while another nipped across Hal's thigh, tearing a patch from his khakis and drawing blood. Neither of the cuts were deep, and neither did any serious damage beyond the instantaneous pain that they produced. Both men knew, however, that they would have sore limbs the following morning, and once returned to the ship, Hal made sure that their corpsman painted both tiny wounds with iodine before he slapped a piece of gauze and a line of sticking plaster over them in an attempt to ward off sepsis.

"Sorry about that," Bender said, once Hal got back up to the bridge. "Once things calm down a mite and you get back to your desk, you're to put both Kawalski and yourself in for Purple Hearts."

"You've got to be kidding," Hal said.

"I'm not," Bender said firmly. "A wound is a wound, and when this thing is done, that's what a Purple Heart commemorates. May not mean much to you now, but one of these days a far piece from now, once you and your draft board get to having grandchildren and they ask you what you did in the great war, you can trot out all your Purple Hearts as proof that you didn't sit at home and try to claim that you had flat feet."

"I'd call it a step too far," Hal said, with a shake of his head. "Nothing to it, if you see what I mean. I could have done the same thing by brushing my leg against a nail or a wire or something."

"Bullshit," Bender said, "and I don't want any bullshit out of you about it either. Just write up the papers for me to sign, Hal, and there's an end to it."

And there, Hal let the matter drop.

On the 14th, after a night of relative rest in the bosom of the offshore fleet, everyone awoke to find that Kesselring had renewed his attack, throwing in whatever armored columns he had left. When he did, every destroyer in the vicinity as well as both the *Boise* and the *Philadelphia* began to hammer the advancing Germans with such an assembly of five- and six-inch naval gunfire that nothing the

Germans tried to advance made it anywhere near the beach. The fighting ashore that day, from the little that Bender and Hal could glean from their communication links, proved bitter, the 36th, 45th, and 82nd Airborne going at it with a tenacity and drive that astonished everyone, with the Brits to the north putting up the same kind of resistance. In the midst of the fighting, out to sea, the Germans got another of their hated glide bombs into the *Warspite*, after the Royal Navy had rushed two of her famous battleships—the *Valiant* and the *Warspite*—up to throw their big guns behind the Allied advance. Once again, it proved a near thing; then, as the day advanced, it didn't. German pressure all along the line was slacking off enough by the middle of the afternoon to lead even the men aboard the *3X* to believe that the tide had turned.

Throughout that day and the next, *ATR-3X* continued to perform routine functions, assisting retrievals from the beach, moving damaged ships alongside salvage vessels so that temporary repairs could be made to them, moving pontoons around various sections of the beach, and assisting this or that ship to make up to them. When the occasion warranted, the *3X* maneuvered to avoid the occasional German artillery shells that still fell into the waters around them. Twice during that time, once on the 14th and once on the 15th, Me 109s had gotten through the air cover that was supposed to protect them and dropped down toward them for a strafe. In each instance, but without success, Yak, Bix, and the other gunners had enjoyed the satisfaction of opening fire on the enemy. The first of those planes had turned away before it could ever come near them, and the second had been blown from the sky by an attending destroyer before it could come within half a mile of them.

Finally, on September 16, after what seemed an interminable wait, Montgomery's Eighth Army sauntered up from the toe of the Italian boot and made contact with the Fifth Army south of Agrópoli. When the linkup showed itself to be both firm and ongoing, General Kesselring, fully aware of what was taking place, made the strategic decision to withdraw north, moving back quickly as the combined Allied armies advanced, and demolishing, as far as he was able, the harbor of Naples as the Germans withdrew. Later, Hal and Bender would learn that the Germans had withdrawn all the way up the boot and across the Volturno, establishing the line that would eventually hinge on Monte Cassino. At the time it was a place only the most committed Roman Catholics might have heard about, the monastery there being revered as the oldest Benedictine monastery in the world. But if no one paid much attention to Cassino then, later months would give them lasting cause never to forget it; the German line which did indeed hinge on the position was destined to lead them to a stalemate that would last for months while withholding the prize that they most sought—the capture and liberation of Rome.

But on September 16, as the battle slacked off, the capture of Rome seemed to be about the last thing to cross Hal's or Bender's mind, and Yak, for all his commitment, could talk of nothing but the times they would all have in Naples when they got there.

"Don't hold your breath," Bender told him as he, Hal, Yak, and Garcia sat down for dinner that evening, leaving Lewis on the bridge and on watch. "I'd guess that there's going to have to be a hell of a lot of work done in Naples before we're ever called up there. From what I've been able to learn, the Krauts are sinking everything they can find in the harbor and wrecking everything on the piers. And to make matters worse, our glory boys in the Air Corps seem to have absolutely flattened everything within three blocks of the harbor. Once we do get in there, we'll be lucky if we can find so much as a single beer without walking inland for miles."

"Now, now," Yak said, "let's not be pessimistic. According to the crew, we'll be met by pushcarts filled with beer, wine, and grappa, all of them attended by attractive Italian babes, none of them wearing bras, all of them sporting knockers to die for."

Garcia broke out laughing. "More likely," he said, "we'll be met by crones in black shawls, all of them begging for food or cigarettes, all of them barefooted, all of them speaking Italian with a German accent."

"See what I mean about war making you guys pessimistic?" Yak said to Hal and Bender.

"If our people can clear Naples within six weeks to two months," Bender said, "I think they will have exceeded expectations. What you'd better hope is that our orders will take us back to Palermo where we'll be miles farther away from Kraut artillery and, I can only hope, those damn glide bombs."

"All kidding aside," Garcia asked, "what seems most likely?"

"To tell you the truth?" Bender said.

"Or something close," Garcia said.

"My guess," Bender said, "is that while the build up goes forward, they're liable to hold us right here. For a while at least, once the Brits in the X Corps cross the mountains, I'm guessing we'll move right up to Salerno. It may be small as ports go, but for the time being, it's all we've got for supporting the Allied advance. Until Naples is occupied and cleared, it's going to have to carry the load, and what it can't carry will go right on offloading over the beaches. It's possible, I suppose, that we might be sent back to Palermo for one reason or another, but it looks to me like the work here is going to be enough to keep every tug in the fleet busy, so this is where I imagine we'll be staying."

"From what I've been given to understand," Hal began, trying to lighten the mood, "as a student of history, Salerno during the Middle Ages and the early Renaissance seemed to be the site of the most important medical school in Europe. Perhaps, in the evenings when he has nothing to do, we could enroll Yak for a short course so that he could fill in for Batcher, if Batcher ever goes down sick."

"Oh, thanks very much," Yak said acidly, "but what I'll tell Batcher is 'corpsman, heal thyself' and give him two APCs to see that he never goes down sick. If your draft board, Mr. Goff, could hear you proposing something so preposterous, I think she might disown you on the spot. Wall Street, that's the place for me after the war; Mayo Clinic is not on my horizon."

"No interest in proctology then?" Bender grinned.

"Absolutely none," Yak said at once.

"With regard to those babes that are supposed to be waiting in Naples behind the pushcarts," Garcia said, "I wonder, in fact, what we ought to expect. This is the first time American troops will have ever set foot on Italian soil, isn't it?"

"No," Hal said. "We've been here before, in the First World War."

"You're kidding," Garcia said.

Hal grinned. "I'm not," he said. "In 1918 we sent a regiment in, the 332nd, a part of the 79th Division. I'm guessing that it was probably for boosting morale and showing Allied solidarity, but according to the history books, they took part in the Battle of Vittorio Veneto and fought well. They weren't in the line for very long, mind, because the Austrians threw in the towel not long after, but they were here long enough to design a special regimental patch showing the Lion of St. Mark to commemorate their service, and some of them were decorated."

"That's the genuine truth?" Bender questioned.

"It is," Hal said, with an affirmative nod of his head, "and if that's not enough, I'll go it one better. In the first place, the U.S. Navy also played a significant role in the whole campaign. Down south, between the heel of the boot and Corfu, our subchasers did major service in manning the Otranto Barrage which attempted to seal off the rest of the Med so that Austrian and German U-boats wouldn't be able to get out of the Adriatic."

"Now I know you're kidding," Garcia laughed. "I've been in the Navy nearly twenty years and never heard anything of the sort."

"When we least expect it," Hal grinned, "life has a way of springing a new fact on us. And just to punch home the truth, I will further astound you by telling you that the Navy, our Navy, also maintained a seaplane base about forty miles south of Venice, for both fighters and bombers, all of them attempting to make life hell for the Austrian fleet in places like Pola, Cattaro, and Split. According to what I read, the Italians, who were our allies for that one, supplied the planes, and if you can believe it, our friends the Macchis with whom we've become all too familiar, turned out a little fighter seaplane, the M5, a pusher of all things, that proved capable of contending with anything the Germans or the Austrians could put in the air."

"Where in the hell are you getting this stuff?" Yak asked, his jaw hanging half open.

"*Ah*, well, I would have read it in a book, wouldn't I?"

"Someone actually reads?" Yak gasped. "Something besides op-orders and messages?"

"Just imagine where such bad habits could take you," Hal said. "Why, if you were to fall victim to the disease of books, you might even wind up reading people like Dickens, Trollope, Homer, or even someone as archaic as Edward Gibbon."

"Here now," Yak protested, "I read a book once, I think it was called *Fundamentals of Risk and Insurance* by Curtis Elliott. Very interesting, that one, and useful."

"An obvious business major," Bender said, his voice dripping with acid.

"Yes," Hal said. "We are wondering, Yak, if, during your ivy-covered years at college, you ever dropped by the library to pick up your library card?"

"Library card?" Yak responded. "What the hell is that?"

"We call it suspicions confirmed," Bender laughed.

❧

To Yak and the crew's displeasure, the babes with the pushcarts and the grappa, not only in Naples but in Salerno, did not materialize in the immediate future. Regardless of the fact that the Fifth Army made good progress in fighting its way forward, none of the ships in the invasion fleet managed to get into the port of Salerno before September 25 for the simple reason that while German combat formations were slowly withdrawing, their artillery observers remained in the hills farther back and turned out to be some of the last people to go, retreating mere yards ahead of the Allied infantry.

The Fifth and Eighth Armies made slow but steady progress as they pressed their attack north through the hills separating the Gulf of Salerno from the Bay of Naples. Rather than sit beneath an afternoon sun drinking grappa at some pleasant taverna in Salerno, the officers and crew of the 3X remained at sea drinking coffee, gallons of it, in an increasingly difficult attempt to remain awake as they labored day and night to handle the volume of traffic that offloaded the two armies' desperately needed supplies onto the beaches south of the port—a beach which remained under fire. Throughout that entire period, as the 3X first moved one Liberty ship in toward the beach and then another away from it, and aside from the occasional enemy artillery round that landed near them, they were never free from attack.

Farther out and away from the beach, a screen of destroyers, subchasers, PCs, and PT boats did stellar duty in their attempt to prevent German U-boats from getting at the supply ships. However, not unlike the supply ships themselves, those vessels also came under threat from continual air attack, even as the larger ships moved heaven and earth to unload, retract, and rejoin the convoys that would scoot south toward safer waters as soon as enough had collected. Some of the attacking German planes the escort vessels were occasionally able to shoot down. Others they were not, and still a few others managed to plant or guide their bombs with enough precision to do damage. On September 14, even as the battle ashore reached its crisis, the SS *Bushrod Washington* was hit, gasoline in the cargo setting the ship on fire before leading to its total loss. And on the 15th, the SS *James Marshall* suffered a similar fate, taking the LCT into which she'd been unloading down with her.

As the infantry began to press inland and farther up into the hills to the north, beginning around September 19 and continuing nonstop, masses of supply ships began arriving. That was when the men on the *3X* ceased to be acquainted with the word "rest," so much so that by the 27th as many as ninety merchant ships had arrived near the beaches, cluttering the seas between them with such a plethora of beaching craft designed to unload those ships that had to anchor in deeper water that it had become difficult for anyone in the Gulf to move. From what Hal would later remember of that time, two events stood out in his mind. First, on the 21st of the month, nine huge transports had come up from the south carrying the 34th Infantry Division—the "Red Bull" as it was called, its nickname drawn from the shoulder patch its men wore which showed a red bull's head against a black background. Then, at about the same time but under the cover of darkness and a blanket of mist, the *Kriegsmarine* had attempted the unthinkable by slipping two E-boats through the screen in an effort to run a torpedo attack against one of the cruisers still in the area. Fortunately for the ships in the Gulf, one of the radar-equipped destroyers in the area had finally detected the penetration in time to make things exceptionally hot for the E-boats. The torpedoes they fired missed their target before both of the E-boats, putting on a flank speed that could easily outrun the destroyers, managed to hug the coast and escape by confusing their own images on radar with the ground return coming off the Amalfi coast. No E-boat that Hal could imagine would waste a torpedo on a tug as small as the *3X*, but the danger of getting blown to smithereens by an accidental hit left every man aboard with a knot in his stomach.

And then, on the 28th, sweeping in from nowhere and unannounced, a sudden gale struck the Gulf of Salerno, packing winds that measured up to 80 mph and creating instant chaos for the fleet. Before the winds blew themselves out, the gale succeeded in beaching or broaching a total of sixty landing craft and no fewer than twenty-seven different beaching craft while utterly disrupting the unloading operations that were underway. For hours afterward, all Bender and Hal could hear over the radios were frantic calls for help as the massive unloading operation tried to recover its bearings and get back underway. The mystery to Hal and Bender both turned on why none of the merchant ships or transports had broken loose and been driven ashore from the positions in which they'd been anchored. Neither bothered to think about that for long, however; given the utter confusion on the beach, all they did for a day and a night and yet another day was to work with the other tugs in the vicinity, hauling their towline to the beach, hooking up to whatever broached vessel seemed next in line, and then working the craft loose and back into the water without so damaging its screw and rudders that it would be useless for the job at hand.

Finally, on the night of September 30, with all of the small boys rescued and re-floated, the exhausted men of the *3X* were permitted to make their way into Salerno's inner harbor, tie up in a nest with their sister tugs, and were given a twelve-hour stand down. Bender, Hal, Yak, Garcia, and Lewis gathered in the wardroom for a late supper, chow for everyone having been delayed by two hours so that the ship could complete the work it had been doing and reach the inner harbor before the PT boats guarding the entrance declared the harbor closed for the night.

"Well Yak," Hal said, as he threw himself into his chair with the salmon cakes, navy beans, and mashed potatoes that Shay had prepared for their meal, "what's it gonna be? The babes and their pushcarts with grappa, or a good night's sleep?"

"Very amusing," Yak said, "as if you didn't know. First things first, I always say. The world is filled with babes, and if the Navy actually wanted any of us to have one, I'm sure they would have issued her to us along with our skivvies, our boondockers, and our jackknives. But a good night's sleep? There's something which had better be snatched while it's available because when we're likely to get another remains a mystery. Considering the way they've been working us, a bird in the hand is better than one with a bush."

"Oh, that's good," Garcia laughed. "Mind if I write that down?"

Lewis merely let out a croak of a laugh and bent his head over his chow tray.

Bender looked to Hal like he was going to say something, but before he could make an attempt, Weatherford, the radioman—an Iowa farm boy with wide set eyes, big ears, and a nose that reminded Hal of an Arthur Rankin gnome—stepped into the wardroom after knocking once, and handed Bender the message boards.

"Thought youse might like to see the news," Weatherford said, his sudden grin revealing a mouth filled with tobacco-stained teeth.

Immediately, everyone perked up. With regard to news and the rest of the world, Hal realized he hadn't given either much of a thought since they'd left Palermo, and it was in that same instant he realized that aside from missing her terribly, he hadn't received a letter from Bea for the last three weeks.

"Hot damn!" Bender said, his eyes lighting up. "The Reds have recaptured Smolensk! That means that the Ruskies have damn near kicked the Nazis right back to Minsk."

"'Nough 'bout them Roosians," Lewis said. "I got money ridin' on the Cards. What 'bout them?"

"Cards took the pennant," Bender read quickly. "Beat the Cubs 2-1, and it looks like the Yanks have the American league, so that oughta make for a hot Series."

"An' thas gonna put money in ma pocket," Lewis said, grinning from ear to ear.

"Anything about the Pacific?" Hal asked.

163

For a minute, while he continued to read, Bender remained silent, but then he spoke.

"I guess the fight on New Georgia's ended," he said finally. "And MacArthur is supposed to be attacking some place called Finschhafen. Where the hell is that?"

"The Huon Peninsula," Hal said, "on New Guinea, well west of Buna and Gona."

"Ah," Bender said.

"Anything else?" Garcia asked.

"The Hollywood canteen welcomed its one millionth guest, and some Army sergeant got a kiss from Betty Grable to mark the event?" Bender said, showing Garcia an expectant expression.

Garcia broke out laughing. "Right," he said, "that's major news for sure. I'll bet that every would-be white hat at the Great Lakes boot camp is salting away his pay in expectation of being able to rush right out there."

"You're probably right," Bender laughed. "None of them have been in the service long enough to have developed Yak's perspective yet."

"And I'd bet money," Hal said, "that there isn't a one of them who doesn't think he looks like Frank Sinatra in his uniform."

"I think I've heard enough," Yak said, asking to be excused. "Not to belabor the pun, but I'm bushed, so if I can fall back on rank for at least once in my life, I'd like to suggest that warrant officers don't wake me when they drift in tonight, coming back from whatever flesh pots and dives they expect to frequent."

"Ha," Lewis grunted, "da dive dis warrant's takin' is the one into da bunk right below youse, an youse betta not step on me gettin' up into that crow's nest of youse neither."

And with that and with no other fanfare, all five officers almost instantly vacated their wardroom, disappearing into their bunks as the *3X* bobbed mildly behind the Salerno breakwater.

9

Units of Mark Clark's Fifth Army finally liberated and occupied Naples on October 1, 1943, salvage crews going immediately to work in what seemed like a hopeless attempt to clear and restore the harbor. With an eye to this endeavor, the *3X* did not participate. Instead, for yet another extended period, she remained right where she was, working without a break to assist the merchant ships and beaching craft in the Gulf of Salerno as they continued to supply the advance of the Allied infantry toward the Volturno.

By the time the Fifth Army readied itself for an assault on the Volturno line, the vagaries of the Italian weather were already beginning to play a role in the campaign; the autumn rains had begun to fall, swelling the rivers and turning many of the roads into virtual quagmires. From what Hal, Bender, and the others were able to learn, snatching a bit of news from the radio scheds here or a well-turned rumor there, the American 3rd and 45th Divisions went into a crossing of the Volturno on the night of October 12. Despite meeting stiff resistance from a skillful German rear guard, they managed to begin pushing the Krauts back into what turned out to be their main defense position around Cassino—the position people would begin calling the Winter Line or the Gustav Line. There, finally, the Allied attack stalled. What no one knew at the time and what the men of the *3X* could never have anticipated was that the stalemate that developed around Cassino would devolve into a numbing meat grinder that would continue to hold up the Allied thrust toward Rome through a long and indescribably bitter winter.

Had Hal and the others been fully cognizant of what took place ashore, they would have lamented it. By the time German resistance fully stiffened, however, they were no longer in the Gulf of Salerno, and without regard to Yak's longings for babes, pushcarts, and grappa, they had not followed the supply fleet up to Naples either. Instead, they were back in Palermo, having been ordered to return there for a period of rest, upkeep, and maintenance.

"Well, it looks like there must be a Santa Claus after all," Bender grinned when he read the order for their return.

"Betty Grable coming over in a sleigh to commemorate our one millionth tow?" Yak cracked.

"You'll think Betty Grable when we get down to Palermo," Bender said. "Sicilian grappa may be stronger stuff than the Neapolitan variety, but my guess is that the Sicilian babes you're going to find down here will be every bit as luscious as anything that Naples has to offer."

"And besides, Yak," Hal added, "given the number of occupation troops in Naples, you'd be reduced to taking seconds. In Palermo, where the occupation has become light, you will probably find the babes lining up on the pier just waiting for you to offer them home-cooked cans of Spam and cartons of Camels in exchange for small favors."

"That's very thoughtful of you, I'm sure," Yak said sarcastically. "But according to my recollections, Sicilian fathers and brothers come armed with long knives and those little sawed-off shotguns called *Luparas*, most of them no doubt supplied by the Mafia for use against anyone like Americans who tread on their turf."

"Catholic, are you?" Bender asked.

166

"No," Yak said.

"Well," Bender said, speaking with a broad grin, "you might want to take it up, attend a few early masses and such. You never know, but I'd almost bet money that any girl you meet in a pew in one of those establishments will be as pure as the new driven snow and as anxious to exchange human warmth as you are."

"You mean with her father, her mother, her chaperone, and her seven little brothers and sisters sitting right there beside her?" Yak grunted.

"A naval officer never allows himself to be discouraged," Bender said.

"Somehow," Yak said, "I continue to think that Naples might be more forthcoming with regard to delivering the fruits of battle."

"Considering the size of the occupation force up there," Hal laughed, "it might also be more forthcoming with regard to a fruit known as the clap."

"Here, now," Yak said. "Bite your tongue."

Once arrived at the repair facility to which the *3X* had been assigned, three Sicilian shipfitters came aboard like a trio of greased streaks and began tearing out the damaged starboard rail where enemy gunfire had shredded it. In the meantime, down below in the hole, Garcia, two or three specialists from a nearby tender, and nearly the entire number of snipes and machinist mates who crewed the space went straight to work overhauling everything they could attend to in the ship's propulsion plant. Topside, with Hal and Bender working in their staterooms while Yak and Lewis bent over the wardroom table, the four officers took in hand the mountains of paperwork they'd been forced to let slide during their time at sea. Aside from the annual, semi-annual, quarterly, and monthly reports which were never-ending requirements in the Navy, they were faced with personnel records which required updates, inventories that had to be completed and sorted, survey reports on damaged equipment that had to be replaced, work requests for additional jobs they wished the repair facility to complete, and changes to official publications that had to be made.

"Sort of makes you wish you'd joined the infantry, as a private, where all a man has to do is march, eat, and try to avoid being shot," Bender called across the passageway from his stateroom.

"There are those who would agree with you," Hal called back. "Privates in the Army's quartermaster corps might have an easier go of it still. Or how about being a mail sorter back there in Bizerte or Tunis or Oran?"

"They also serve who stand and wait," Bender said. "Speaking of mail, what do you hear from your draft board? I can't be sure, but from what I saw in this morning's delivery, you finally hit the jackpot."

Earlier that morning, when a mail sack finally reached the ship, Hal had been pleased to pick up as many as nine lengthy missives.

"My draft board is as busy as a bee," Hal laughed. "According to the latest reports, school is back underway, red meat is being rationed, people are walking more than ever with gas and tires in short supply, and she is immersed in one good course on the early English novel and another about which she is less enthusiastic regarding American romanticism."

"That sounds like Hawthorne, Emerson, and Thoreau," Bender said.

"Exactly," Hal said. "Not quite my cup of tea either, I'm afraid."

"I was once forced to read some Thomas Carlyle," Bender said, "and as I recall, Carlyle and Emerson were friends, and each helped the other to get his books published. I think they were supposed to have visited when Emerson toured England, and when I tried to imagine what a conversation between those two might have amounted to, I found it gave me a headache."

Hal laughed. "From what little I know, I think it would take a road map just to decipher their syntax."

"Between the two of us," Bender said, "for late night reading, I think I'd prefer to fall back on Hemingway or even Dashiell Hammett."

"I can't say I haven't gotten a kick out of Dickens and Trollope from time to time," Hal said, "but on the whole, one of those monster novels a year is about my limit."

"Change of subject," Bender said. "Want to see if we can't go ashore and rustle up a worthwhile serving of calamari this evening?"

"I'm game," Hal said, remembering the taste of fried squid the first time he'd tried it. "Yak and Lewis included?"

"Absolutely," Bender said. "Garcia can't go because he's up to his elbows in the overhaul he's doing, so he said he'd be willing to stand as command duty officer for as many days and nights as the job takes."

By 1800 that evening, Bender had acquired the use of a jeep from somewhere, so it was into a battleship gray Navy jeep that all four of them piled. Bender took the wheel and drove like a maniac as they skirted the immense piles of rubble that continued to obstruct some of the streets. This cleared, they emerged onto the north road which would take them around Mondello to the tiny port of Isola delle Femmine where, according to Bender, he'd been told about a former tourist hotel that could still put together a meal fit for consumption.

"On the whole," Yak observed, "I've been more than satisfied with what Shay has been cooking for us, but you've got to admit that the combinations of ground beef, canned salmon, and Spam to which the Navy continues to confine him do seem a bit limited. If this place you're taking us to can break that routine, I won't complain."

"Good of you," Bender said. "Perhaps you'd care to write a culinary review, once we're back on the ship. Tourism is bound to start flourishing around here once we leave, and you might do wonders for the trade with a well-honed article in one of the travel magazines. 'Haute cuisine served amidst assorted removed land mines, disabled Italian tanks, and burned-out Nazi vehicles with the lingering scent of gun cotton in the air.' Just imagine the number of tourists that could draw. You'd become world famous with the mere stroke of a pen."

"Thanks very much," Yak said. "I think I'll stick to trading stocks and bonds if you don't mind."

"What?" Hal said, "And miss out on all the high-toned babes an article like that might draw in?"

"Ha," Lewis chuckled, intoning another of his reverberating grunts, "if it's high-toned babes he's after, like as not, wavin' a ten spot in the air somewheres 'round that opera house in Palermo will draw 'em like flies."

"Well yes," Bender said, "there's always that, of course: the direct approach."

"You continue to be pessimists," Yak said acidly, "the whole lot of you."

The Hotel Isola del Vento, named for the land spit flanking the tiny bay where Bender took them, turned out to be a relic of the 19th century which had apparently retained the same décor and furniture with which it had first been equipped around the time of the *Risorgimento* when Garibaldi had first invaded the island.

"Well," Hal said, as the four were ushered inside by a genuine doorman, "it's sure got atmosphere, I'll give you that."

"This is what's called immersing yourself in the culture of the country," Bender quipped. "It's a trifle shop worn, I'll admit, but if the chef is as ancient as the surroundings, he will have acquired mastery by now."

"Which will be fine," Yak said, "as long as the food doesn't come to us petrified with a side serving of fossilized dinosaur eggs."

"Here now," Bender said. "Where's your spirit of adventure?"

"Him squandered it in Palermo," Lewis said, "searchin' for the babes."

"Fat chance," Yak said. "What with ten million reports to write, when would I have had the time?"

"Why, I don't know what you're talking about," Bender laughed. "What with two little burn reports to write and no more than monthly and quarterly ammunition inventories to submit? It wouldn't surprise me to learn that you'd set up a lawn chair and were out on the pier somewhere, sipping grappa, chatting up the babes, and taking the sun for five hours every afternoon."

"Those burn reports came to over fifty-five pages each," Yak protested, "and with more than thirty line items per page, each of which I had to copy by hand before they could be typed! I ought to be in hospital for the writer's cramp I developed. I'm only surprised that you didn't put me in for a Purple Heart for that job!"

"I fear the lad exaggerates," Hal said.

"So it would seem," Bender said as they came to the door of the dining room.

Unlike the trattorias in which they'd previously eaten, the dining room at the Isola del Vento came equipped with upholstered chairs—the upholstery worn but nevertheless comfortable—clean white tablecloths, and genuine silver tableware that had somehow been hidden from the Krauts before they pulled out with the rest of the loot they'd confiscated all over the island.

"This looks like living of the finest kind," Hal observed. "How the hell did you find out about this place?"

"Guy I went through OCS with," Bender said. "He's the communications officer over on the tender, and he apparently got onto it. Said the food's good and the service better."

The service turned out to be meticulous, every waiter who came near the table a thorough professional, his skills honed through long service, and as far as Hal could judge, there wasn't a man in the lot who seemed any younger than Methuselah.

"If their profession allows for it," Yak said, "these guys must all be warrants by now."

"Stand to reason," Lewis beamed. "Widout us dats got da expertise, where'd youse youngsters be? No offense intend, Cap'n."

"None taken." Bender smiled.

The calamari, garnished with a sprinkling of red pepper flakes, and the crab lasagna that they had that night, both dishes washed down with Lágrima de Cristo, an Italian white wine imported from the mainland, proved more than satisfying. When two of the waiters actually came to the table and peeled plums to go with the cheeses that they'd asked for in place of desserts, all four of them found themselves astounded by the precision with which the operation went forward.

"This has been an experience," Hal said. "There's no getting around it."

"Wishing your draft board were here?" Yak prompted.

"Yes and no," Hal said. "If I could have my draft board off to a table by ourselves, yes; if I had to subject her to the leers of you three, no, decidedly *no*."

"That's really big of you," Yak said.

"I know," Hal said, "you might even call it generous. I shouldn't like to throw temptation in your way or generate the antics you might get up to in her presence. I'd hate to be called responsible if one or another of you swooned dead away."

"I'll remember that," Bender said. "The mere thought is going to make yet another good story to tell her when we meet her one of these days. Now, what about a good shot of cognac to go with the espresso?"

Save for Bender who latched onto the cognac he called for, the other three elected to stick with grappa, expecting the best, and none of them were disappointed.

"Dis stuff a sight different than dat firewater we gets in town," Lewis said, his eyes lighting up at the first taste.

"Boy, I'll say," Yak exclaimed, coming to the edge of his seat. "The grapes that produced this must have been raised with loving hands."

Hal could not dispute them. The grappa was excellent and as smooth as glass, so much so that each of them called for a second.

"Watch it," Bender said. "I don't want you falling out of the jeep and becoming war casualties on the way back."

"Speaking of war casualties," Hal said, "did you collect any war news when you were over picking up the jeep?"

"Some," Bender said, "and some of it's surprising. I guess Patton is in hack."

"What are you talking about?" Yak questioned.

"*Hack*," Bender said, "just like if I were to throw you in hack aboard the *3X* and order you into confinement in your bunk room without allowing you to come out for one infringement or another. I don't know exactly what happened, but in addition to shooting off his mouth here and there—and that apparently has given Ike fits—Patton is rumored to have slapped a couple of soldiers. Whether that's true or not, I don't know, but according to what I heard on the beach, he's in the doghouse for doing it."

"Thas a stretch, for a general to be doin' it," Lewis said, "but you boys should a been in the ole Navy for a few days. 'Bout the time I join up in '18, if a man started causin' trouble somewhere and didn' stan correction first time his chief tole him, like as not the chief would take him up ta the foc'sle an' use 'im for a punchin' bag. Personally, I don't cotton to that kind of discipline, but I ain't sayin' it weren't effective."

"Sort of a replacement for flogging, was it?" Hal asked.

"Exactly," Lewis said. "An' if a man didn' straighten up quick, the next stop on da line was da brig or Portsmouth Naval Prison."

"Sounds a mite tight," Yak said.

"Was," said Lewis.

"Hear anything else?" Hal asked, turning once more to Bender who happened to be in the process of savoring his cognac.

"Yes," Bender said. "Monty's across the Volturno line, just like us, but same as us, he isn't setting any records for moving fast. I think the Brits have captured the big air base at Foggia, but according to the scuttlebutt I heard, the Air Corps' is having second thoughts about trying to get their bomb loads over the Alps, so for the time being, they may be concentrating their attentions on Greece, Albania, and other points east. And there's also a rumor about the Krauts having massacred an entire Italian division on one of the islands in the Adriatic, in retaliation for Italy's surrender."

"Shit, that's going a piece against a former ally!" Yak said.

"No question," Bender said, "if the rumor is true. Personally, and I'm not trying to sound like a defeatist, but I have real reservations about us getting up north and trying to break into Austria and Germany through the Italian Alps."

"Concur," Hal said. "That front produced a bloodbath during the First World War, and I can't imagine our people being able to manage a penetration through those mountains any easier in this one. If what I've read is true, that seems to be one of Churchill's pet projects, and frankly, if it is, I think he's dreaming."

"Rome first and the Alps later?" Yak asked.

"Yes," Bender said, "Rome first. Anyone want to place bets on how long it will take us to get there?"

"No," they all said in unison.

"Hear anyting else?" Lewis asked.

"Corsica—the Free French have retaken it, and I gather that the Krauts have also withdrawn from Sardinia," Bender said quickly.

"What might that mean for us?" Hal asked. "Think we'll be going up there?"

"I don't have a clue," Bender said. "I guess the Air Corps will put bases on those islands, for bombing all points north of Naples. Ought to be tailor-made for sending over medium bombers. But whether or not there will be much of a naval presence up there, I can't say, and I didn't hear a word about it in Palermo."

"Food for thought then?" Yak said.

"That's about it," Bender said, making a sign to the waiter and calling for the check.

After returning from the Isola del Vento in one piece and hugely satisfied with the meal they'd taken, they were able to make the trip twice more before their period of upkeep, rest, and maintenance ended, and on none of those occasions did they come away dissatisfied. Yak, in the meantime, failed utterly to make contact with any of the babes or pushcarts on the beach. One or two of the crew did, but they were sorry for it later when they were forced to have a series of injections while waiting to see if they were going to undergo courts martial for having contracted VD. The remainder of the crew went ashore when they could, drank more than their share of Sicilian beer and wine, did their work without complaint, participated in a couple of softball games, won a pickup touch football game with another of the tugs in the harbor, and restored their energies after the grueling ordeal they'd been through around Salerno. Finally, after three weeks in port and after inspectors had come aboard and pronounced the 3X once more ready for sea, they sortied near the beginning of November, steamed south for half a day, and took a

Liberty ship in tow which had been struck by a torpedo and left dead in the water halfway back to Bizerte.

"Why didn't the U-boat sink her, I wonder?" Yak asked on the bridge as Lewis, back aft, took the slack out of the towline and began to take the Liberty ship in tow.

"Maybe that was the Kraut's last torpedo," Bender said.

"And the U-boat didn't have a deck gun with which to finish the job?" Yak said.

"That Liberty ship's got a 5"/38 and a Navy gun crew aboard," Hal said, pointing out the gun tub forward, "so I'm guessing that the U-boat skipper wouldn't have wanted to take the risk. And beside that, with the bigger ship burning the way that it must have been at the time, judging from the scorched sides that are showing, maybe the Krauts figured it would sink without any more help."

"Point taken," Yak said, examining the Liberty ship through his binoculars. "Fire clearly burned right up the port side and around the pilot house, so she may well have looked like she'd sink. I wonder how they got the fire out?"

"Grit, I'd guess," Bender said, "and nothing much else. Good crew over there, obviously."

"They give medals to merchant sailors?" Yak asked.

"I have no idea," Bender said.

"At this speed," Hal said, standing at the chart table, "we ought to make Bizerte around 0200 in the morning."

"That's just dandy," Bender said, sarcasm dripping from his every word. "What that means is that we will have to cool our heels until at least 0500 when the port authority will finally get off their ass and allow us to haul this bird in."

Later that day, the 3X remained in Bizerte only long enough to work the Liberty ship alongside a salvage pier, take on a few stores, top off with fuel, and sign whatever papers were required to report on the tow she'd undertaken and completed. By noon, she was already back at sea, heading for Naples.

"Well Yak," Bender said to him as the *3X* steamed into the Tyrrhenian Sea east of Trapani, "it looks like your dreams are about to come true. Stand by for babes, pushcarts, and grappa in Napoli."

"I'd about given up hope," Yak said.

"Just be careful they aren't dashed," Bender said, "because if there isn't one Army division in residence waiting to go up to the line, there are probably two."

"Your pessimism is reaching epidemic proportions," Yak said.

Strangely, Hal thought, three days later Yak virtually stumbled into exactly the encounter that he sought. After a day spent moving merchant ships in and out of the slowly recovering harbor, while walking down the south side of the Palazzo Reale di Napoli, Yak had occasion to snatch from disaster a small boy who had gotten away from his grandfather's grasp and angled into the street directly in the path of an oncoming six by six hauling supplies away from the piers. Seizing the lad by the back of his shirt, Yak managed to yank the kid back onto the sidewalk mere seconds before the truck would have run him down. In gratitude and nearly fainting with relief, the boy's grandfather, who had some English, invited Yak to take a glass of wine with him. Then, on the basis of that exchange, the old man invited Yak to accompany him home so that the remainder of the family could take a glass of wine with him and thank him for saving the life of their pride and joy.

To hear Yak tell it, the old man's family—an extended one harboring several more prides and joys, not to mention a cousin or two—inhabited what turned out to be a six-room apartment seven or eight blocks back from the harbor in the old medieval portion of the city, close enough to have been frightened out of their wits by the bombing, far enough away to have escaped any direct hits. The wine, Yak told Hal, was nothing to get excited about.

"Lágrima de Cristo it was not," Yak said. "More like a thick red that smelled and tasted of the barrel, but after being introduced to one of the Cicciano cousins, a really lovely girl by the name of Anna, I didn't care. Nice girl," Yak continued, "modest, reserved, very pleasant to talk to, although her English is a trifle Victorian, probably because she reads Dickens and someone who I think she mentioned as Andy Hardy."

"I think you may mean Thomas Hardy," Hal laughed. "You're mixing the author up with that character Mickey Rooney plays in the flicks."

"Oh," Yak said, a reflective expression suddenly showing itself on his face. "Yeah, you're probably right. Mistake there. I'll have to be careful the next time I visit."

"You intend to go back?" Hal quizzed. "What about the babes and the pushcarts and the grappa?"

"I'll be leaving them for the crew," Yak said. "Anna is a nice girl, Hal, no kidding, and both the grandfather and Anna's grandmother invited me back. Her father is apparently missing in Russia with whatever Mussolini sent out there to help Hitler against Stalin, but as long as I see Anna in the apartment and in company with her family, I seem to have their seal of approval."

"And so, after all of the song and dance, you really hit the jackpot?" Hal grinned.

"Yeah," Yak said, turning serious after a moment's hesitation, "yeah, I guess I did."

With regard to meeting someone with whom he could keep company, Yak, Hal thought, had indeed hit the jackpot, just as long as he would be willing to confine his attentions to meeting Anna within the well-supervised atmosphere provided by her family. With regard to receiving from her the kinds of benefits provided by the girls with the pushcarts and the grappa, Hal imagined that Yak would remain out of luck. Those girls might be ubiquitous on the streets of Naples, but the girl named Anna Cicciano was not one of them nor likely to be. What amused Hal turned out to be the simple fact that after all of his talk about rushing the babes with the grappa, Yak didn't seem to mind. After months at sea and after the actions they'd been through, Yak, like the rest of them, was simply lonely for a little female companionship. While the 3X was not in port with time off so often that Yak risked wearing out his welcome with the Ciccianos, the ship did put in often enough that the family seemed to enjoy seeing him when he arrived. The fact that Yak also took them cans of Spam and salmon, not to mention packs of Camels, probably helped to grease the wheels for him. As the weeks slipped by, judging from the things Yak said and the improvement of his morale, Hal thought that Yak's relationship with the family looked to be developing into something more satisfying for both parties involved in the relationship. For his own part, Hal began feeling Bea's absence more than ever, so much so that the high point of each day the 3X returned to port seemed to turn for success on whether or not the mail clerk could hand him a letter when the mail had been sorted.

If the 3X managed one liberty night in Naples out of three or four, everyone aboard felt more than satisfied. During the remainder of their time, when they weren't working large merchant ships in and out of the harbor in company with subchasers and an occasional LCI(G), they found themselves shepherding heavily laden LCTs, LCMs, and other light supply craft from the piers in Naples up to the mouth of the Volturno. Rations, ammunition, and gasoline could be quickly unloaded there, put on trucks, and dispatched directly to the front line without the necessity of becoming lost in the octopus of alleys, streets, and roads that defined Naples' complicated and difficult road network. If going by sea proved to be much faster than going by land, it also proved more dangerous, for while Naples remained under what Hal thought of as fair air cover, the coast north of the city did not. Allied planes were in the air there, and often, but those not involved in what the Air Corps continued to call "strategic bombing" inland were in large part offering tactical air support to the infantry, which kept trying to advance but could not. As a result, air cover for Allied traffic at sea remained minimal, every convoy in which Hal and Bender took part having to rely on its own guns to protect itself.

Across a period which extended until the week before Christmas, with the weather always becoming worse and the rains colder, Hal wrote up for Bender's signature no fewer than nine separate after-action reports. In one case, they'd been bombed by two Stukas down from some Kraut landing field to the north. Both of them dropped their bombs wide, one of them plunging straight into the sea owing to a lucky shot or series of shots from a 40 mm on the LCI gunboat that accompanied them on that trip. In three other instances, single Me 109s had strafed them without effect, and in the middle of November, two Heinkel 111s had attacked them with bombs, flying in on their convoy from two different directions. Again, both dropped their bombs wide of the mark, Bix getting a splatter of rounds into one of the bomber's engines which sent it away trailing smoke. Then, at the beginning of December, to everyone's dismay, yet another Stuka managed to plant a single fifty-kilogram bomb dead center on an LCT carrying gasoline. The entire LCT exploded on contact, killing every man aboard while hurling burning debris for hundreds of yards in every direction.

"*Shit!*" Bender said, struggling to breathe in response to the shock the explosion had given them.

Hal didn't say a word. He couldn't. He was as breathless as Bender.

"*Shit!*" Bender said again. "You think we should look for survivors?"

"No," Hal said, when he finally managed to regain control of himself enough to get a word out. "There won't be any. Saw a man in the air, Jos. Musta been a hundred feet up 'fore he dropped straight back down into the fire. *Jesus!* If I live to be ninety, I'll never get rid of it."

The last attack they endured came while they were retrieving a grounded LCM from near the mouth of the Volturno. The LCM's coxswain had cut a corner at the entrance, running an entire cargo of winter overcoats and galoshes aground, and then been unable to back himself off of the sandbar which held him fast. Hal, merely to break the routine he'd been maintaining, had gone forward with the crew of the whaleboat in order to help them take over the fiber towline they intended to use in pulling the Mike boat free. Not fifteen yards out in front of the *3X*, with at least another seventy or eighty to go before they could throw the messenger up to the stern hook on the Mike boat, Hal and the others suddenly became aware that they were under fire. Machine gun bullets plowed into the water all around them.

With no place in which to take cover, Hal and the others knew that the Me 109 making the strafe had never intended to shoot at the whaleboat; it was after the *3X*, but for whatever reason, the bastard's aim was off. Before he passed over the both of them, getting only a few rounds into the prow of the *3X*, he also passed out a single 7.2 mm round which came within inches of Click's knee before gouging out a piece of the whaleboat's gunnel not more than a foot away from where Hal happened to be standing.

"I'll tell youse, Mr. Goff," Click roared, "I've had about all this war I want!"

181

Before Hal had time to say a word, the outbound Me 109 exploded inland by a few hundred yards, Yak's three-inch gunners having caught it with a VT fused round before it could make its escape. And in that second, with every man in the whaleboat, the Mike boat, and aboard the *3X* erupting with cheers, the air filled with more joy than Hal thought he might expect over a Navy win in the annual Army–Navy classic.

"Well," Hal said, when the cheering finally died down and his heart had stopped pounding, "that change your perspective, Click?"

"No Sir," Click said at once, "not one bit."

"Mine neither," Hal grinned. "On the whole, I'd say, I'd rather be home for Christmas."

"Thas for sure," Click said. "Thas for damn sure!"

"*Buon Natale!*" Bender said, coming into the wardroom to join Hal, Lewis, and Garcia, all four of them wearing blues for Christmas dinner. "Seats, gentlemen. Yak, of course, will not be joining us, sitting for Christmas dinner with the Ciccianos as he will be, all of them no doubt preparing to make pigs out of themselves over the chickens with which Yak has supplied them in lieu of something better. I regret, I must say, that Shay will not be supplying you with the turkey and trimmings that traditionally go with this meal; those treats as you know are to be served on the front line, probably in the rain. You and I will have to tough it out on the T-bone steaks that Shay has assembled in place of a bird."

"The sacrifice we make for the good of our troops almost defies description," Hal said, a wry smile curling his lips.

"Remind me," Garcia said with a grin as broad as Texas, "what *is* a T-bone steak? It seems just possible that I crossed the path of one at some time in the past, but after the Spam and the canned salmon, I'm having trouble visualizing one."

"Not me," Lewis grunted. "Suppose we say grace so as we can get at the fixins."

They said grace, and moments later, the mess cook tending to the wardroom brought them each a well-grilled T-bone and baked potato served on a genuine china plate.

"Boy," Hal said, "Shay has gone all out for this one!"

"Not only do we have actual china," Bender said, picking up his knife and fork, "but if you will look closely, that is genuine butter for the baked potato. My only hope is that Shay didn't trade someone our sextant or binoculars in order to get it. Dig in, lads. Henceforth and for the rest of your lives, you will always remember this moment as one of the high points of the war. Just think," he said, "an honest-to-God T-bone steak, coming to us all the way across the Atlantic from some distant slaughterhouse in Nebraska, Iowa, or even Kansas! The miracles that a modern Navy can produce know no bounds."

The steaks, grilled to perfection by Shay's able hands, met their every expectation, and the taste of genuine butter on their baked potatoes simply underscored their delight.

"Given a feast like this," Hal said, "one might almost expect a plum pudding to follow."

"Those are probably restricted to admirals with names like Pickwick, Cratchit, and Tiny Tim," Bender said, "but I'll tell you what, when I came through the galley on my way in here, I could see pumpkin pies coming out of the oven, and if you don't mind me saying so, I can't imagine any of us wanting to chuck one of those overboard."

And Bender was right.

As Shay's mess cook cleared the plates away, Hal reached into his pocket and produced a small cardboard box containing four Toscano cigars.

"Merry Christmas," he said, taking the first cigar for himself before handing the box to Lewis so that it could be passed around the table.

"If those are real Toscanos," Bender laughed, "we're all liable to be cross-eyed five minutes after lighting up. As far as I know, those are the strongest cigars ever fashioned by the hand of man."

"That's what my draft board told me too," Hal said. "She said that her father and grandfather cut them in half and only smoke one half at a sitting. Christmas present, those. Purchased with loving hands and mailed with promises for the future."

"And what, if I might ask, did you send your draft board for Christmas?" Garcia asked, taking a Toscano from the box and cutting it in half with the sharp blade of his case knife.

"A cameo," Hal said, "showing the Three Graces."

"Considerin' the cost of dem tings, youse must have a ting for dis draft board of youse," Lewis said.

"I'd call that an astute observation," Hal said, as Lewis nearly choked after lighting up his cigar.

"Holy crimney!" Lewis barked. "Dis ting's stronger den rope."

"Told you," Bender laughed. "In another minute or two, your head will be swimming."

"Speaking of swimming," Garcia said, "where do you expect the 3X to be swimming next?"

For perhaps thirty seconds, Bender didn't say a word. But then he did, speaking so quietly that the others had to bend themselves toward the table in order to hear him.

"According to what I hear on the beach," Bender began, "this thing at Cassino is damn near beating the shit out of us, and no one—not us, not the British, not the French, not even the Poles—is getting anywhere against the place. Aside from the fact that the approaches seem to be knee deep in mud from these rains that bedevil us, the Krauts are sitting up there with an array of forward artillery observers and pounding the hell out of us every time we make a move on the place."

Thus far, Bender hadn't said anything that the rest of them didn't already know or thought they knew.

"And?" Garcia prompted.

"Well," Bender said, "I can't say for sure, but every time I go ashore, I hear another rumor, and almost all of them point to the same thing. Any guesses about what that might be?"

"The only thing that would make any sense," Hal said, feeling himself becoming lightheaded from the draw of the Toscano, "would be an end run of some kind."

"Right," Bender said. "And some weeks or months back, I guess we were thinking about making one, and then, owing to a lack of shipping or for some other reason, the operation was called off."

"On again?" Lewis asked.

"According to this week's rumors," Bender said, "yes."

"Where?" Garcia asked.

"Ah," Bender said. "That's the mystery, isn't it? The boys on the tender think we'll go in somewhere north of Rome. Secondhand word from some of those types on the *Biscayne* where the admiral's supposed to be holding up are talking about the Pontine Marshes, as though we could get in there and outflank the Krauts without the Krauts being able to get to us. Sounds bogus to me, but what do I know. And if you want a third possibility, how about an invasion as far north as Point Ercole which is southeast of Elba?"

"That would be a stretch," Hal said. "That sounds way too far north."

"Sounded that way to me too," Bender said, "but that's what I mean about the rumor mill. It's out of control for the moment."

"So we'll just have to wait and see what comes when it comes?" Garcia said.

"As always," Bender said, "with this single caveat: with whatever comes along, we'll probably be the last to know."

"Goes with our size," Lewis laughed. "Das da Navy way."

"Pick up anything else while you were over on the beach?" Hal asked.

"Yes," Bender said. "Rommel's apparently been sent up to France, which means that Kesselring is now running the whole show in Italy."

"Das way 'bove my level of expertise," Lewis laughed. "I don't even know who in our Navy we'se supposed to be answerin' to most of da time."

"If it makes you feel any better, Chief, neither do I," Bender joked.

"Any news of the Pacific?" Hal asked.

"Ever hear of Makin, or Tarawa?" Bender asked.

"I think those are in the Gilberts," Hal said.

"Well, wherever they are, we've invaded 'em," Bender said, "and from the sound of things, it wasn't pretty. From what I heard, the army lost about seven hundred men taking Makin, and Tarawa must have been an absolute bloodbath. Little bitty island apparently, but the Marines lost a thousand dead and another two thousand wounded in order to take it, and according to what I heard they had to kill close to five thousand Japs in order to secure the place."

"Sounds to me like for casualties that would put Tarawa right about on a par with Salerno," Garcia said.

"Das gonna make for a lot of misery at home," Lewis said.

"Yes," Bender said, "it is."

Once the mess cook set coffee before them, the whole table took to talking about more festive subjects—new movies they'd read about but hadn't yet seen, Lena Horne's recording of "Stormy Weather" which had just become a hit with the fleet, and Tommy Dorsey's "Boogie Woogie," the title of which they all found amusing.

"Bet dat Mr. Yaakov ain't getting' no boogie woogie dis afternoon," Lewis joked. "More like, dem Ciccianos gonna drag him out to an afternoon mass somewheres."

"As long as they let him sit beside Anna and don't try to sandwich him between the grandmother and one of the other prides and joys," Hal laughed, "I doubt that he'll complain."

"You know what would really top off Christmas dinner?" Bender said.

"Speak," Garcia answered.

"A really good grappa," Bender said.

"Long as we don't have ta buy it off one of dem pushcarts from one of dem so-call babes," Lewis said, "I'se game."

And with that, leaving the remains of their Toscanos in an ashtray on the wardroom table, they stood, buttoned their blouses, picked up their hats, and left the ship to spend the remainder of their Christmas afternoon in the mildly quiet interior of the Taverna Amicizia.

10

In and around Naples, January 1944 turned out to be colder, wetter, and more miserable than anyone could have imagined, and according to what the men on the *3X* heard, the so-called front had turned into a virtual sea of mud, leading to everything from pneumonia to trench foot among the troops. Muffled against the cold, the *3X* twice escorted supply convoys to the mouth of the Volturno and back, but in each instance those convoys ran at night and therefore, miraculously in Hal's opinion, avoided air attack. For the remainder of that period, they found themselves assisting or moving the immense array of shipping that had suddenly jammed the Naples harbor, most of it consisting of LSTs and LCIs. It was then that the officers and men on the *3X*, while not privy to any of the details, recognized that an invasion of some kind seemed to be impending.

Finally, on the evening of January 18, 1944, Bender found himself summoned to a conference on the beach. When he returned around midnight and found his officers drinking coffee and waiting for him in the wardroom, he didn't hesitate to dump an immense op-order on the table and deliver his announcement to them with a straight face.

"It's called Operation SHINGLE," he said. "It's Anzio."

No one that Hal could remember had even mentioned Anzio for an invasion. Anzio was directly north of the Pontine Marshes, south of the Alban Hills, and within striking distance of Rome. Would they be attempting to steal a march on the Germans, capture Rome when the Germans weren't looking, and completely bottle up Kesselring's army at Cassino by cutting off its avenues of retreat? Hal didn't know.

"You're going to tell us what this is about, I hope," Yak said, looking at Bender.

"For what it's worth," Bender said, "but you're going to have to judge for yourselves to see if you think it's feasible. Not that anyone is going to pay a lick of attention to anything we might think, of course."

"Which goes without saying," Garcia said.

"Well, for my money," Bender began, "we're going in weak, with only two divisions—the U.S. 3rd Infantry Division and the British 1st Infantry Division—as well as three battalions of Rangers, two battalions of Commandos, and a regiment of paratroops. Subordinate to Mark Clark, Major General John P. Lucas will be commanding, and whether he's going to try to consolidate the beachhead or hit the beach running for Rome I don't know because we ain't privy to whatever orders Clark has given him. According to the scuttlebutt about the way this thing was first planned, three or four months back, this kind of end run wasn't supposed to have been tried until the advancing Fifth Army had moved to within twenty miles of wherever the invasion was to go in. Right now, the Fifth Army is stopped dead in front of Cassino, and that's more than 120 miles south of Anzio, so as far as I'm concerned, that's really tossing the invasion force out on a limb. I guess Clark is planning a big advance against Cassino in hopes of breaking through, but whether that will succeed or not is anyone's guess. With the roads in the condition that we've heard they're in, it would seem to me that it would take a miracle for the Fifth Army to get up to Anzio in a hurry, and that's if they can score a breakthrough in the first place. I don't like to sound like a pessimist, but I'm not all that hopeful."

Hal didn't feel hopeful at all. For weeks, the Battle for Cassino had been grinding up men like hamburger. What made Clark or British General Sir Henry Maitland Wilson—Wilson having taken over from Eisenhower when the great powers had suddenly decided to ship him off to England—think that yet another attack would break through the Kraut's Winter Line proved something that Hal couldn't measure, and because he couldn't, he doubted that it would happen.

"So, how are we to be organized for this one?" Garcia asked.

"Nothing irregular there," Bender said, stopping to feel the stubble along both sides of his long jaw. "Rear Admiral Lowry will be in the *Biscayne* commanding VIII Amphibious Force under the U.S. Eighth Fleet. The way I see it, we'll be back with the LCIs, escorting them up there and then waiting to retrieve whatever can't retract from the beach or take in tow any ship that is damaged and unable to move under its own power."

"Nasty beach, is it?" Yak asked.

"No, not according to air intelligence and the subs that have surveyed it," Bender said. "According to the photos that they screened for us, it looks like the kind of place that has served the Italians for a resort in the past. Clean sand, easy slope, that sort of thing."

"What about inland?" Hal asked.

"There's a plain that runs inland for several miles," Bender said, "but if the Krauts get their guns up into the Lepini Mountains, this could develop into a second Salerno. I'd guess it all depends upon how fast Lucas moves and how fast Kesselring moves to stop us."

Hal didn't consider himself a strategist by any means, but by the time the Anzio invasion was announced, he'd read enough military and naval history to measure the risks. Without speaking his mind, he thought that someone—FDR, Marshall, Churchill, or

Wilson—was taking a gamble, and from what he knew about the way the campaign in the Mediterranean had developed, he imagined the real risk taker, the man who had pushed for Anzio, to be Churchill.

Later, after the wardroom meeting had broken up and Hal and Bender were about to turn in, Hal looked at his captain and said, "I don't have a particularly good feeling about this one."

"Nor do I," Bender said. "Looks to me like someone is trying to grab a headline while snatching Rome quick."

"Much like that time on Sicily when Patton threw that battalion too far up the east coast in advance of the rest of them and nearly got the shit kicked out of him," Hal said.

"Yes," Bender said, "that's about the size of it."

Amphibious Force VIII rehearsed for the Anzio landing in the Gulf of Salerno. To Hal and Bender, the rehearsal conducted amid rough seas seemed so screwed up and confused that they didn't see how it could give anyone any confidence. Nevertheless, the entire Anzio force departed Naples on January 21, and while the Air Corps was supposed to be sealing off the Anzio beaches by bombing roads, bridges, marshaling yards, and air fields inland, the task force diverted into the Tyrrhenian Sea by a distance of over one hundred miles in order to mask their final intentions. With LSTs, LCIs, and LCTs accounting for most of the troop lift, Hal and Bender remained on the alert for collisions and breakdowns. In fact, the small fleet made the journey without hindrance, arrived in position exactly on time for the 0200 H-hour, and in a development that shocked everyone, carried out a night landing without preparatory bombardment that caught the Germans totally by surprise, resistance on the beach and for several hours afterward consisting of nothing more serious that desultory rifle fire that resulted in few casualties while putting as many as 36,000 men ashore.

Not long after daylight, six Messerschmitts managed to penetrate Allied air cover, made a run on the beach, and, regardless of the amount of anti-aircraft fire thrown up by the surrounding ships, managed to set a store of supplies on fire. Then, to what seemed to Hal like no more than an hour or two later, a pack of strafing Focke-Wulfs raced in at low level, dropped bombs over a cluster of LCIs and LSTs making up to two pontoon causeways on the beach, and succeeded in destroying a single LCI. Farther out, the USS *Portent*, one of the larger minesweepers assigned to the invasion, struck a mine and sank within a matter of mere minutes. At the time, the *3X* was not called to search for survivors; with the LCIs she'd been shepherding now empty and already retracting from the beach, she found herself fully engaged in collecting them together so as to begin retracing her path toward Naples. In the event, not five miles south of Anzio, she and the LCIs came under air attack from a single Heinkel 111 which attempted to come in from the sea and unload a bellyful of bombs over the tiny contingent.

Hal did not stop to count the number of three-inch, 20 mm, and 40 mm guns with which the collection of LCIs happened to be armed. Once the Heinkel had started its attack and been spotted, it seemed clear that the Kraut pilot had made a mistake; with every gun in the little fleet firing, the plane did not come within a thousand yards of dropping its bombs before it exploded in the air as what seemed to Hal like thousands of rounds and tracers converged on the plane.

"And good riddance," Bender said, once more turning to the pelorus to take a bearing on the explosion. "Damn fool, that one!"

"Yes," Hal said, immediately sensing his own relief. "If he'd tried dropping on us from eight or ten thousand feet, I doubt that we'd have got him, but coming straight in at low level like that wasn't a good idea—steady target all the way."

Back in Naples before nightfall and without having to undergo another attack, the LCIs swiftly took on more troops with the result that they were once more headed north shortly after sundown, carrying yet more men up to the beaches.

During the four days that followed, remaining in almost continuous motion when they weren't either taking on fuel, stores, or ammunition to replenish what they were expending, the *3X* made multiple trips to and from Naples and Anzio, lending its support to an effort which had upped the numbers of men on the beach to more than 70,000. By that time, it seemed clear from the rumors they'd picked up that General Lucas did not intend to "run for Rome." Instead, he'd apparently set about consolidating his defense of the beach. In response, and in contradiction to all the Air Corps claimed to have done, Kesselring had apparently thrown in everything but the kitchen sink in an attempt to surround the beaches at Anzio and bottle up the invasion. To make matters worse, Mark Clark's assault on Cassino had failed, leaving the Anzio force out on the limb that Hal, Bender, and the others had anticipated. It was at that point, according to word which leaked back to them from ashore, that something like all hell broke loose. German artillery in the Lepini Mountains opened up on them en masse. The troops on the ground fought back as best they could but for the most part had to sit tight and endure unending bombardment, all of it made infinitely worse by the fact that with considerable rain, even their foxholes and dugouts were filling up with water, forcing them to shelter in the open but behind sandbags.

On January 26, the weather became so foul that aside from a British LST that had exploded after drifting into a minefield that had not been swept and an LCI that had suffered the same fate and sunk, the rain, sleet, and fog, not to mention the mounting waves, all contributed to such confusion near the beach that both Hal and Bender broke into a full sweat under the tension of trying to get in safely to help some of the troop carriers retract after they'd broached. The word "misery" came nowhere near providing an apt description of that time as the air attacks continued and

German artillery exploded around them. When they finally got out and back to Naples for a well-earned night of rest, no one in the wardroom of the *3X* even wanted to mention the day they'd just concluded.

Somehow, regardless of the confusion and mayhem on the beach, using whatever troop lift became available to him, Admiral Lowry managed to evacuate most of the civilian population of Anzio to Naples. By that time, the strength of seven divisions had crammed itself into the beachhead which had expanded only a few miles inland before coming up against an impenetrable Kraut defense, so keeping the troops supplied with everything including water, food, and ammunition had become an immense problem. But Lowry, equal to the task, had found a solution. For the invasions of Sicily and Salerno, it had sometimes taken whole days to unload individual LSTs. What Admiral Lowry managed to do was reorganize the supply stream so that rather than carry up straight cargo from Naples, the LSTs were filled with pre-loaded trucks and DUKWs so that the minute their ramps dropped, every vehicle aboard could begin driving straight off and straight to a supply dump without anyone having to worry about collecting stevedores to unload the vessels. As a result, the unloading time for an LST dropped from as much as a day to as little as an hour, and the turnaround time for each convoy that went up was reduced to a minimum. Not only were the troops receiving their supplies faster, but the exposure of both ships and supplies to air or artillery attack had been reduced almost beyond measure.

Frequently, of course, if a Kraut air reconnaissance went undetected, the Germans knew when a particular convoy might be arriving and could plan their air attacks accordingly. Prodded continually by Army and naval commanders, however, the Air Corps had started picking up its pace, supplying the beach with more air cover and interdicting the German's reconnaissance flights. As a result, only three times in four weeks did the *3X* have to defend herself from air attack during one of her swift turnarounds after escorting a herd of LSTs to and from the landing beaches.

German artillery, on the other hand, turned out to be a different matter altogether. Once up into the battle zone, one kind of shell or another was apt to raise a geyser anywhere around them. A few of those shells, when they struck the sea east, west, north, or south of the ship, looked to Hal like they might have counted for spent rounds of the 40 mm variety. The geysers raised by German field artillery and what the men took to calling their dreaded 88s left an entirely different impression. The damage caused when one of those larger shells did hit an LCI, LST, or one of the larger Liberty ships that made the trip every ten days left all of them with their mouths agape, stunned by its enormity.

For Hal, Bender, and the others, the last days of January and virtually the whole of February seemed to creep by at a snail's pace, save for those hair-raising moments when they were actually up off the beaches at Anzio; then, every terror-stricken moment seemed to race by, nearly paralyzing them but never doing so as they went about their work with a dispatch and urgency that all of them knew they were never again likely to experience once the war ended and they could go home.

"Life ain't supposed to be like this," Bender said, glancing forward to where a round from the beach had landed no more than fifty yards in front of them.

"No," Hal said, "it isn't, and the sooner we can get out of this and be done with it, the better I'm going to like it."

"Tomorrow, and tomorrow, and tomorrow creep in the petty convoys?" Bender said.

"And we'd just better hope this won't turn out to be a tale told by an idiot signifying nothing," Hal said, feeling a bitter wind blow straight off the beach and into his face. "Jesus, it stinks out here! What do you figure?"

"Feces and dead bodies, most like," Bender said. "Some of those wounded the long boat brought out for evacuation on that LCI said things were so bad ashore that they weren't leaving their holes to bury the bodies, and when they did, they were just throwing them into shell holes, piling on some dirt, and leaving them for graves registration to pick up later."

"Those would be the boys from the band? The graves registration people?" Hal asked.

"So I've been told," Bender said, "but who knows. I have no earthly idea how the Army details that duty."

"Hard to imagine worse duty," Yak said, catching the end of their conversation.

"Not really," Bender said. "For me, at least, trying to dodge machine-gun fire up on the front line seems a lot worse."

"Writing burn reports excepted," Yak tried to joke.

"Well," Hal said, managing to register a grin, "there is that, I'll have to allow. Which makes me think, O Master Gunner, don't you have one to write for January?"

"Not to worry," Yak said. "If you'll be willing to take it in Italian, I'll have one of Anna's little brothers put one together for us the minute we get back to Naples. I'd be willing to lay odds that the esteemed staff officers on the *Biscayne* would never notice before initialing it and passing it on to the Navy Department."

"You're probably right," Bender said, "but nevertheless, don't try it."

Yak might have said something in response, but before he could open his mouth, something big crashed into the water not one hundred yards to the west. Taking it for a bomb and apprehending that they were suddenly under air attack, Yak went straight over the forward rail, dropped onto the catwalk around the pilot house, and from there dropped once more onto the deck behind the 3"/50 which had already put out two rounds as yet another lone Focke-Wulf 190 blasted over the convoy and disappeared to the east.

"Where the fuck did that bastard come from?" Bender roared, his whole body shaking.

"From right up our tail," Hal said, when he got control of his stomach which had tried to turn over.

"Son-of-a-bitch!" Bender exploded. "What the hell is the after lookout doing? Race back there, Hal, and kick some ass!"

The trouble, when Hal managed to get back to the fantail, turned out to be that the after lookout was dead, killed instantly by a machine-gun round from the Focke-Wulf before, according to Lewis who was helping the corpsman to remove the body, anyone knew the plane was in the vicinity or making an attack.

"Dead?" Bender said, shocked when Hal brought him the news. "*Benson*?"

"Yes," Hal said, feeling his entire body shake. "Benson."

They both knew the kid, a farm boy off a small dairy farm in Wisconsin. Hal had helped the boy, who couldn't have been six months beyond the age of eighteen, to arrange an allotment for his mother. "Ta help out with expenses, Mr. Goff," Benson had told Hal when he signed the papers. "'Taint a large farm, Ma's, but with me gone and the old man drinkin' again, 'taint easy for her. Takes all she's got to keep the place goin.'"

"You probably won't believe it," Hal said quietly. "I didn't myself, but Vega, for all his supposed machismo, was actually crying when the corpsman covered Benson up."

"Believe it or not," Bender said, "for once, I can sympathize with Vega. I feel like crying myself. I'd held out hope that we might get through this without casualties and get everyone home safe."

"Yes," Hal said, "I'd hoped for the same thing, but if it's of any comfort, I've been through this before, and there isn't a damn thing we can do about it. That's the horror of it. None of us could have seen this coming, and if it ever happens again, I doubt that any of us will see that coming either."

Later, before the *3X* entered port in Naples and while Hal stood watch on the bridge, Bender read a memorial service on the fantail for those men not on duty. They did not bury Benson at sea. Instead, as with Anzio's other dead—those who could be moved—they kept Benson aboard until he could be transferred and buried beside his brothers at arms who were steadily filling up the American cemetery near Naples.

Later that evening, once the ship had tied up, and the crew and officers assembled in the mess and the wardroom for their evening meal, a sound of almost utter silence prevailed.

The *3X* did not return immediately to Anzio. Instead, the following morning, taking in tow a Liberty ship which had seen her shaft unseated by a near miss from a 500-pound bomb and could not get underway by means of her own power, Bender, Hal, and the others headed for Palermo where the Liberty ship would go into the yards for what her captain hoped would be a swift repair. Given the winter seas through which they steamed, they did not have an easy time of it, Lewis back on the fantail and on the capstan working overtime in order to manage the tug's big wire rope so as to keep slack out of the line and ensure a steady pressure that would not cause the line to go suddenly so taught that it would snap. As a result, by the time they finally reached Palermo near nightfall, Lewis felt so bushed from what he'd been doing that all he wanted to do was throw himself into his bunk to sleep. The others, not rising from the supper table quite so fast, mulled over the possibility of going ashore for a grappa.

"Think your draft board will look benevolently upon your indulging in an occasional grappa when you return?" Garcia asked Hal, a weasel's smile appearing on his face.

Hal laughed. "On the whole," he said, "I'm doubtful that I'm going to have any difficulty with that issue. As far as I know, both her father and her uncles brew the stuff every year, once they've made their wine and have the grape husks with which to distill it. Theirs is a small still, I'm told, but it does the job and allows them to put up between forty and fifty bottles."

"Better than the stuff we get on the beach here?" Yak asked.

"That I can't say," Hal said, "because I haven't been able to try it yet."

"So instead, you can only hope?" Bender said.

"Ah, there you have it," Hal grinned. "But if it's half as good as the stuff we got out there at the Isola del Vento, you won't hear me complain."

"Yes," Yak said, "that was a sight better than what Mama Galdoni had to offer."

"Amen," Bender laughed. "There are those who would say that turpentine does not go down as well as the genuine article."

"Still," Yak said, "a bird in the hand is worth more than two in the bush, so if you're up for Mama Galdoni's, I'm for making the run."

They made the run, sat for two hours over their grappas, poured themselves into their bunks upon their return, and slept better than they had for days, well out of the action for the moment and sheltered beneath an anti-aircraft umbrella that was supposed to be the pride of the Mediterranean. The following day, escorting yet another heavily laden Liberty ship, they were on their way back to Naples nursing the kinds of hangovers that only Mamma Galdoni's grappa could produce.

Once returned, Bender left the ship to report himself to the service force commander who held the secret of their next assignment, and when he returned, Hal could see dismay written all over his face.

"Apparently," Bender said, pouring himself a mug of coffee and seating himself across from Hal at the wardroom table, "there's been a battle up at Anzio that defies description."

"Go ahead," Hal said, "I'm listening."

"Well," Bender continued, "I guess Lucas tried to push an attack up in the direction of Cisterna. Krauts must have found out about it and set an ambush. Of the 767 men that went in with the 1st and 3rd Ranger Battalions, 761 of them were killed outright, wounded, or captured. Only six of them came back whole."

"*Shit*," Hal hissed, the shock of the thing nearly seizing him by the throat.

"I'll tell you what," Bender said, "the atmosphere over there on the beach right now is grim, and I mean grim. Listen to what they're saying, and you'd think that every man's mother had died."

"And I'll bet that the Cassino front hasn't moved an inch either," Hal said.

"Not an inch," Bender said. "We're in a hell of a fight, and that's certain. Clark, Churchill, FDR, and God-only-knows who else have bitten off more than we can chew, and the Krauts have us stopped dead at every turn."

"I hate to ask," Hal said, "but what's in it for us?"

"Same-o, same-o," Bender said. "We're going up tonight with six LSTs, under the apparent cover of more rain because the weather people are predicting a pip."

"Just our luck," Hal said.

"It could be worse," Bender said. "We could be in the infantry. The only thing I heard ashore that could even approach being funny was some wag on one of the service desks talking about issuing snorkels to the 45th Division so that they could survive the high water in their foxholes."

"Some joke," Hal said.

"Yeah, isn't it," Bender replied.

With twelve- to sixteen-foot waves throwing green water all the way up to the flying bridge and the ship pounding like a hammer, their night trip to Anzio seemed to run just this side of hell. Thrown from his bunk when he failed to strap himself in, Kawalski cracked a rib that resulted in so much pain that Hal saw to it that the man was relieved from his watch. Shay in the galley, unable to cook, fed the men nothing more than apples, all that they could eat, and dry sliced bread for breakfast. Inside the ship, the constant tossing that everyone endured led to an epidemic of seasickness that they hadn't seen for weeks, if not months, the two warrants riding herd on the crew to clean things up as rapidly as the men threw up but having nothing available with which to damp down the smell.

"What are things like below?" Bender asked Yak when he came up to relieve Hal from the watch.

"Smells like a perfect shithole," Yak said, refusing to dress up his facts. "Up forward, they're sticking to their bunks, but that doesn't mean they aren't throwing up over the sides, and if the man in the top bunk tosses his cookies, you'd better believe that the guys down below him are quick to follow."

"Sounds ugly," Bender said.

"It is," Yak said. "I took one look in that forward compartment and fled from it."

"You going to hit the sack?" Bender said to Hal as all three of them were suddenly lashed by a wall of spray.

"No," Hal said, "I'm staying right here, cold, wet, and miserable, but it beats trying to go horizontal and feeling the whole stomach come up the minute I turn in. Here at least I can see what's coming and try to meet it."

"Well," Bender said, "you can do what you want, but I've got to lie down for a few minutes, not so much for my stomach as my head."

"Go ahead," Hal said, once more shielding his face from a sudden blast of spray. "Yak and I will mind the shop. When do you want us to get you up?"

"First light," Bender said, "and make sure the boatswain in the pilot house empties the barf buckets down there. I don't want that crap swilling over the sides and mucking up the deck."

"Right," Hal said. "It'll be done."

With Bender gone below for what didn't promise more than an hour's rest in which to recover, both Hal and Yak looped safety lines around the pelorus, loosely lashing themselves to the ship.

"I'll bet you'd rather be home with your draft board," Yak said, planting his feet to compensate for a sudden roll.

"In a heartbeat," Hal said. "And you? Things go well in Naples, do they?"

"They do," Yak said. And then, after a moment's hesitation, "You know, Hal, when the old man first invited me over to their place to meet the family, I didn't think a thing about it. I know that I'd been talking about the babes and the pushcarts, but that was just the normal bullshit that goes with the turf we're on, so about the last thing I could have imagined was meeting anyone I might take an interest in."

"But you have?" Hal said.

"I have," Yak said, "and in the backstreets of Naples of all places."

"You think something serious is underway?" Hal asked. "With Anna, I mean?"

"Probably against my better judgment, yes," Yak said, "I do."

"You know, of course, that we might get jerked out of here and sent anywhere at any time," Hal said, "even to the Pacific?"

"Yes," Yak said, "and that's the rub. I don't seem to be able to go forward, and I sure don't feel like going back. I don't want to sound sloppy about it, but I know the difference between what's shallow and what's not, and what the two of us have going over there isn't shallow."

"I don't know what to tell you," Hal said, catching yet another blast of spray in the face. "Not to wax poetic, but it's a good bit like this damn storm. Sudden moves can spell disaster. We've got no choice but to ride it out and hope for more settled times in calmer waters."

"As long as we're still around to take advantage of them," Yak said, a lashing of green water nearly drowning his words.

"As long as we're still around to take advantage of them," Hal agreed.

◠

Owing to the storm, they did not, as they had hoped, make Anzio in the dark. Instead, with Bender back on the bridge more steady than in the hour when he'd gone down, they finally arrived off the beaches after what had been designated as sunrise but which remained obscure owing to the rain, the low clouds, the high spray, and the wind. The pontoon causeway to which the LSTs were supposed to make up had broken loose sometime in the night. So, for the first two hours that they were near the beach, by means of hastily rigged blocks on the shore and the use of both their fiber as well as their wire rope, the men on the *3X* wrestled with the pontoons, helping to move them back into place by means of the tension on their capstan while one of the tiny yard tugs in the area butted straight up against the beast in order to push it back into position. The Army engineers ashore, working with a few Seabees, did their level best to secure it to its moorings.

Once that job was done, the first of the LSTs came in and somehow made up to the causeway. Then, quick as a lick and as soon as the ship's ramp came down, the loaded vehicles aboard raced to escape their confinement, one or another of the drivers stopping only to barf out of the side of his truck or over the side of whatever DUKW he happened to be driving.

Given the fury of the storm, all of them might have hoped that the Kraut artillery would give them a lull, but it didn't. No one thought that the German observers in the hills could see what they were shooting at. Instead, with the entire beach zeroed in, Hal imagined that they were simply firing on pre-arranged sectors, hoping to impede whatever was going on around the beach by means of nothing more than harassing fire. When one of the rounds struck a vehicle unloading from the second LST to go in, causing yet another delay in the operation while the burning vehicle was cleared from near the ramp which it had just left, Hal, Bender, and Yak knew that the Kraut gunners were, to some extent, achieving their aim.

"This sucks," Yak said, a grim expression tightening his jaw.

Before any of them could utter another word, they were thrown off their feet when yet another German round threw up a geyser not thirty yards distant, the impact and the amount of water that came down on them shaking the ship like a leaf.

"Get down below, Hal, and check for damage!" Bender ordered as swiftly as he could get the words out. Pulling himself together, Hal shot down the ladder and into the pilot house on the run.

Topside spaces, Hal quickly discovered, were free of damage, but up forward, along the base of the crew's compartment, both Hal and Garcia found that a seam had indeed been worked loose by the explosion and enough so that seawater had started to seep through.

"Well?" Bender said, once Hal returned to the bridge.

"We popped a seam near the base of the crew's compartment, and that's just below the water line, so seawater's starting to seep in," Hal said at once. "Garcia already has the repair party working on it, but to close that thing up tight, he told me, we're going to have to put the ship in dry dock."

"What about the storage compartment directly below the crew's quarters?" Bender asked, the urgency in his voice immediately apparent.

"We were both down there, and the seams are tight," Hal said. "No damage in that compartment or the one below it."

Hal could see relief spread across the man's face.

"All right," Bender said, more or less recovering himself. "Get down to your desk and get the work requests written up, and then draft a message that we can get off to Naples. And once we get that off, we'll all live in hope that they can get us into dry dock before we sink."

"I don't think there's much danger of us sinking," Hal grinned, "but if the pumps can't keep up with the water we're taking on, the crew is going to have to wade to their bunks for the next day or two."

"They're sure to be thrilled," Bender said.

"And just try to imagine how that story will grow by the time we get them home," Yak said. "I'd be willing to guess that inch of water will have grown to two or three feet, with one or another of them having been forced to rescue a buddy because he couldn't swim."

Finally, Bender grinned. "Yes," he said, "that's bound to be the outcome."

"As long as we don't sink," Hal laughed.

"As long as we don't sink," Bender said.

Around noon, about the time the LSTs finished unloading and the little convoy prepared to start back, the storm finally began to abate. Cloud cover remained low, but with the wind slacking and the rain ceasing to fall, the seas began to moderate as well. Before either the LSTs or the *3X* could fully retract, at least two more of the big shells from the Kraut guns fell within fifty yards of them. Aside from rattling the nerves of everyone aboard, neither of those did any damage, so by 1300 that afternoon they were all moving south at something that approached flank speed for the LSTs and out from under an immediate threat from the German guns. For a while, everyone continued to scan the skies for German aircraft, but with the weather socking things in the way it had, threats from the air did not develop. By 1900 all of the ships had returned to Naples, where the LSTs were preparing to take on cargo during the night. When Bender returned from his visit to the service force dispatcher, he came back with the news that the *3X* would not be going out the following day, that her proposed escort duty would be assigned to yet another tug, and that she would remain tied up alongside the pier all day until she could go into dry dock one day later.

"What's our leak doing?" Bender asked Garcia as everyone sat down to supper in the wardroom, a welcome serving of Shay's meatloaf accompanied by butter beans and mashed potatoes.

"The deck in the crew's compartment is wet," Garcia said quickly, "but that's about all. Our shipfitter drove some fiber into the seam with some temporary caulking, so most of it is sealed, but there's a six-inch gap back near the after bulkhead and behind a stanchion that he can't get to, and that's where the water's still coming in."

"So there's no danger of our sinking while we're all asleep?" Bender tried to joke.

"No Sir," Garcia laughed. "Our pumps are working just fine, and if the water in that one corner gets over half an inch deep, I'd be mighty surprised."

"Good job, Chief," Bender said.

"I'll pass the word to the fitter," Garcia said. "All in a day's work, if you see what I mean."

The minute supper ended and the mess trays disappeared, with both Lewis and Garcia going to their bunks and Yak disappearing onto the beach, Hal and Bender lingered over their coffee.

"Look to you like Yak is getting serious about the Cicciano girl?" Bender said.

"I don't think he saw it coming," Hal said, "but yes, I'd say he is."

"As serious about her as you are about your draft board?" Bender asked.

"I think it's beginning to look that way," Hal replied.

Bender looked away toward one of the wardroom's portholes. "I wonder how far things have gone between them?" he said.

"I doubt that there's been much physical contact," Hal said, "not with all of the rest of the Ciccianos riding herd."

"That could be both good and bad," Bender said.

"Agreed," Hal said, "although, as I say that, beyond holding hands and some very pleasant necking, Bea and I didn't get very far along those lines either. Not with the little time we had together, and not with the living arrangements we had."

"Maybe that's best," Bender said. "My wife and I took things a little farther than that before we tied the knot."

"You're married?" Hal gasped, the shock of Bender's revelation striking him like a bolt of lightning.

"I was," Bender said "but I'm not now. She was German and, as I later found out, a member of the Bund, you see, so when I joined up before the war started, we got into a fight and she left me. We're legally separated, and I haven't seen her in two years. Whether her views have changed or not, I don't know, but mine have, and if she doesn't divorce me, I intend to divorce her. In looking back, it was a mistake on both our parts."

"Sorry," Hal said, "I had no idea."

"No," Bender said, "I've kept it pretty private. The rest of them don't know, and I'd prefer that they didn't."

"Understood," Hal said.

"So, that brings me back to my original subject. What do you suppose Yak has in mind?"

"If we aren't snatched out of here and sent off to God knows where and if things continue with the girl the way they seem to be going," Hal said, "I think he may consider trying to marry her, with the object of taking her to the States after the war."

"That would mean a raft of hurdles to get over," Bender said.

"I think he's trying to measure those right now," Hal said. "In his mind, if you take my meaning."

"I'll help him if he asks," Bender said, "but otherwise I mean to stay out of it."

"Right," Hal said, "none of our business. He asked me a couple of questions last night, and I gave him straight answers, but I have no intention of meddling."

"Nor do I," Bender said, "and if he talks to either Garcia or Lewis about it, I would imagine that they will talk to him like Dutch uncles."

"Probably," Hal said.

"Want to play some chess?" Bender said, changing the subject.

"Why not," Hal replied.

11

When the *3X* came out of dry dock two days later, fully repaired and shipshape, she did not immediately go back on the Anzio convoys. Instead, across the three miserable weeks that followed, she four times towed badly damaged LCIs to Palermo for refit and twice towed equally damaged LSTs to Bizerte for the same reason. What made the weeks particularly miserable turned out to be the weather—a mixture of harsh Levanters with cold Mistrals that blew up seas with so much turbulence that Hal and the others thought their knees would never recover from the constant flexing they put themselves through to compensate for the pitch and roll they were taking as they labored to remain on their feet.

"I've been told," Bender said during one particularly trying transit, "that the Great Lakes can whip up ungodly weather in the winter, but for the life of me I don't see how it could be any worse than this."

"Not exactly the crystal blue water and white sands that are supposed to surround the Greek islands, is it," Hal observed, snatching at the rail to keep himself from being hurled over the side.

"If a Kraut U-boat surfaces out here and comes at us with a deck gun we're toast, because with all that green water coming over the bow, Yak and the three-inch gunners can't get near our mount."

"Believe me," Bender said, "that's one thing we don't have to worry about. Any U-boat that tries to surface in this will have its gun crew swept away before they can even bring up a single round."

"And their E-boats are too far away to worry about," Hal said, ducking to avoid the remains of a sudden wave that made it all the way up to the rail.

"Unless I miss my guess," Bender shouted over the crashing of the wave, "those damn things are all hiding up around Genoa somewhere. Last I heard, no one has seen one around Anzio for weeks."

"And let's hope things stay that way," Hal shouted back, suddenly struck by yet another blast of seawater that came hurtling up from the port side and nearly threw him off his feet.

"That's enough of this," Bender said, struggling to regain his own upright place beside the pelorus. "It's getting too dangerous to stand up here. We're going to have to go down and stand the rest of this one in the pilot house."

In the pilot house where they no longer had to fear being thrown over the rail or knocked from their feet by the sudden lashings of a wave, they were nevertheless cramped by having to share the space with the helmsman, the lee helmsman, a phone talker, a quartermaster, the supposed lookout, and the boatswain's mate of the watch. Standing in the proximity of what everyone referred to as "the duty coffeepot" seemed an advantage, but with so many men crammed into such a small space, both Hal and Bender found their movements confined to a six-foot strip of deck-tread immediately behind the forward portholes, all of them thoroughly awash with spray and nearly impossible to see through.

"If we come up on a mine floating somewhere out here, we're not going to see it through this muck," Hal said.

"Probably not," Bender said, "which is why, for once, we're going to have to rely on prayer."

It wasn't that Hal was a non-believer. Somewhere, he thought, some kind of divine or superior intelligence had to be at work. At the same time, whether or not the entity that men referred to as the Almighty intervened directly in immediate human affairs was something he couldn't fathom and suspected that whatever deity existed pretty much expected men and women to help themselves. Trying to remain alive by scanning the seas ahead through a wall of seawater didn't qualify. To Hal, it simply seemed too dangerous.

"Captain," he said to Bender, "this isn't going to cut it. Like it or not we're going to have to climb back up there, lash ourselves to the pelorus, and ride this thing out."

"Yes," said Bender. "I'd hoped for better, but there's nothing for it, is there?"

"No," Hal said, "there isn't."

Reluctantly, after finishing their coffee and replacing their mugs in the cup holders welded to the forward bulkhead, both men cracked the starboard hatch, thrust themselves onto the wing, and once more climbed the ladder to the flying bridge. They lashed themselves to both sides of the pelorus and rode out the remaining six hours of the voyage—soaked to the bone regardless of the foul weather gear they'd gotten themselves into—and arrived in Bizerte, exhausted. Without taking time to eat, they crashed into their bunks along with the remainder of the officers and crew, utterly spent.

By late March, the *3X* had returned to duty with the Anzio convoys. Twice each week and at night, she escorted as many as six LSTs north to the Anzio beaches, and in between she often helped to take up as many as fifteen LCTs, also at night. At intervals of what seemed to Hal to be eight to ten days, she occasionally helped to screen the four Liberty ships that were sent up in the same way. For a part of that time, as March extended into April, the weather moderated;

when it didn't, everyone aboard returned to Naples feeling like they'd been bounced like a ball and slammed from a paddle at the end of a rubber string like one of those toys with which small boys were apt to entertain themselves. The number of bruises and contusions that the corpsman treated during that time seemed extensive. As if that weren't enough to worry about, even at night after getting in and out with ever increasing speed, the number of Nazi rounds that came down around them and continued to come down while they were waiting to help the supply convoy retract turned out to be more than enough to unsettle every man's stomach. After every escort voyage, it remained Hal's duty to draft the ship's after-action report; in the middle of April, when he finally thought to make a count, he tabulated a total of thirty-two German rounds that had fallen within a hundred yards of them during the times they'd been out after their last run to Bizerte.

"I'll tell you what," Yak said, coming up to relieve the watch on their way back from Anzio in the early morning of April 16, "my hands are beginning to shake."

"Welcome to the club," Hal said. "Not only are my hands starting to shake, my right eye has developed a twitch. Bender isn't a lick better off, and according to what Lewis said at supper last night, the corpsman is mixing up about a gallon of some kind of goop every day in an unsuccessful attempt to help the crew settle their stomachs. And that includes Lewis himself."

"Nerves, do you think?" Yak asked.

"*Christ* yes," Hal said. "Stress, tension, call it whatever you like. The simple fact is that the whole lot of us are scared shitless and with good reason. And there isn't a damn thing that any of us can do about it other than try to keep our heads down, do our jobs, and hope we get through it."

"If the boys down at Cassino could break through and get up here," Yak said, "I think that might go a long way in easing things."

"No doubt," Hal said, "but don't hold your breath. From what Bender said when he came back from service force HQ yesterday, the Fifth Army at Cassino isn't getting anywhere fast, and just like here, their casualty figures are climbing through the roof."

"I guess that puts us right in the crapper," Yak said.

"I guess that keeps us in the crapper, more like," Hal said. "The only good thing I can think of is that Kesselring doesn't seem to have enough strength left to pull the chain and flush us all the way down. Looks to me like Anzio is as much of a stalemate as Cassino."

⌐

Finally, on a night near the end of April, as the *3X* sortied from Naples in convoy with six more of the daily LSTs, Hal and Bender looked up to find the skies clear, a moon shining, and stars twinkling. Not only were the seas calm, but the air had actually warmed enough so that, for once, they could unbutton their foul weather gear enough to feel genuine spring breezes blowing against them.

"What do you reckon?" Bender grinned. "Think the foxholes at Anzio will begin drying up?"

"I wouldn't be surprised if those boys don't break out shovels and start planting gardens," Hal quipped. "The earth up there has certainly been turned enough."

"And if things carry on drying out," Bender said, "maybe our lot down at Cassino can finally get moving, those who don't already have trench foot or pneumonia."

"After what this past winter's put everyone through," Yak said, stepping up beside them, "we're about due for a good turn. I asked Anna to marry me this afternoon, and she said 'yes,' with her family's blessing, so I can guarantee you that our luck has changed."

"You're kidding," Bender said, turning suddenly, surprised by the news.

215

"I'm not," Yak said. "We'll be seeing the base chaplain on Monday to get the paperwork started."

"Congratulations," Hal said, showing Yak a broad grin and shaking his hand. "Looks like you're going to get hitched even before Bea and I get the chance. Planning to stick around Naples after the war?"

"Not on your life," Yak said. "Once this thing is ended, I intend to get Anna back to the States about as fast as the government will allow for, and then, I wouldn't be a bit surprised if her entire family didn't try to immigrate. One of her uncles is already set up in Queens where he apparently runs a bakery, and with what that guy already knows about immigration and what I'm sure I can learn, I don't think we're going to have a problem."

Hal didn't imagine that things would be as easy as Yak anticipated, and about their luck having turned, he knew that he could only hope. And then, later that night, as the fifth LST in their convoy made up to the causeway, their luck did turn, but not in a way that any of them could have foreseen.

At around 0300 that morning, just as the fifth LST in their convoy dropped its ramp, a shell from one of the Kraut field guns landed directly on the ship's foc'sle, penetrating the main deck before exploding on the well deck where it immediately set several pre-loaded trucks on fire before they could make an exit. Fortunately, none of those trucks were loaded with ammunition or gasoline, save for what they were carrying in their gas tanks, so subsequent explosions did not follow. Nevertheless, the damage control parties aboard the LST, faced with the possibility that those tanks might blow, made an extraordinary effort to put the fires out before they grew out of control. In that effort they succeeded, a commandeered tank finally managing to haul the smoldering trucks from the well deck onto the beach before they could ignite the entire ship.

But with regard to the convoy's movement and its return to Naples, they were delayed two hours. This meant that by the time the fifth LST had fully retracted, allowing for the sixth to go in and unload, sunrise had already taken place, Bender had ordered the guns manned, and everyone aboard not actually inside the skin of the ship had started scanning the skies for a possible air attack.

The air attack, when it came, caught everyone by surprise. Rather than come from the sea, from the north, west, or south, it came at them straight out of the morning sun, from the east. Two of the dreaded Focke-Wulfs dropped straight down from over the crest of the Lepini Mountains, hugging the deck regardless of the ground fire that the troops threw up at them, and boring straight in on the LSTs and their escorts for a strafe. Hal and Bender never heard them coming; the lookouts scanning to the north and the west at the time never saw them. The first indication that the ship was under fire came when Hal, glancing forward, saw Yak and two of his gunners go down while more machine-gun rounds splintered the deck around them. And then, even as Hal turned to warn Bender, Bender was thrown backwards by a sudden shower of splinters thrown up from below, yet another round catching him in the thigh, spinning his whole body into the rail and breaking his leg, something Hal knew at once when he heard the bone crack.

Shouting down the voice tube to the pilot house for a corpsman, Hal snatched the first aid kit from its stowage, but before he could take two steps in Bender's direction, he was himself slammed to the deck—and hard. The last thing he remembered before he lost consciousness turned out to be the burning pain that seemed to bore straight into him from somewhere behind, dissolving proof as he passed out that yet a third Focke-Wulf had followed the first two.

When Hal finally regained consciousness, he had no idea where he was. What he did know was that his head hurt, that he seemed to by lying on his stomach, and that when he tried to move his arm so that he could massage his headache away, more pain instantly resulted. Up and down his arm, he felt like someone had started trying to stab a clutch of needles into him.

"*Shit*," he groaned.

"Ha," he heard from behind him, "coming around, are we? And it's about time, too, because we don't tolerate slackers around here."

Hal could not see the owner of the voice which sounded vaguely feminine to him because the speaker seemed to be somewhere behind his back. When he first attempted to turn over so that he could look the owner in the eye and speak the sharp retort that came first to his mind, his slightest effort shot so much pain across his back and up his side that he found it a wonder he didn't black out.

"Who are you?" he said flatly, once his mind had cleared. "And where the hell am I?"

"Where you are," the voice answered back sharply, "is right where you ought to be, Mister, in a hospital bed for the un-walking wounded aboard the USS *Respite*, a first-rate U.S. Navy hospital ship sitting right alongside the pier in the Bay of Naples. I am Lieutenant Commander Julia Hill, the head nurse around here."

"Does that mean that I'm to call you *Sir*?" Hal answered back, matching the woman's tone.

"If you do," Nurse Hill answered back tartly, "I'm liable to give you a slap on that wounded ass of yours that will bring you right out of that bunk screaming."

"Is that why I'm here, because I've been hit in the ass?" Hal asked.

"And I'll bet you're going to expect to collect a Purple Heart for it too, aren't you?" Nurse Hill said.

"I've already got two, maybe three," Hal said acidly, "so the last thing I need is another. Suppose we stop horsing around, Commander, while you tell me what's wrong with me."

"Well, for starters," Nurse Hill said, moderating her tone only slightly, "aside from the machine-gun round that passed through your right cheek and which seems to have chipped your hip bone, including the surgery that was required to repair that, the surgeon apparently dug a total of fourteen tiny shell fragments not to mention another four sizable wooden splinters out of your right bicep, sewed up a gash alongside your left thigh, and yet another on your left forearm. If you ask me, I think you're lucky your testicles are still intact, not to mention number one."

"Thanks for the good news," Hal said, his headache seeming to intensify. "I know someone who will be relieved to hear it. So, Commander, if I don't tax your patience, how long do you intend to keep me here before I go back to my ship?"

"If you really do have two or three Purple Hearts," Nurse Hill said, her tone once more hardening, "and you haven't had enough of the war by this time, you must be a damn fool. But fool or not, you're done. I've already seen the surgeon's report on you, and it isn't pretty. If you had in mind a career in the Navy, Mister, I'd start thinking about insurance, or law school, or something even more tranquil. My guess is that the Navy Department will discharge you just as soon as we get you back to the States and out of the hospital, and if they don't, you're sure to ride a desk for the rest of your days."

Suddenly, without Hal doing a single thing to encourage the response, his entire body seemed to go slack as what he realized to be tension melted straight away from him.

"What about Bender, and Yaakov, and the others?" Hal asked as he felt himself relax. "What about the 3X?"

"Try to speak English," Nurse Hill said. "I don't know what you're talking about."

"My ship," Hal replied, "and the officers I served with."

"We don't know the first thing about your ship or any of the men aboard her," Nurse Hill said at once. "That kind of thing is right beyond our brief. You boys come in here wounded and cut up, and we do our best to sew you up and keep you from catching infections. We had an air raid down here two weeks ago, and that's as close as any of us have come to the war. What kind of a ship did you come off? Cruiser? Destroyer?"

I came off a rescue tug," Hal said before Nurse Hill could continue, "the *ATR-3X*."

"Good God," Nurse Hill said. "I didn't even know we had such things. Sounds like a canoe."

"Good for you," Hal said, "you're getting close."

"And you're getting close to that slap I threatened you with," Nurse Hill said at once. "But I have just the medicine with which to take care of that. Now that I can see that you have your faculties back and that we don't have to consign you to the psycho ward, I'm going to give you a little something to help you sleep, and when you wake up again, I'll keep my hopes up that you'll know how to talk to someone who outranks you by two grades."

"You know what?" Hal said. "I might be wrong, but I'll bet that there will be no one in that insurance line you mentioned or in that law school that will give two hoots about such things."

"Probably not, and more's the pity," Nurse Hill said. "*Tweekie, tweekie* now." And in the next instant, Hal felt a jab in his left cheek and faded straight out.

❧

Two days later, not long after an attractive nurse, a lieutenant, had finished feeding him soup over the top of his pillow, Hal found himself surprised to see Lewis suddenly appear in front of his bed, pull up a stool, and sit down where Hal could see him.

"How's youse pullin'?" Lewis said, showing Hal a grin.

"I'd shake hands with you but I can't raise my arm yet," Hal said, trying to show the warrant a smile in return.

"Consider it done," Lewis said. "Got a lot a hurt, does ya?"

"Not much," Hal said, "'cause I think they've been giving me something."

"Thas probable," Lewis said.

"So," Hal said, "give it to me straight. How many of our people are down. And what do you know about Bender, Yak, and Garcia?"

"Sure you want to hear it?" Lewis asked.

"Yes," Hal said.

"Hefling and Spense dead on the fantail, Vega and Cullen dead on the gun mount. And both Click and Bix wounded," Lewis said. "Captain Bender took two rounds and a fistful of splinters, an' his leg's broke. Amblance took him to 300th General Hospital once we's back here. Army got them splinters outa him, put him in a cast on that leg, an' flew him down ta Bizerte, for him ta recover."

"And Yak?" Hal asked.

"Round through the calf and a couple a splinters," Lewis said. "Da Army kept him. He's still up ta the 300th, an dat girl a his been up there seein' to him ever day."

"And what about you and Garcia?" Hal asked.

Lewis laughed. "Garcia, him didn't get a scratch," he said. "Got me a couple splinter, but I pulled 'em out on the spot. Didn't have no choice. Corpsman seen to me soon as he got to the rest of youse, an' all he did was pour in iodine, slap a bandage round the wounds, and make smart ass remarks. We got outa dere fast after that an' didn't have no more trouble. Bender was in enough pain so dat da corpsman put him out, and youse was already out cold with a goose egg on the side of youse head, an' Mr. Yaakov they carried up da wardroom where the corpsman could lay him on the table and clean out his wound."

"Surely Yaakov didn't take us back?" Hal asked.

"Oh no," Lewis grinned. "I tole him he was in command, but I took the con and brought us down. Piece a cake, Mr. Goff. I done horsed tugs around before, both in Boston and New York, so there

221

was nothin' to it. Knowin' we had wounded, the skipper of the leading LST dispatch us from escort, so I got us back here three hour before the Ts come down."

"Thanks," Hal said. "So what happens next? The Navy give you command with the rest of us gone?"

"Ha," Lewis said, giving his head a knowing shake. "Dat wasn't in da cards. We got back ta Naples 'bout 1300 dat afternoon, and by 1800, we had us two new ones an' a chief gunner's mate aboard. Lieutenant Patelli, him's the new CO, and dis little bitty j.g. name of Hewlow is the XO, an' we'se supposed to be gettin' another ensign to ride herd on the guns 'fore we go out again."

If Hal had needed confirmation for what Nurse Hill had told him, Lewis had delivered it.

"Chief," Hal said, realizing that he would probably never see Lewis again, or any of the other men with whom he'd served on the *3X*, "I want to thank you for everything you've done for us, and I know I speak for Mr. Bender when I say that. It gives me a bit of a sinking feeling knowing that I'm done with the ship and won't be going back, but from what I've been told here, I gather that they're shipping me home, probably for desk duty if not discharge."

"Mr. Goff," Lewis said, "ain't never been no man left a ship that didn't feel a wrench. For a while it makes ya feel hollow-like, like youse leavin' some of youseself behind. Dat'll pass. Personally, I'se glad youse goin' home. Youse done enough. Youse got stuff to look forward to, an' dere ain't no point in sticken around and gettin' killed. It's time for someone else to step up to da plate."

"Good of you to put it that way," Hal said. "Thanks Chief, and when you get back to the ship, thank Garcia for me as well, and the both of you keep your heads down."

"Youse can bet on it," Lewis said, grinning as he stood up and pushed the stool back against the bulkhead. "Keep well, Mr. Goff, and when you see that draft board of yours, tell her dat the *3X* sends her der best."

"Thanks for stopping," Hal said, "and smooth sailing."

In the next second, Lewis disappeared through the hatch into a passageway, the last man from the 3X that Hal was ever to see.

The *Respite* remained alongside the pier in Naples for six more days collecting wounded to be returned to the States. During that time, Hal also had a visit from Garcia, Morris, and Kawalski with whom he'd often manned the whaleboat, and of all people, Prince, whose gambling habits he'd done his best to curtail. From what they reported, the repair facility in Naples had done all that could be done to put the 3X back in shipshape condition, a new ensign, a man named Rivers, had joined the ship, and very shortly, they would be going back to sea, towing an LST down to Bizerte for overhaul. In fact, on the same morning that the *Respite* got underway for New York, Nurse Hill reported to him that the 3X was rumored to be pulling out right behind them.

"Saw that boat of yours," Nurse Hill said. "Not much to it in my opinion."

"Small though she seems," Hal said, "she was a good home."

"That's what they all say," Nurse Hill said, coming quickly back.

"And as well they should," Hal said, not to be topped.

"Looks to me like your arm's healed up enough so that you ought to start moving it," Nurse Hill said, instantly changing the subject, "and I think it's about time we start rolling you over off of your balls and your number one for a change. You're going to feel it, of course, but there is no progress without a little suffering."

"Oh thanks," Hal said. "And which inquisition was it that you trained with? I'm afraid I've forgotten."

"And that, Mister, is something you'd best go right on doing," she said, instantly rolling Hal onto his side and causing him to screech from the sudden stab he felt as a result. "Yes," Nurse Hill continued, "that's just about what I imagined it would feel like."

223

"Your tender ministrations seem to know no bounds," Hal said, acid dripping from his every word.

"Oh good," Nurse Hill said, "you're finally getting the idea."

Hal was not yet on his feet to see Gibraltar as they passed through the Straits, but aside from a prickly feeling that continued to arise whenever he moved his arm, he looked forward to the time when the surgeon would remove the stitches from his gashes that had been sewn up. About halfway across the Atlantic, once the stitches had been cut and removed and the hole in his hip had closed and stopped seeping, they finally permitted him to sit up and begin taking something other than the bland, half-liquid diet that he'd been forcing himself to endure.

"What would go well with this," Hal said, speaking to the nurse who brought him the first thing that resembled a hamburger, "is a good shot of grappa."

"Never heard of it," the nurse said.

"You're kidding," Hal said. "You've been to Naples, and you don't know what grappa is?"

"I don't know what Italian wine tastes like either," the nurse said. "We were alongside for sixteen days, and they didn't let us off the ship once."

"Probably afraid you'd be assaulted by our sex-crazed troops," Hal laughed.

"Ha," the nurse said. "If you think sailors are any better, you've got another think a comin'. Just in the past week, I've been pinched twice, squeezed twice, and propositioned more times than I can count. And that's from men who've been mostly confined to their beds, just like you."

"The world is a more dangerous place than I ever imagined," Hal said.

"You don't know the half of it," the nurse said. "Idle hands are the devil's workshop. From everything I've been able to gather, that Naples over there must be a regular sink of promiscuity, most of it probably fueled by that grappa you're talking about. Don't say I said it, but our VD ward is crammed to overflowing."

"Naughty boys," Hal said.

"Right you are about that," the nurse said, "and all of 'em should have known better. Now, Mr. Goff, if you'll just lie back, it's time for me to give you a sponge bath."

"Ha," Hal said, "aren't you afraid that might raise a problem somewhere?"

"Ha, yourself," the nurse said, "one flick of my finger, and you'll go as limp as a wet noodle."

"Good Lord," Hal said, "perish the thought. I certainly hope you haven't taught the sisterhood ashore that trick."

"The sisterhood can take care of itself," the nurse giggled. "Aboard the *Respite*, we are dedicated to enforced moderation in all things."

Their crossing of the Atlantic, which Hal was told they were making in company with empty Liberty ships and a few destroyer escorts to screen them, turned out to be something they accomplished in ten days. Their voyage included one stop in Puerto Rico, where thirty-six wounded soldiers from a Puerto Rican national guard unit were unloaded for transport to one of the Army's hospitals on the island. Then, without any other stops along the way, the *Respite* and the other ships in the convoy steamed north, arriving in New York near the beginning of June 1944. There, finally, Hal was taken off the ship on a stretcher and transported to the Brooklyn Naval Hospital, and it was in that facility, mere days later, that he finally learned that the Fifth Army had broken through at Cassino, relieved Anzio, and taken Rome. One day later, that good news was consigned to the shade when the radios and the newspapers announced the landings at Normandy.

"Looks to me," said the man in the bed next to him, a lieutenant, junior grade by the name of Harrison, "like this is the beginning of the end for the Krauts."

"Let's hope," Hal said.

"Where'd you get it?" the man asked.

"Off Anzio," Hal said. "A trio of Focke-Wulfs strafed us, and none of us moved fast enough to get out of their way."

"That's where I got it too," the man said, "acting as a forward observer ashore, if you can believe it. One of those damn 88s landed not ten yards from the hole in which I was cowering, and the concussion must have blown me straight up into the air. Broken leg, broken wrist, and broken ribs, not to mention shrapnel. You?"

"Shot right in the ass," Hal said, speaking with disgust, "not to mention the splinters and the shell fragments."

"And ain't we the lucky ones," the man said. "I can't say much for the food here, but this sure beats the hell out of Anzio."

"Oh, doesn't it just," Hal said.

"What do you figure our chances are for being sent back once we've recovered?" Harrison asked.

"Slim," Hal said. "Just off the top of my head, I'd say we're home to stay. The head nurse on the *Respite* told me that she'd seen my record and thought I'd be either discharged or consigned to riding a desk for the remainder of the war. If they'd intended to use us again, I think they would have kept us over there. They shipped my CO to a hospital in Bizerte, and as far as I know, they kept our gunnery officer right there in Naples at the 300th General. My guess is that my former CO was too shot up to send home right away. About our gunnery officer, I can't say. He might go back to duty after he's released, and because he intended to marry a Napolitano, I doubt he'd mind staying."

"Not one of those babes off the streets, surely!" Harrison exclaimed.

"No," Hal laughed. "Not one of those. Nice girl, the one he met, and guarded like gold by her family. As far as I know, if they ever got beyond holding hands in family gatherings, I'd be mighty surprised. Guy I'm talking about apparently saved a grandson from being hit by a truck, and the grandfather took him home to meet the family, and that's where he met the girl."

"Minor miracle, that," Harrison said. "B-girls and whores were the only ones any of us ever came in contact with. What about you? You married?"

"Engaged," Hal said, "sort of. You?"

"Same," Harrison said. "Mine's supposed to be waiting for me in Fargo."

"And thawing out after a long winter?" Hal laughed.

"Let's hope," Harrison said. "She's supposed to be earning a teaching certificate at North Dakota State."

"Mine's supposed to be working on an M.A. at the University of Illinois," Hal said. "And if or when they finally discharge me, I'm thinking about doing the same thing in history. What's on your plate, if they let you go?"

"My old man's got an Ag business up there, in Fargo," Harrison said. "Before I joined up, he wanted me to come in with him, but at the time I couldn't abide the idea because I thought I wanted something active, something exciting, if you see what I mean. Well, as far as I'm concerned, I've had enough excitement to last me a lifetime. I guess I must be an example of that crack that Mark Twain is supposed to have made about getting home and finding out how smart his father had become during his absence."

"I take your meaning," Hal said. "That's why I'm looking at the history thing. A quiet life in some college town teaching history suddenly looks just right to me, and if both my wife and I can get on at the same college, so much the better. And if we can do it on a quiet street and behind a white picket fence, so much the better again."

"I guess the war has changed us a lot, hasn't it?" Harrison said.

"You can bet on it," Hal said.

C

Although Hal had written to Bea from Naples, from the *Respite* on their way home, and from Brooklyn once he'd arrived, none of Bea's letters caught up with him until more than a week after he'd settled into the hospital. Then, finally, he did receive a letter which, regardless of the fact that he had described his condition in glowing terms, left him in no doubt that she seemed beside herself with worry and felt desperate to come to New York to visit him.

"Don't do it, Love," he told her when he finally managed to get a telephone call through to her. "I'm laid up in bed and will be for at least another month, and they only allow visitors in here at rare intervals and for no more than an hour at a time. I'm fine. I'm healing nicely, and in a month or two, after some rehabilitation, I'm sure they'll send me on convalescent leave, and I'll come straight to Urbana. And then, if you'll still have me and if you can swing things with your family, we'll go down to Herrin and get married just as soon as you'll be willing to say 'I do.'"

Their phone conversation came close to being their first fight, but Hal finally convinced Bea to be patient and wait for him to come out of the hospital. After getting off the phone with her, Hal set himself to recover, regain his strength, and wrangle his discharge from the hospital.

C

All told, Hal was not discharged from the Brooklyn Naval Hospital until the Americans had secured a victory in the Marianas and until two days after the Allies had liberated Paris. Then, finally able to walk without the aid of the cane that he'd been using, Hal reported to the hospital's personnel office, cooled his heels for ten minutes on a bench, and was shown into the office of Commander Clemec who, apparently, the Navy intended to speak for the hospital's medical board.

Judging from the gray in his hair and the ribbons on his blouse, Clemec was a reserve officer and retread from the First World War. He greeted Hal with a smile and pointed to a chair in front of his desk.

"Enjoy your stay with us?" Clemec asked, raising an eyebrow to indicate a slight degree of irony in his question.

"Yes Sir," Hal said, "about as much as I could under the circumstances."

"None of the nurses try to seduce you?"

Hal laughed. "No Sir," he said. "I'm getting away whole."

"Good," Clemec said, "and getting away is just what the Navy has in store for you." The man became serious. "Your country is in your debt, Mr. Goff, and the four Purple Hearts you're wearing attest to the fact. Put simply, you've done your bit, and more than your bit, and unless you wish to contest your discharge, the Navy is ready to let you go. Think you can live with that?"

"Yes Sir," Hal said.

"Thought you might," Clemec said. "If you were a regular, they'd probably find desk billets for you, but we're so full up with reserve officers in your grade right now that your departure will in no way endanger the war effort, and it is thought best to let you get on with your life. You will be advanced to the rank of lieutenant with your separation pay to be computed accordingly, and as of this moment, you are on sixty days' convalescent leave, after which you will return here for final separation and discharge under wholly honorable conditions. Understood?"

"Yes Sir," Hal said.

"Very good," Commander Clemec said. "So, Mr. Goff, if you don't mind me asking, what are your plans?"

"Marriage first," Hal said, "and then graduate school at the University of Illinois."

"Good for you," Clemec said, rising from his chair and extending his hand to indicate the interview had ended. "If it's teaching you're after, I can recommend it. I taught biology at Wyoming until Pearl Harbor and I was recalled, and I intend to go right back to it the minute the Navy lets me go, so all the best to you and your young lady."

"Thank you, Sir," Hal said, and he meant it.

And then, Hal walked straight out the door, caught a taxi, filled out a telegram at the train station, and boarded a train for Chicago. Once aboard, regardless of the condition of his hip, he found he would be sitting pretty much on his B-four bag for the length of his journey.

12

As the train from Chicago pulled into the Illinois Central station in Champaign, filled to overflowing with airmen returning to duty at Chanute Field on the heels of their three-day passes, Hal could see that an August rain had started to fall. He wondered if Bea would wisely have waited for him at Mrs. Frear's rather than risk having to stand under an umbrella—if in fact she had remembered to have carried one. Once on the platform, however, with airmen swarming in all directions around him, he knew that his worries in that regard had been foolish. There she was, standing back from the crowd in the shelter of the awning and looking straight at him. Wearing a new do that he had never seen before and a svelte suit that made his blood race, Bianca Colombo looked a picture of everything that Hal had thought about and looked forward to while he'd been away.

"Hello sailor," she said to him without moving as he approached her beneath the awning. "Home at last?"

"You are without a doubt," Hal said, standing stock still, "the most sophisticated, delectable lovely that I have seen anywhere since I last left you."

In the next second they were in each other's arms, kissing so passionately and hugging so tightly that they were breathless by the time they began to ease their grip on one another.

Outside the station in a taxi, before Hal could give the driver Mrs. Frear's address, Bea laid her hand on his, stopped him, and gave the driver an address that Hal knew to be three streets over and a block farther to the east.

"You've moved?" Hal asked.

"I have," Bea said. "Mrs. Frear's niece is starting school, so I offered her my room. My new place is only a block farther away from things, but I think you'll like the landlady. She has ... well, what should I call it? Spunk, perhaps."

Hal wondered what that might mean but didn't ask, and after a ten-minute drive down Green Street and a turn onto South Lincoln, he knew that he was going to find out fairly quickly. The driver took only a minute or two more to turn east onto Iowa and pull into the drive of a high Victorian pile with a rounded turret on one corner and a long gallery that looked like it extended all the way around three sides of the house.

"Quite a palace," Hal said, as he paid the cabbie. "Live in the turret, do you, with visions of letting down your long hair so that I can climb up and through the window?"

"Not quite," Bea said, opening the door and thrusting out her umbrella before stepping out into the drive. "Not that way," she called as Hal hauled his B-four bag from the trunk and started for the gallery. "Back here."

As the two of them sheltered under the umbrella and darted down the drive toward the back of the house, Hal spotted the enclosed garage which he immediately realized had been converted into a studio apartment.

"Welcome home, sailor," Bea said, as she thrust her key into the lock and threw open the door so that both of them could hurry inside out of the rain. "I won't say it's big, but I will say it's comfortable. Living room and studio kitchen here, bedroom and bath in the rear."

"When did you move in here?" Hal asked, glancing around what looked to him like a well-organized room containing a sofa and two easy chairs as well as a small kitchen table with two straight-backed chairs on the edge of what passed for a kitchenette. "I've been sending all my letters to you at Mrs. Frear's."

"Mrs. Frear is a dear," Bea said, setting down her purse and closing the door behind them. "I moved over here and set up housekeeping about two weeks after you settled into that hospital in Brooklyn, but Mrs. Frear and I agreed to keep the secret so that I could surprise you when you came back."

"Have a telephone?" Hal asked. "I guess I ought to call Mrs. Rogers to see if she can put me up until we get down to Herrin."

For half a moment, the room went silent.

"Oh, my dear," Bea said, suddenly turning and looking him in the eye, "you will never be staying with Mrs. Rogers again. It's raining outside, and according to this morning's weather report, it is going to rain right on through the afternoon and well into the evening, but you and I are not going to notice it. Instead, what I hope we're going to do is spend the entire afternoon in bed where I can give you the homecoming you deserve and that I've been waiting months for, and then, I hope I'm never going to let you out of my sight again. Think that will suit?"

Hal grinned. "Oh," he said, feigning a laconic delivery, "I think it probably will."

Three days later, Mario and Caterina Colombo met Hal and Bea at the Illinois Central station in Carbondale and drove them the fifteen miles to Herrin, to a pleasant, four-bedroom house on 10th Street, about four blocks north of the immense Norge factory. The house, as far as Hal could decide, looked like it had been lifted directly from somewhere in Italy and set down on the street, much like two or three others which came into his view. And the resemblance did not end there; behind every house on the street, he noticed that the walks leading to the outbuildings which flanked the alley were shaded by overhanging grape arbors all of which were bordered by vegetable gardens that seemed full to overflowing.

"It's the grandmothers," Bea told him when Hal asked about the gardens. "There isn't a one of them living on this street that couldn't outcook the best New York chef, and you'd better believe that when they cook, they cook with their own fresh ingredients."

"So it would seem," Hal said.

Once inside the house, Hal was introduced to the grandmother that Bea had spoken to him about, Lena Colombo, and Hal instantly recognized a resemblance between the woman and her son. The difference seemed to come with stature. Whereas Lena Colombo couldn't have stood much over five feet in height and seemed about as big as a minute, Mario Colombo, Bea's father, although only around five foot nine in height, looked as solid as a rock, with muscular arms and a chest that seemed as thick as a beer barrel. Caterina, like Bea, remained shapely, slender, and attentive. When Hal met the remainder of the family, he found Bea's aunts, Maria and Stephana, to be cast from the same mold as Caterina while Bea's uncles, Julio and Gino, both looked enough like Mario so that anyone might have mistaken them for triplets, although Gino seemed to have been born with blonde hair unlike his two older brothers, both of whom had gone already to salt and pepper.

Noticing a photo on a free-standing side table, Hal asked, "A relative?"

"My brother," Bea said, "Franco. He's joined the Air Corps and is in training as a bombardier at some place he finds quite godforsaken called Deming, New Mexico."

"And how is it, I might ask, that you never mentioned a brother to me?" Hal asked, swiftly raising an eyebrow.

"Didn't want to scare you off," Bea said. "Franco was a golden gloves boxer before he joined up, and once or twice while we were in high school, he gave the heave ho to more than one of my potential suitors and in each case without my consent."

"Good for Franco," Hal said. "I must remember to thank him when we meet."

Conversation around the table when all of them sat down to eat turned out to be something that Hal realized he would have to get used to. Grammo Lena spoke English, but her English was very broken, so most of the rest of the family spoke to her in Italian. Among themselves, they relied on English, which all of them spoke without a trace of an accent, a clear indication that they had grown up in the States and been through American schools.

The meal they sat down to that evening turned out to be a treat that Hal thought he would never forget. In place of pasta and in keeping with Lombard tradition, they started with risotto, prepared by Bea's grandmother and far and away the best that Hal had ever tasted. The main course for the evening turned out to be veal scallopini that, in a manner of speaking, Hal thought he could die for.

"You know how to make these dishes?" Hal asked Bea as the two sat side by side making pigs of themselves.

"Ha," Grammo Lena chuckled. "Yousa gonna haveta wach it 'Al, or dat girl gonna make youse fat."

"Our father started cooking for monks in a monastery near the St. Bernard pass when he was about twelve years old," Mario said, "and used to entertain everyone with the lie that he taught Mamma all his secrets. Mamma, of course, learned her own secrets from our grandmother, so once you and Bea are settled, I think Bea will treat you to some of what she's learned from both Caterina and Mamma."

"I can only hope," Hal said, putting away another bite of the scallopini. "What I'm waiting to find out is if she knows how to distill grappa or if I'm going to be reduced to trying to buy it off the shelf somewhere."

"You know grappa?" Uncle Julio asked, his eyebrows rising.

"I was first introduced to it in Palermo," Hal said, "where to be honest most of the stuff tasted like turpentine, but we did find a place out on the coast where it wasn't half bad, and once or twice in Naples, we found something almost as good."

"After dinner, I'll give you a taste of ours," Mario beamed. "Grappa from the occupied provinces is bound to be bad, and their cooking down there is bound to have been worse."

"Occupied provinces?" Hal said. "Do I take it you mean the areas the Allies have moved into?"

Most everyone at the table laughed. "What my brother means," Gino grinned, "is the areas which the Camorra and the Mafia have taken over—Sicily and the foot of the boot. I know we're prejudiced, but for Lombards, everything south of Rome might as well be considered foreign territory and would be if any of us lived in Italy and still considered ourselves Italians, which we don't. About half the folks living around here are Lombards from around Milan, so it isn't too much of a stretch to say that Sicilians and Napolitans aren't real popular here."

Hal realized that there was a lot he didn't know, a lot that Bea would probably wind up explaining to him.

"When we were children growing up here," Caterina said, "I don't remember hearing a word about either the Mafia or the Camorra. All of that seems to have started with Prohibition, and now, from what we read in the papers about people like Al Capone and that Luciano, people hear the word Italian and think we're all that way, and we aren't."

"It's a curse, no doubt about it," Mario said with distaste. "My hope is that our grandchildren will survive long enough to outlive it."

The grappa, when it came at the end of the meal and after the men had adjourned to the front porch, exceeded in quality anything that Hal had ever tasted before.

"I think you could bottle this and sell it for a premium price," Hal said, smiling after his first taste, "and the same goes for the wine we had with supper."

"Those are two things we picked up from our father," Julio said. "In the village from which he immigrated, I think everyone made their own wine and distilled their own grappa. We don't grow our own grapes around here, so each year, a number of families go together, order grapes from either New York or California, bring them home in stake trucks when the grape train arrives, and then spend two or three days putting up the wine. From what I've been told, in a lot of the western states, tradition allows for the same kind of time off from work or school during hunting season. Franco knows the procedure, but I don't think Bea does, so one of these days, you're going to have to join us and learn how to do it for yourself, if you like to have wine in the house, that is."

"Not a bad idea," Hal said, "and a skill well worth learning, although where the two of us might eventually be able to practice it, I can't say."

"And what *are* your intentions in that regard, if you don't mind me asking?" Mario said, his brows suddenly knitting with a more serious expression. "I'm well aware that Bea is her own woman now, and I don't intend to interfere, but Cat and I are still her parents, and we'd like to have some idea about where your road leads."

"For the moment," Hal said, speaking straightforwardly, "I'm on sixty days of convalescent leave. That will coincide with the start of school at the U. of I., so what I intend to do is enroll for a graduate degree in history, make a fast run back to Brooklyn at the end of my leave to take my discharge, and get straight back for classes as soon as the train can turn around. I've got enough saved to finance at least two years of school, and once the two of us have our degrees, I hope we can both get on teaching at the same college somewhere. The Congress has just passed this thing they're calling the G.I. Bill, and from what I hear, it might even provide us with enough in the way of subsistence and housing to allow me to stay in school longer. If it does, I might try to go for a PhD. From what I know of the academic world, that would provide us with the kind of secure future that Bea deserves, and if it seems possible, I mean to see that she gets it."

"If you're able to swing that," Mario said, "we'll see Bea through a PhD of her own; that'll be our wedding present to the two of you."

"That's generous beyond words," Hal said, genuinely surprised by the offer.

"We've talked about it," Mario said, "Cat and I, and we think it beats offering you a set of china, an assortment of silver, or the furnishings for a bedroom. Stuff is easy enough to come by once you have a salary to fall back on. Education is altogether different and far more secure. Bea seems to love what she's doing, so from our point of view, it seems like the best gift we can give the two of you."

"Understood," Hal said, "and Bea will be thrilled."

"I can't say for sure," Mario grinned, "but I think getting you back from the war in one piece is the biggest thrill she'll ever get. You will never know the relief we felt once we knew you were back in Brooklyn and recovering. If you'd checked out over there, and from what I understand, you damn near did, I don't think she would ever have recovered."

"Thanks for the thought," Hal said. "I can't say I didn't feel a degree of the same relief myself."

Three days later, before more than one hundred of Bea's family and friends, and with Bea's own parish priest officiating, they were married in a Roman Catholic manner with a modest reception to follow. Then, as swiftly as the two of them could change, Mario and Caterina helped them load their bags back into the car for the drive to Carbondale where they could catch their train for Champaign. For the time being, the two of them had agreed to forego and postpone anything resembling a honeymoon. Registration for fall classes would be taking place within thirty-six hours of their return to campus; already well acquainted with the enormous lines that attended that event, neither wished to miss it. So rather than honeymoon at the Palmer House in Chicago, the Mark Hopkins in San Francisco, or the Waldorf in New York, Hal and Bea honeymooned in the studio apartment that Bea had found for them and never knew the difference, emerging only on the afternoon following their return in time to snatch a quick meal at Pren's before swiftly returning to the bed which neither had bothered to make.

To Hal's surprise, on the day that he enrolled for the fall semester, he found that the Veterans Affairs on campus was already up and running, that his tuition, subsistence, and housing would be covered for four years, and that, matched with the money he'd saved from his Navy pay as a result of having absolutely nowhere to spend it during his time overseas, he and Bea would be sitting prettier than most of the people he knew. Two nights later, then, in partial celebration of their good fortune, Hal booked a table at Skaggs and took Bea our for a celebratory dinner.

"You're tired of my cooking already?" Bea said, feigning outrage.

"I am not," Hal said. "I want to let the people at Skaggs get a good look at you, so that if we fall on hard times, I can take you down there and get you a place as their head chef with the promise of improving their menu."

"Does that mean that you intend to sign on as their dishwasher?" Bea teased.

"No question about it," Hal said, "as long as they give me adequate instruction about how dish-washing is done."

"Oh, that won't be any problem at all," Bea said. "I'll begin giving you instruction the minute we finish dinner tomorrow night."

"So," Hal asked, as the two of them touched glasses and took their first sip of Skaggs' wine, "how did classes go today?"

"The Milton class was brilliant," Bea said. "My teacher is a woman—a very precise, very sharp North Carolina Scot who has apparently had considerable orthodontia but who, in my estimation, has the best mind that I have yet encountered here. We're starting with Milton's sonnets, but I cannot wait for her to tackle *Paradise Lost.*"

"And your seminar on the Romantics?" Hal asked.

"That one looks like it is going to turn out to be something of a dud," Bea said. "Young prof, not many years out of grad school who apparently won't lecture. Instead, he's assigning papers, and if I can actually see what's coming, it looks like all we're going to do in there is write papers and read them to each other."

"That does sound dull," Hal said.

"Doesn't it just," Bea said. "What about you? How did your day go?"

"It was interesting," Hal said. "Good opening lecture on the causes of the American Revolution, although I've studied that before, and in depth, but my afternoon seminar, the one on Modern European History, proved absolutely excellent. That one is starting right off with the causes of the First World War, and frankly, some of the parallels between that one and the one I've just come back from seem stunning."

"A lot of papers to write?"

"I suspect the two of us are going to be haunting the library to the point where we'll almost want to take up residence there," Hal said.

"Perhaps we can get carrels together over there," Bea joked, "make up a little bed for ourselves, and only leave the place for meals."

"I think it would take them ten minutes to throw us out for conduct unbecoming," Hal laughed.

By the middle of October, both Hal and Bea were deep into their studies, with Bea writing a paper about the first three books of *Paradise Lost* while Hal had only just received one back on the Battle of Tannenberg.

"There are times," Hal said to Bea as the two of them sat down that evening to nothing more than a plate of Bea's risotto, "that you wonder how the Russians survive. For starters, the Russians lost close to 200,000 men at Tannenberg and seemed to go right on losing in those kinds of numbers for another three years."

"From all reports," Bea said, "their losses in this one, military as well as civilian, are ungodly."

"Hardly surprising," Hal said, "when you consider that they are fighting about four-fifths of the German army. Biggest gift Hitler ever gave us was attacking Russia. It looks to me like it's swallowed him."

"Hearing anything about that in your course?" Bea asked.

"From time to time," Hal said. "The general consensus seems to be that while the Russians are doing a lot, they're also going to want a lot once they reach Germany and this thing ends."

"Stands to reason, doesn't it," Bea said, making a statement rather than asking a question.

"It does," Hal said. "What that will mean for the post-war period, of course, is anyone's guess."

"Which makes me think," Bea said, "when does your post-war period officially begin?"

"I'll catch the train to New York on Friday night," Hal said, "with the expectation of being back here as a loving husband and an official civilian on Sunday evening."

"Maybe we can come back early from the library this evening," Bea said, "so that we can start making up ahead of time for the nights you'll be away."

"Why, what thoughtful foresight you are gifted with," Hal grinned, squeezing her hand.

"Let it never be forgotten," Bea said, "that Athena, deity of wisdom and forethought, was a female."

The following Friday, as planned, Hal hopped on a train to New York, received his discharge with a suitable advancement to the rank of lieutenant USNR-R on Saturday, and was back on the train before the October sun set, arriving tired but as an official civilian and, indeed, a loving husband before noon on Sunday. Then, hand in hand, rather than spend their afternoon in bed, the two of them once more treaded their way to the library where they spent the remainder of their day curled up in their carrels with research materials.

A week went by and then two, and near the beginning of November, Hal returned home one afternoon to find a copy of the *Chicago Tribune* sitting on the edge of his chair.

"Where did you find this?" Hal asked, immediately sitting down and picking up the paper.

"On the doorstep," Bea said. "My guess is that the paperboy left it as a means of tempting us to subscribe. Why don't you sit down there and read it while I get up some *casoncelli* for our supper."

"You're kidding about the *casoncelli*, aren't you?" Hal said, his eyes lighting up.

"I'm not," Bea said. "I had the afternoon off, and it seemed like a good time for me to prepare you something special in exchange for that lovely night you treated me to at Skaggs."

"You are more than a sweetie," Hal said, throwing himself into his chair and picking up the paper.

As a matter of course, Hal turned first to the war news. Reports seemed sketchy, but apparently the Navy had fought and won a major Pacific naval battle at a place called Leyte Gulf while in Europe the Canadians had taken Zeebrugge, and Patton's army had crossed the Moselle and seemed to be honing in on Metz. Then, near the bottom of the page, in a single tucked away inch-long column carrying the headline SHIP SUNK, Hal suddenly felt himself kicked in the stomach as he read that the *ATR-3X* had struck a mine west of Genoa and gone down with all hands.

For a moment, Hal thought he might be sick, but after taking a few deep breaths, he managed to get control of himself. Then, he simply felt dazed, like someone had walked up to him and, without a warning of any kind, socked him on the jaw. West of Genoa? What the hell had the *3X* been doing there? Why wasn't she down in Palermo or in Naples where she belonged?

How was it, Hal wondered, that he and Bender and Yaakov had gotten off in time? How was it that they had survived but the others had not? Hal didn't know and knew he never would. When Bea finally called him to the table that night, Hal stood, took one look at her, and thanked whatever lucky stars had brought them together. And then, silently cursing the vagaries of the war, Hal walked to the table and sat down to the feast that Bea had promised him.